A Study in Desire

Jane Maguire

Cover design by Erin Dameron-Hill
Edited by Nevvie Gane

ISBN: 978-17778926-8-5

www.janemaguireauthor.com

Also by Jane Maguire

To my third grade teacher, for encouraging me to keep writing. Thanks, Mr. B.

A Study in Desire

THE
ROCKLIFFE
DYNASTY

By Jane Maguire

Prologue

Beatrice Prescott, the Dowager Marchioness of Rockliffe, would have thought she'd made enough peculiar requests over time to no longer cause her man of business to bat an eye. Yet no sooner had she explained what she needed done than Mr. Adolphus Clare's eyes widened, and his mouth began quivering at the corners.

"But, my lady, that's ..."

The dowager sat stiffly in the chair behind the vast oak desk that technically belonged to her son, resisting the urge to drum her fingers against its surface as she waited for Clare to select the appropriate adjective. *Uncharitable*? *Wicked*? *Illegal*? Perhaps what she'd asked of him was all those things. But oh, did she have her reasons. Reasons that Clare, or anyone for that matter, could likely discern if he only took time to stop and think. If he was too shortsighted to recognize the implications of the situation that unfurled before his eyes, though, she certainly had no intention of voicing them aloud.

"Spare me the lecture on morality." She gave a dismissive flick of her hand, ignoring the painful jolt that came from what had to be the onset of rheumatism. "While it may not appear so, I *do*, in fact, have everyone's best interests at heart. I regret that we couldn't have come to a resolution using less drastic measures, but sometimes, these things cannot be helped. In the end, Theodora and the boys will be happier for it. As for you, Clare, I'm sure it goes without saying that your cooperation in this matter will not go unnoticed. In fact, I'll consider myself quite in your debt."

Clare's forehead wrinkled, and he reached up to swipe away beads of perspiration that had accumulated near his receding hairline. He shifted uncomfortably in his leather chair on the other side of the desk, making a great show of indecision. However, was there really any question as to whether he would comply? He'd been her—well, the former and then current marquess's—man of business for more than three decades, and old habits died hard. Especially when one received handsome compensation for these habits.

For a moment longer, he looked at her with a face etched with tension, his boots making irritating scuffing noises against the floor. But then, his feet stilled, and he made a quiet sound, one that had the air of a poorly repressed sigh. "If you're certain that's the best course of action, my lady."

"Good." The dowager made a weak attempt at feigning relief for the concession she'd already known he would make, although whether it showed through her satisfied smirk was doubtful. Not that it mattered. She had already turned her attention elsewhere, to the many preparations she had to make for what was to come. "The sooner you can see this done, the better. In the meantime, though, I suppose I'll have plenty to occupy me. I should arrange for Theodora to acquire a new wardrobe, so that when she's ready to cast aside her mourning attire, she can go about *without* looking like a strumpet. Then, there's the matter of a tutor for the boys, for Lord only knows what sort of education, or lack thereof, they have received thus far—"

She broke off, cognizant that her man of business had resumed his infernal fidgeting and made another low sound. A chortle? "Is something the matter, Clare?" She didn't bother concealing her irritation.

He pulled himself upright in his chair and cleared his throat, this time with purpose. "Regarding the debt you feel I'm rightfully owed ..."

"So soon?" She arched an eyebrow but then stilled, restraining herself before her expression turned to one that had been known to make grown men cower. After all, assuming Clare saw to the successful completion of the task she'd requested—and he would, because Clare always did— she would, indeed, owe him a favor. Best see to it at once before he had the opportunity to develop any further misgivings. "Very well. What can I do to make this an even exchange?"

"You said you're in need of a tutor for your grandsons, and I'd like to propose a candidate." He paused a moment, eyeing her evenly. "My son, Jeremy."

She peered at him in return, processing the request. Of all the things he could have demanded of her, that was the last she would have imagined. Had she even known that Clare had a son? The topic must have come up a time or two, although they usually eschewed personal matters in favor of business. Which presently, happened to be family business.

"He's more than qualified for the position," he rushed to say before she could make a comment one way or another. "A scholar. Until recently, a fellow at Oxford, and under different circumstances, he would have become a vicar. The boys could ask for no finer instructor, and I'm certain that, as you always do, you would provide generous compensation to partake of such skill."

"Ah." The dowager took great pains to keep her expression passive. There were numerous points on which she could interrogate him. Primarily, why he wished, above all else, for his son to have this position. One that would bring him little prestige, even if well paid. However, did it really matter? She could do her own delving into the character of Mr. Jeremy Clare later. For now, it was best she agree, so she could at least ensure her man of business held up his part of the deal. "Send him to me, then, for an interview, and I'm certain we can come to some sort of arrangement."

"Very good, my lady." Clare clasped his hands together, his mouth twitching in something resembling a smile.

"That is, after you've seen to the successful completion of the task I asked you to do." She reached for the brass bell on the corner of the desk and gave it a shake, the indisputable sign that their meeting had come to a close.

Clare's grin vanished, his shoulders slumping as he pushed himself up from his seat. Already, the butler, Flynt, had appeared in the doorway, ready to escort him out. Leaving him with no additional time to negotiate or protest.

And Clare—good, loyal, dependable Clare—lifted his shoulders and nodded. His face may not display enthusiasm, but at least it showed decisiveness. "Yes, my lady. I'll see to it right away."

He bowed and made a hasty exit because he'd worked as the dowager's man of business long enough to know that was the only acceptable course of action. Leaving her, once more, alone in a silent study.

She gripped her chair's arms, pushing herself upward amidst the protesting ache in her joints. The reminder that, while she may still know how to take charge of a situation with the same sharpness she'd possessed thirty years prior, her body wasn't infallible. She should have brought along her walking stick, the decoration that accompanied her more and more frequently of late. In a baseless display of optimism—and strength, too, if she were being honest with herself—she'd left it upstairs in her bedchamber this morning.

She hobbled to the window in an effort to walk out some of the stiffness, gazing at the bustling Mayfair street below. What sense was there in dwelling on how old age crept up on her a little more each day? After all, it happened to everyone, eventually. The main thing was she was getting her affairs in order. Yes, the past months had been horrible —perhaps even worse than the time when she'd changed from marchioness to dowager fifteen years prior—and more than she'd care to admit was in shambles. One son dead and buried. Another gone half a world away, grasping at something that was already lost. And to add insult to injury, an uncooperative daughter whose status as a spinster solidified itself more with each passing day.

But there was nothing that couldn't be fixed. By the time she was through, she *would* have a reputable heir and spare. A future Marquess of Rockliffe respectable enough to make the ton forget the scandals that had come before him.

The first step was to summon the tutor to see what improvements could be brought about by the instruction of Mr. Jeremy Clare. She could only hope his father hadn't exaggerated his merits.

Her mind drifted back to the old schoolroom two floors above her, long in disuse now, and her lips twitched upward at the thought of the two curly heads that would soon occupy it. Hellions, both of them, of that she had no doubt. But that could be remedied.

The momentary twinge of affection for her grandsons

evaporated as another dark, curly head slipped into her thoughts. The mother—*Theodora*—who had passed so many of her features onto the boys. The woman who had bewitched the spare to the marquessate and ruined everything. Had it been possible to foresee the future—namely, the consequences of Nicholas's ... the marquess's ... accident —Beatrice would have taken far greater trouble to prevent that chit from wheedling her way into Samuel's life in the first place. However, she'd lived long enough to realize regrets changed nothing. A person's time was far better spent learning to deal with a situation as it was rather than how one wished it could be.

"Theodora." Without meaning to, she uttered the ridiculous name aloud, grimacing as the sound echoed off the windowpane. Young boys could be easily molded, but as for a grown woman who'd spent her life devoid of propriety and social graces—well, that was another matter entirely, and a troublesome one at that. However, Beatrice knew enough about a mother's stubbornness to recognize that trying to remove her from the picture was an exercise in futility. No, she would just have to find a way to live with her. To mold her, too.

If the dowager had been the type of woman to clutch her forehead and sigh at the faintest sign of distress, she would have surely done so now. Instead, she squared her shoulders and continued to gaze at the faceless crowd while that particular troublesome face stayed in her thoughts.

"Theodora," she repeated with quiet steeliness. "Who will instruct *you*?"

1

April, 1805

Theodora Prescott wished she could say that having a hackney barrel up alongside her as she walked, narrowly avoiding a collision and splattering her from head to toe with mud not twenty paces from her front door, was the worst thing to happen to her this month. Alas, what did the cold, mucky drips that ran down her cheeks and stained her pale gray skirts signify beyond another inconvenience after a long string of calamities?

Nonetheless, she glared up at the coachman as he pulled to an abrupt halt beside her, uttering an oath too quiet for him to hear but she hoped he could read on her lips. Just because she'd experienced worse hardships didn't mean she would stand by meekly while a coachman drove recklessly enough to endanger anyone in his path while rendering her filthy besides. And all this after she'd taken care to bring along an umbrella to protect her from the driving springtime rain.

At least the coachman, a man of middling years with

puffy eyes and a drooping chin, had the decency to look sheepish. "Apologies, ma'am. I—"

"I am *profusely* sorry." In a sudden flurry of sound and movement, the hackney's door flew open, and a decidedly male voice called out to her as its owner sprang to the ground. "You're not hurt, are you?"

She glanced from the coachman over to his passenger, who, for some reason, felt the need to apologize on his behalf. The passenger stepped toward her, his eyes filled with concern. Eyes the most attractive shade of light green she'd ever encountered. Even the shadows beneath them, suggesting he was lacking in sleep, didn't detract from their appeal. They were evenly spaced in a face composed of a pleasing combination of lines and angles, set above a tall, lithe frame. A man who no one could mistake for a barely grown schoolboy yet still exuded youth. His age probably wasn't that much lower than hers, really. Although lately, she often felt one hundred years old instead of thirty.

She stiffened and gave a brisk shake of her head, appalled at the way she'd let her mind wander, and under such circumstances. "No, I'm not hurt." At least, nothing was hurt beyond a bit of her pride, and that had taken such a beating recently that this incident was hardly enough to faze her. Regardless, that didn't change the fact that his coachman had been dangerously careless. She turned back to the coachman where he sat upon his perch, fixing him with another scowl. "However, you should really take better care."

Another oath formed on her tongue as she brushed at the mud on her skirts, which only helped to spread it and stain her gloves besides. Ultimately, though, she choked the vulgar word back with a sigh. At least the incident had happened when she was alone rather than with the dowager beside her, ready to criticize as if the mishap were somehow her own fault. Or, even worse, with the boys in tow, rambling about the street carelessly, oblivious to the possibility of sudden danger. The very thought made her stomach drop.

The passenger took the brief silence as an opportunity to rush forward and mutter something indecipherable to the coachman as he handed him up some coins. Then, after a final rueful inclination of the coachman's head, the hackney rolled back into motion, at a sensible speed this time.

Leaving her free to carry on her way as if the whole incident had never happened. Except for the mud that still covered her from head to toe. Oh, and the passenger with the too-green eyes, who hadn't gotten back into the hackney but remained beside her, continuing to look apologetic.

"I really am sorry." He was staring at her now, his gaze traveling along the length of her body before coming to rest on her face. The way his lips twitched suggested she must look every bit as frightful as she imagined. "When I emphasized my need for haste to the coachman, I didn't intend for him to abandon caution altogether. But perhaps in my desperation not to be late, I was a trifle too insistent."

Without looking away, he reached into his coat pocket, producing a crisp white handkerchief and extending it to her. "Here, take this. You have a little something on your—"

"Thank you," she muttered brusquely, snatching it under the shield of her umbrella before it could become drenched by rain. She was covered in more than a *little* mud, far beyond what a lone scrap of linen could remedy. But despite it being a lost cause, she swiped at her cheeks and forehead, desperate to return to at least some semblance of normalcy. Then again, maybe leaving the mud there would conceal how her face heated from his continued scrutiny.

She thrust the handkerchief back into his palm and used her free hand to pull her cloak more tightly about her shoulders. If she had any sense, she would use that as her cue to depart and carry on with her task. But she couldn't. Not when those green eyes kept resting on her like that.

"What is it?" She didn't mean for the words to come out as prickly as they did. However, he seemed to be drifting nearer to her, as close as the wide brim of her umbrella would allow. Close enough for her to detect the faint smell of shaving soap.

"It's only …" He stayed with his hand held in midair, clutching the bunched-up handkerchief. And then, he was gliding it along a spot on her left cheek, his gloved fingertip brushing against her skin as he went. A shiver threatened to course through her body, and she quickly tensed. He may not be covered in mud, but in the few minutes he'd spent here on the street with her, the deluge had soaked him through. Water dripped from the brim of his hat, and droplets coated his eyebrows and lashes, making them a darker brown than they must usually appear. Making the green irises beneath look even more vivid.

She wrenched the handkerchief out of his grasp and pulled it away from her face, jerking backward a step. "What are you doing?"

"Apologies." He staggered backward, too, as if suddenly hit by the untowardness of performing such an intimacy with a stranger. "You missed a spot. There was still some mud …"

Despite the chill of the rainy day, her face grew hot once more. Of course there was still mud! The only way she would rid herself of it all was after a good scrub in a hot bath. But even if she did, would she be able to wash away the tickle of his fingertip as it traced over her skin?

"It's nothing over which you need trouble yourself," she snapped. "I thought you said you were in a hurry, as was I before your hackney nearly knocked me to the ground."

It wasn't true. Her errand had no particular direction or purpose beyond making her feel like she hadn't resigned herself to an unwanted fate. At the end of the day, though, she knew she was fighting a losing battle. Still, the lie was necessary if it served to extricate her from this situation without delay. She was a widow. A mother. She could *not* continue to stand here, noticing these trifling details about a strange—and altogether too handsome—man. And worse, letting them affect her.

"You're correct, I am," he said. With a couple quick gestures, he straightened his hat and smoothed his topcoat, although given how sodden the articles had become, his efforts to neaten his attire were for naught. "However, I couldn't rush off without assuring myself you were unharmed. As that seems to be the case, I should bid you farewell and be on my way, Miss ..."

"Yes, well, good day." With that, she spun on her heels and marched off, lowering her umbrella close to her face to provide an extra shield against unwanted scrutiny. There was no point lingering to tell him her name. Or to explain that given her status as a married woman turned widow, she was *Mrs.*, not *Miss*.

Her first thought was to take off running as fast as she could without drawing additional attention. However, her legs had other ideas, for they propelled her forward with slow, measured steps. No matter, as long as she was moving, her feet beating out a rhythm as she went. *Don't look back. Don't look back.*

She looked back. Her traitorous neck twisted, allowing her to survey the scene she'd just left. The man had already departed, of course. Yet presumably, the fact he'd paid the coachman and sent him on his way meant he wasn't far from his destination.

No, he wasn't. Even from a distance, with his back

turned to her, she spotted him right away. He'd gone only about twenty paces from the sight of the near-collision, stopping before one of the stately brick town houses and knocking on its glossy black door.

The same door she'd emerged from not so long ago. The front entrance to *her* home. Rather, the dowager's—her mother-in-law's—home. But her place of residence as well, until she could find a way to make it otherwise.

Suddenly, her eyes darted down to her fist, to the crumpled handkerchief she still clutched within. She opened her palm and shook the scrap of linen until it unwrinkled enough for her to read the monogram she'd previously detected in the corner but hadn't paid much heed. *JC.*

The conversation she'd held with the dowager over breakfast that morning—if one could call a one-sided lecture a conversation—came drifting back. *The tutor I've hired for the boys arrives this morning. Mr. Jeremy Clare, the son of my man of business and a respected scholar. I certainly hope the boys do not do anything to deter him from the position, for if anyone can prepare them for Eton in short order, I have every confidence it's Mr. Clare.*

Jeremy Clare. *JC.* She scrunched the handkerchief into a ball again, shoving it into her reticule.

She'd done as the dowager had requested and given the boys a halfhearted lecture of her own before stepping out on this ill-fated errand. *Ben, Alex, I expect you to be on your best behavior when Mr. Clare comes. Your grandmother will give us all no end of torment if you are not.*

It had been difficult, though, to put any true feeling in the words. Because maybe, if the boys' behavior grew appalling enough, the dowager would lose patience and decide she would rather keep them all at a distance. Provided for, but not under her roof. Then again, if she grew so angry that she cut them off entirely, where would that leave them?

No better off than in the months following Samuel's death, when they'd found themselves destitute and then hungry, facing one catastrophe after another. Until finally, she'd had nowhere left to turn but the Dowager Marchioness of Rockliffe, the mother who'd cut Samuel off while he was still living.

The dilemma worked in a relentless cycle, one from which she had no way of breaking free. At least not yet.

She turned her head back toward the house, but in the time she'd taken to examine the handkerchief, a servant must have allowed Mr. Clare entry, for the step was now deserted. As if she'd imagined his presence there, and she could almost begin to believe she had. After the few brief times she'd encountered the dowager's man of business, a lanky man whose pinched lips made him appear as though he were constantly dealing with something unpleasant, she'd just assumed his tutor son would be equally as sour-faced. Not a man who may share his father's height but was otherwise totally different, with a frame that was all perfectly proportioned and eyes that shone intently—

Enough. It was time for her to stop gawking in the street, still a target for any other reckless hackneys that might come racing by, and carry on with her outing. Except where was she going, really?

To visit another of Samuel's starving artist friends and beg for money they didn't have? To plead with a shopkeeper to give her employment despite her lack of experience, so she could earn a salary that would barely support her alone, much less two boys? Back to the printshop as if her last hope of salvation hadn't been destroyed? As if she wouldn't find a burned-out shell of a building with a printing press that had been reduced to ash and the copy of Samuel's final manuscript along with it.

She'd performed all these activities enough times to

realize they led nowhere. Perhaps today, she'd be better off turning her attention elsewhere. Especially because, even after Mr. Clare's best efforts to clear her face of mud, her clothing remained coated in thick brown splotches.

She could go home. Despite how she tried staying out of the dowager's path as much as possible, she really needed to return to the house and change her clothes. It was only natural that after doing so, she would also peek into the schoolroom to see how the boys fared. And the tutor. Would he feel so bold once Ben and Alex were through with him?

If this arrangement was to work out, he would become a fixture within the household, at least until the dowager deemed the boys ready to be sent off to school. She may as well get used to seeing him, until the greenness of his eyes and the memory of his unexpected touch didn't cause her to so much as blink.

She was a widow. One who'd learned enough hard lessons to have gained some common sense. And that's all there was to it.

2

Jeremy Clare had hoped the day would bring about a promising new beginning, although the dead mouse nestled in his desk chair made that possibility seem increasingly unlikely.

Two sets of eyes—one brown, one blue—regarded him intently, their owners sitting straight in their chairs, hands folded atop their desks. They were the very model of attentive young scholars, ready to learn. Jeremy, however, wasn't born yesterday. Upon entering the schoolroom on the top floor of the resplendent Mayfair town house, he'd thought it wise to keep his guard up, at least a little. And with good reason, apparently. To the boys' credit, he had yet to teach students who welcomed him with a mouse carcass.

He quickly turned away from the chair, giving his audience a placid half-smile. The boys could likely smell discomfort, and he didn't plan on giving them the satisfaction. Besides, he had no particular need to sit and could just as easily teach while standing.

He stepped toward the desk in front of him where he'd laid his satchel, intending to retrieve one of the books from within, and felt his foot slide out from under him as it connected with something exceptionally slippery. He grabbed the edge of the desk to steady himself, but not quickly enough to prevent both boys from simultaneously clearing their throats in a poor attempt to conceal laughter. He refused to look down to see if he could determine what substance they'd used to make the floor so slick. Whatever they chose had served its purpose.

So that's how it was to be, then. He'd never taught children before, and based on his experience thus far, he was ill-suited to the task. Then again, certain undergraduates—particularly some of the sons of peers—could also be accused of mischievousness and immaturity, and he'd always survived those lectures unscathed. Why should this be any different?

He took a large but careful step to the other side of the desk. Given that was the way he'd passed after entering, and it had thus far proven free of traps, it seemed the safest choice. He half-seated himself atop the desk, just in case the slickness extended farther than he expected, reaching for his satchel again with all the nonchalance he could muster. Now, he just needed to open it without his fingers fumbling, for the satchel was still damp from the rain. A reminder of what had happened in the street.

The hackney screeching to a halt. The irate but fortunately unharmed woman who stared at him with fire in her eyes. The dark curls that hung below her bonnet. And that speck of mud covering a flawless, scarlet-tinged cheek that he'd somehow felt the need to remove ...

He plunged his hand into his satchel, turning his full attention to retrieving the appropriate book. It was bad enough that he'd overslept, nearly been involved in a collision, gotten drenched, and earned himself a powerful look of censure from the Dowager Marchioness of Rockliffe for his lateness and dishevelment. Oh, and that he now had two boys who seemed hell-bent on his downfall. The last thing he needed was to get distracted by thoughts of a woman he'd encountered briefly, through a stroke of what she'd consider extraordinary bad luck, and would never see again.

"Here we are." He cleared his throat, chasing away the sudden dryness that had accumulated there, as he pulled out the leather-bound volume he'd been seeking. "I thought we could start with classics. Have you read the story of Odysseus?"

The older boy—*Benedict*, his grandmother had supplied when the boy himself remained silent—regarded him with a scowl. "We already know classics. Our father read to us."

Jeremy shouldn't have permitted the rudeness—especially after the Dowager Lady Rockliffe had insisted he was to place the same emphasis on deportment as scholarship—but he didn't have it in him to object. The dowager had explained a small bit about the boys' situation during his initial interview, and his father, the dowager's longtime man of business, had supplied the rest. The boys were the offspring of an estranged second son. One who'd shunned polite society in favor of a group of low-class artists, writers, and vagabonds—or something to that effect—until he met an untimely end. Leaving his sons fatherless and his widow saddled with such insurmountable debt that she'd turned to the dowager for help.

The boys had grown up around "unsuitable influences," the dowager had informed him in a voice like iron, and it was imperative they be taught the rules and manners befitting a marquess's grandsons without delay. After some proper instruction, they would come to realize how much better off they were for having left a life of squalor and unruliness behind.

Nonetheless, Jeremy couldn't ignore the underlying

truth of the situation. The boys had recently lost their father. Life in the dowager's home, while perhaps an improvement from a financial perspective, was foreign to them, and adjusting to these new surroundings would take time.

Which was what prompted him to remain leaning against the desk, displaying what he hoped passed for calmness. "Perhaps you can also teach me something, then." It seemed an inopportune time to point out how he'd been a tutor of Greek language and literature back at Oxford.

If looks could kill, he would have expired on the spot, for both boys glared at him as if wishing for his demise.

They waited for him to do *something*. To stomp along the slippery floor and go flying onto his face. To shout at them, or fetch a strap, or flee to their grandmother in indignation and announce that he quit.

Perhaps a different man would have done those things. However, if the boys expected him to do them, too, they'd miscalculated. Yes, they could cause him all manner of torment, bodily harm, mental anguish, and a vast list of other afflictions he didn't care to contemplate. Regardless, there was one key fact they didn't understand.

Nothing would be worse than the shame of crawling back to Oxford and asking to be reinstated as a fellow because he wasn't to become a married man, after all. Nothing could bring him lower than having his father pull strings in an attempt to secure him another living, given the last one wasn't meant to be. And *anything* was better than continuing to sit alone in his newly acquired bachelor's lodgings, scribbling away fruitlessly, while forced to confront the fact that he'd filled his adulthood with mistakes and poor choices.

It was there, in this deadlock with his new pupils, that he held the advantage.

"I brought along a few other books, too, if you would find starting with something else more agreeable." An impressive book collection filled shelves lining the schoolroom's walls as well, although, for the moment, it was probably safest that Jeremy *not* leave his position of safety to peruse it. He rifled through his satchel instead, trying to decide what might best appeal to boys who had no intention of learning. Some of the pages were still damp from the rain that had soaked him through, giving him another jolt back to his encounter in the street. To the dark, fiery eyes, the smooth cheek, the mud coming away with a brush of his finger—

"Ahem."

The noise caused his neck to snap upward and his gaze to dart toward the open doorway.

It was her. The woman who leaned against the doorjamb with her arms folded across her chest, eyeing him mildly, was the one from the street. She wore different attire now, a simple mauve day dress without a hint of mud. But she had the same deep brown eyes and the same thick dark hair, which, without the confining influence of a bonnet, looked ready to burst from its knot and go cascading down her back.

Except it couldn't really be her, could it? Perhaps his drifting thoughts had combined to form an illusion, or—

"Mama!" The younger boy—Alexander—jumped from his seat, his glower becoming a grin. Something within his coat pocket wriggled. And then croaked.

Lord, grant him patience. And more importantly ... *Mama*? Jeremy glanced from the two boys, both on their feet and exhibiting decidedly more enthusiasm than they had thus far, to the woman in the doorway. He tried very hard to appear collected, although he had doubts as to his success. If nothing else, the morning was shaping up to be far from dull.

"Good morning again, boys." She sauntered a few steps into the room, and for the first time since he'd laid eyes on her, a smile crossed her lips, making her lovely face turn exquisite. "I returned early from my errand and thought I'd peek in to see how you're getting on."

"Fine," they mumbled in unison, refusing to look at Jeremy. Alexander pressed both hands against his coat pocket, trying to contain the commotion within.

Her smile disappeared, and for the briefest of moments, her eyes flickered up to his before returning to her boys. "You know, when I returned to the house, I couldn't help but notice that a tray of currant buns had just come out of the oven. I imagine you'd be allowed to have one if you go down to the kitchen and ask politely. And if your tutor has no objections to a short break, of course."

Three stony gazes fell on him now, daring him to object. Not that he was foolish enough to have any such notion. "By all means."

The boys scrambled across the room in a tangle of limbs. A promising sign that whatever they'd put on the floor was concentrated to the area around his desk. "And," he called out in his lecturer's voice, one that caused them to halt just steps from the doorway, "when you return in a quarter hour's time, I imagine you'll be in better form to see to the few things in the schoolroom that require tidying, after which we can begin our lessons."

They both looked at him from over a shoulder, and there it was again: the death glare.

"As he says, boys." It turned out that the woman—their *mother*—had mastered a commanding tone of her own. Not that that came as any great surprise. She motioned toward her younger son's wriggling pocket, arching an eyebrow. "And Alex? *Outside*."

With the vaguest of nods, they bolted away, their arguing over who was going to get to the kitchen first floating down the corridor. Leaving him alone with the woman. Their mother. The widow, whose clothing in the colors of half-mourning he should have noticed right from the start.

And here he was, still reclining atop a desk while clutching a wet satchel.

He pushed himself to his feet, taking care to jump outward a little, keeping to the right side of the desk. Judging by the way she raised an eyebrow again, he must appear ridiculous, although he would take it over the alternative of having his feet slide out from under him. It was her place, as the wife of a marquess's son, to address him first. Fortunately, she didn't make him wait long.

"Mr. Jeremy Clare, I presume?"

"Indeed." He inclined his head and hurried in her direction before she could approach him and find herself entangled in some other prank the boys had devised. Hopefully, the area nearest the doorway remained safe.

She bobbed her head in return, a clipped, irreverent gesture. "Theo Prescott."

Theo. While he'd known of her existence from the moment his father came to him with the job opportunity, it occurred to him that no one had ever spoken her given name in his presence. Now, he had a name to pair with the heart-shaped face and fiery eyes. It suited her.

"Forgive the interruption," she continued, putting his musings to an abrupt end, "but I was hoping to speak with you for a moment. Alone."

"Certainly." He swallowed, hoping the next time he spoke, his voice wouldn't come out so raspy. They were indeed alone. Even more so than on the street when, for a moment, the world surrounding them had seemed to melt away. An umbrella no longer shadowed her face, and her body was positioned even closer to his, so close he could almost imagine her warmth—

"Before you proceed with this arrangement, I would like to make something clear." She folded her arms across her chest again as if creating a shield. "The Dowager Lady Rockliffe hired you, and it's true that you are in her employ and hers alone. However, while I may have no say in the goings on under this roof, that doesn't change the fact that I'm Ben and Alex's mother. As such, their welfare is of the utmost importance to me. They are not gently bred young boys, accustomed to growing up in a marchioness's household. I cannot imagine they'll make this easy on you, Mr. Clare. And however you choose to deal with that, I will *not* stand by idly if I know they've become unhappy. I will *not* watch you take whatever spiritedness they have left and crush it."

Initially, he'd thought that fire raged only in her eyes. Yet on closer reflection, he could detect it burning upon much of her face. In the plump, pursed lips. In the cheeks stained by a sudden flush. His mind nearly wandered to what that passion would look like in a moment of intimacy. However, he gave himself a discreet but powerful pinch to the leg, forcing himself to remain in the present. The fervor she displayed was that of a mother wanting to protect her children. It was his job to reassure her.

"Few things in life are ever easy, Mrs. Prescott. As for breaking their spirits, that isn't my intention, I assure you."

Her fingers squeezed inward, pressing the mauve fabric of her bodice tight against her chest. "I confess, upon first impression, you aren't what I expected."

He took a small step closer to her. He didn't mean to,

but his feet seemed to have ideas all of their own. "And what did you expect?"

She eyed him, her heated gaze causing an odd prickling to wash across his skin beneath the layers of wool and linen. Until abruptly, she gave a sharp shake of her head. "I understand that you were at Oxford for quite some time."

He nodded, trying to pretend that this were as trivial a conversation as he'd hold with a nondescript acquaintance he passed on the street. "Ten years. First as a student, then as a fellow and instructor."

"I see. And why would you leave such a position in favor of tutoring two unruly boys?"

It was the last question on earth he wished to answer. Yet it was also a perfectly reasonable one.

"Events didn't transpire quite that linearly," he said, choosing his words carefully. "I left Oxford with the intention of becoming a vicar. It turned out, though, that certain arrangements didn't come to pass, and I decided to return to teaching. Albeit in a different way."

Her dark eyes bore into him, making him relentlessly aware of her presence just inches away. "And is teaching your passion, Mr. Clare? Even when facing difficult pupils?"

"I like it well enough." At least he could provide that answer honestly. "Even when facing difficult pupils."

"But still, it's not your passion." She flashed her teeth, though the gesture didn't fully come across as a smile. "Does that lie with the church and the vicarship that has thus far eluded you?"

"No." If only it did, perhaps he wouldn't have found himself in this situation in the first place. Perhaps he should have lied and saved himself any unwanted explanations. Yet she seemed far too adept at reading between the lines for that to do any good. "I find myself most motivated when I have a quill between my fingers and an inkpot nearby."

"Ah, so you're a writer?"

"Only an amateur one. I enjoy novel writing, when the mood strikes."

He cursed inwardly the second the words left his mouth. Before he'd first come to Rockliffe House to interview for the tutor position, his father had emphasized the fact that he should *not* mention his writing hobby. Judging by Theo Prescott's face, it had indeed been the wrong thing to say.

He needed to divert the conversation away from him at once. Could he ask where *her* passions lie? For she definitely had them; the fire radiating from her made that much plain.

"What's this, then?"

He jumped at the unexpected harsh voice, and the distance between them that had grown increasingly smaller turned into a large gap.

Theo—Mrs. Prescott—startled back as well, both of them turning toward the source of the interruption in the doorway. The Dowager Marchioness of Rockliffe strode stiffly into the room, her eyes narrowing at them both. "Theodora, what are you doing up here? And Mr. Clare, where on earth are the boys?"

Theodora—for now that he'd heard her name spoken in full, he most definitely could *not* think of her as plain Mrs. Prescott—straightened her spine, her silky voice becoming tight. "As Mr. Clare is to tutor *my* sons, I wanted to make an introduction."

"As for the boys," he added without delay, "we decided a brief repose was in order. They'll return shortly to carry on with their lessons."

He had no intention of becoming like his father, a man of admittedly weak will who went around in a perpetual state of unease over what the dowager might demand of him next. Almost as if he feared her. With that said, Jeremy was beginning to understand why she might at least inspire awe.

Not because she was particularly large of stature or boisterous in her speech, but because she had a certain way of carrying herself—of looking at people—that commanded attention.

And presently, her focus was on him, her expression nothing short of a disapproving frown. "I hired you to teach. Not to grant reposes after presiding over the schoolroom for scarcely half an hour."

Now it was his turn to draw his shoulders upward. To look her in the eye, after which he may or may not be turned to stone. "Oftentimes, I find that a change of scene and a chance to stretch their legs put pupils in a better frame of mind to concentrate on their studies."

A muscle in the dowager's jaw twitched as, from beside him, Theo made a sound in her throat that quickly became a cough. Maybe he really was going to morph into granite beneath the dowager's icy glare. Except then, her eyes flew to Theo, who became the new recipient of a potent scowl. "Come along, then, Theodora. It would be best if you're not here to interfere when the boys return. Besides, I would like you to accompany Amelia and me to the modiste's. We'll want to ensure you have everything you need for our upcoming soiree."

"Thank you, my lady, but you have already been more than generous in providing me with a wardrobe." The fire in Theo seemed to melt away, turning her words into a brittle murmur. "I couldn't impose on you further."

"Nonsense." The dowager either didn't notice Theo's reluctance or didn't care, for she gave her wrist a slight flick. "This will be your first time out in society, so of course you must show yourself to full advantage. You desired this opportunity, did you not?"

Before Theo could answer one way or another, the dowager pivoted in a stiff half-circle, returning to where she'd first appeared in the doorway. "Come along," she repeated. "I'll call for the coach."

He hadn't meant to stare at Theo, yet that's exactly what he was doing. For somehow, the idea of her bowing meekly to a command was incongruous with what he'd seen of her so far. Nonetheless, she bit her lip and did just that, following in the dowager's footsteps without a single glance back.

In a way, his encounter with her had been agonizing, but now that she walked away, it seemed to be ending much too soon. If only she could have stayed a few minutes longer. If only he could have had a short time more to take in the fire in her dark eyes.

"Theodora." The dowager barked out her name as soon as Theo came up alongside her, and apparently, he was to get his wish, for it caused her to stop just short of the doorway. The dowager stared at her, her forehead creasing. "Why is there mud in your hair?"

Theo's hand flew to the side of her head, running over the spot where Lady Rockliffe's glower rested. As her fingers slid down, they revealed a splotch of pale, crusted mud he hadn't noticed before. One that he may have been foolish enough to reach out and wipe away had it come to his attention earlier.

For the briefest moment, her head twisted to the side, enough that her eyes locked with his. But then, just as quickly, she snapped her attention back to the doorway. "A small mishap," she uttered curtly, maneuvering around the dowager so she could exit the room. "Shall we be on our way?"

The dowager remained planted on the spot, a protest forming on her lips. Ultimately, though, she merely gave a heavy sigh, as if she, too, had dealt with much to try her patience that morning. "You should really take better care.

One can hardly go shopping on Bond Street looking like a disorderly urchin. But never mind. In the interests of not delaying our excursion, I suppose you can find a bonnet large enough to cover it."

He caught a fleeting glimpse of the side of Theo's face as she fled wordlessly into the corridor. Just enough to detect the color that spread over her cheeks.

An uncomfortable knot formed in his chest. Judging by the brief confrontation he'd just witnessed, her life in the dowager's house—under the dowager's command—was far from easy, and adding to her difficulties was the last thing he'd want to do. The profuse need he'd felt to apologize back on the street magnified tenfold. But even more so ... he wished he'd noticed that spot of mud earlier so he could have run a finger through her hair and brushed it away.

"Mr. Clare?"

Lady Rockliffe's voice cut through him like shards of glass, and his neck heated as the realization dawned on him that the dowager hadn't gone marching after her daughter-in-law but remained behind, and she was now looking at him expectantly.

He cleared his throat. "Yes, my lady?"

"I trust that when I happen upon the schoolroom in the future, I'll find the boys hard at work as you preside over their lessons. Which, might I remind you, is the sole reason you were brought into this house."

She didn't give him the opportunity to reply before she made a sharp turn and strode away, her crisp skirts rustling as they skimmed along the floor behind her. Just as well. He would have been hard-pressed to answer with the appropriate level of politeness. Besides, what he'd told Theo was true. Despite what the dowager may wish, he didn't intend to break the boys by imposing a strict schedule of lessons, enforced by even stricter discipline. If he were foolish enough to try, they might break him first.

He sauntered back across the schoolroom, and because his own desk was fraught with perils, he collapsed into the seat of Alexander's child-sized desk instead. This morning's events *almost* made the thought of returning to Oxford appealing. Almost.

He dropped his elbows onto the rough wooden desktop, letting his forehead rest against his fingertips. And promptly caught sight of movement from within Alexander's tin of slate pencils. He snapped his head up, leaning in for a closer look. The tin was half filled with dirt and crawling with earthworms.

Wonderful.

He plucked the dirt-covered pencils out and set them aside, then cupped the tin in his hands. If it stopped raining, perhaps they could bring it outside and turn the excursion into a lesson on zoology. Or something to that effect.

With a sigh, he turned to gaze at the doorway. To check for the reappearance of the boys, obviously. Except as he did, he couldn't help but imagine the dowager's pinched face, peering at him as though she highly doubted his competence. Followed by another face that flashed through his mind with even more vividness. One with dark, glittering eyes and cheeks flushed pink. One that looked at him as though ... as though ... he really had no idea.

As the dowager had so aptly reminded him, he'd come to this house to act as a tutor. Why, then, did it feel like he was the one who'd been given examinations?

Examinations on which his performance had been deemed pitiful at best.

3

"Oh, Theo, I'm hopeless."

Theo glanced up from her drawing, turning to where her sister-in-law, Amelia, sat beside her on the grass of Hyde Park. Amelia pursed her lips, letting her pencil tumble to the ground as she studied her sketchbook. They'd been attempting to draw the weeping beech tree, with its new springtime leaves, that loomed on the other side of the pathway from them, but Amelia's representation of the sprawling branches had turned rather bloblike.

Theo attempted to sound reassuring. "Perhaps you just need to do more ... shading."

Amidst all the miseries that came from living under the Dowager Lady Rockliffe's roof, Amelia provided a surprising spot of light. With her shock of red-blond hair, long-limbed frame, and mouth always ready to turn up in a smile or utter a kind word, she was the opposite of her mother in so many ways—physically and otherwise. Over the years, Theo had heard scattered whisperings about her that could be considered less than flattering. *Peculiar. The plainest of the family. Unmarriageable.* Yet in Theo's opinion, Amelia was delightful—her biggest fault being her willingness to remain at the dowager's beck and call—and she didn't like seeing her grow discouraged.

"Ha!" Amelia's sharp laugh came out more like a grunt. "All the shading in the world couldn't save this drawing."

Fortunately, no true unhappiness clouded the brightness in her eyes, and it was best to keep it that way. Theo flipped her sketchbook closed, dropping it into the unfashionable but practical satchel she'd pilfered from Samuel's old bedchamber. "I've had enough sketching for one day. Shall we continue with our walk?"

"Please." Amelia tossed her sketchbook and pencil into the satchel as well, then scrambled to her feet and began brushing grass from her yellow skirts. Outside the gloom of Rockliffe House, beneath the afternoon sun, her reddish hair and pale skin nearly sparkled. The fact that she didn't have her mother nearby, ready to issue a biting comment at any moment, surely added to the sunniness in her demeanor.

Theo rose as well, making a halfhearted effort to smooth her serviceable gray muslin before sauntering back to the walking path. In a wordless agreement, they linked arms and headed in the direction of the Serpentine, taking leisurely footsteps along the path filled with other visitors who likewise appeared in no hurry. The fashionable hour hadn't yet arrived, but after days on end of dreary springtime rain, the sunshine had drawn people who sought to bask in its warmth out early.

In a stroke of luck—it felt unkind to call it that, but what better word was there?—this rare afternoon of pleasant weather fell on a day when the dowager had kept to her room, saying she was indisposed with a megrim. Meaning that any shopping trips, etiquette lessons, or whatever else the dowager may have planned fell by the wayside.

Not only that, but Theo had managed to invite Amelia along for the outing to Hyde Park without enduring any quips about being a poor influence or unsuitable chaperone. Which was a ridiculous notion in itself, given that Amelia had already reached the age of eight and twenty.

Theo let out a long exhale, tilting her face upward so the sunrays connected with her face beneath the brim of her bonnet. "I feel like I've just escaped from prison."

Amelia gave a little laugh as she mimicked the gesture, allowing the sun to beam down on the dusting of freckles across her nose and cheeks. Yet another action that would have gained them reproach in the dowager's presence, for she was forever emphasizing the need to preserve a flawless complexion.

"Poor Theo. I hope life at Rockliffe House hasn't proven unbearably miserable for you." Amelia lowered her head to look at Theo again, her smile becoming rueful. "I know Mother isn't the easiest person to live with, and she may not always express her opinion or go about getting what she wants in the best ways possible. She really does mean well, though."

Theo choked back a lengthy sigh. "I know." And while it might pain her to admit it, she *did* know. She could think all the uncharitable thoughts she liked about her formerly estranged and now all-too-present mother-in-law, but at the end of the day, the Dowager Lady Rockliffe was the reason she and the boys hadn't ended up on the street.

She swallowed away the bitterness at the back of her throat. "I owe your mother a great deal, and I don't mean to sound ungrateful. I suppose I'm short of patience lately. Forgive me."

"Of course." Amelia gave her arm a light squeeze. "I understand."

Instead of looking up at Amelia, who towered several

inches above her, Theo brought her eyes to the ground below them with a sudden stab of guilt. Despite Amelia's propensity toward cheerfulness, she would have been fully justified in displaying behavior to the contrary. After all, Samuel's death wasn't Theo's burden alone. Amelia, too, had lost an older brother, albeit an estranged one. Not only that, but around the same time, her oldest brother, Nicholas —the current marquess—had taken off for India with no plans to return. Chasing after an errant wife who had run off along with their young daughter, apparently, although no one would breathe a word of it to Theo beyond that. Regardless, the family Amelia had once known was gone, and as she hadn't yet started a family of her own, she'd been left with mainly a demanding mother for companionship. A hard fate indeed.

"Are you looking forward to our soiree next week?" Amelia changed the subject before the brief silence between them could grow heavy, the airiness in her voice betraying none of the hardships Theo had just been contemplating. "I know you expressed trepidation, but I think it might be nice to have a small gathering after our time in mourning. I looked over the guest list, and Mama hasn't thought to include anyone too horrid. Although I should warn you that it contains a disproportionate number of unwedded gentlemen."

"Oh?" Theo felt her cheek twitch. "And is that for my benefit or yours?"

Amelia let out another brittle laugh. "Yours, to be sure. I'm already well acquainted enough with the gentlemen of the ton to know I won't find a suitor among them. Nor do I wish to. That's not to say they're all bad sorts. Only that I'm past the point of desiring that. But for you, Theo, it could be different. If you feel ready, that is."

"I ... perhaps." For Amelia's sake, Theo tried to sound at

least a little enthusiastic, although her assertion fell flat. The soiree had become a daily topic of conversation at Rockliffe House, yet nothing about her involvement in it felt right.

Being a dowager marchioness, Lady Rockliffe could rewrite history as she liked. She could act as the grieving mother coming out of mourning, welcoming a small circle of friends back to her home and introducing them to her darling son's widow. All the while ignoring how said darling son had left his aristocratic family and become a dissipated, excessively imbibing poet while his widow was a lowborn, entirely inappropriate woman who caused horror from the moment he'd first uttered her name within Rockliffe House.

The soiree was likely to be the first of many events in which Theo mingled with high society as if she belonged there. Because, for whatever reason, the dowager had decided to embrace her rather than cast her aside like an unfortunate accident one wished to forget. Theo should be grateful for the outward display of forgiveness and inclusion, yet she couldn't help the suspicions that caused little pangs deep in her chest. *Why*? The question reverberated through her over and over. However, it had to come second to the fact that she and the boys now had a home—and clothing, and food—where they otherwise might not. Besides, if she managed not to botch it entirely, her introduction into society might prove a means to an end where so many of her other plans had failed.

She gave a hardier attempt at mustering enthusiasm she didn't truly feel. "The soiree will provide a welcome diversion, I'm sure. Perhaps you could remind me again of the guest list, so I can begin to learn names ..." Her voice died off as a shout, accompanied by a flash of movement in the distance, caught her attention. They'd drawn nearer to the Serpentine now, where crouched down near the water's edge, on the side of the lake opposite to them, were two boys. They talked animatedly over a pile of unidentifiable materials, accompanied by a man whose nondescript black and gray articles of clothing did nothing to mask the appeal of the tall, lithe frame they covered. The boys' tutor.

"Oh, look." Amelia gazed into the distance as well, although not in the same direction as Theo. Instead, she focused on a spot farther down a side path, where an elaborate barouche containing three young women had stopped so the occupants could wave at her. "It's Lady Rollins and her sisters. They're a decent enough sort, if somewhat silly. Come, I'll introduce you."

"I see Ben and Alex," Theo mumbled, turning her attention back to the opposite bank of the Serpentine. Her boys grasped at materials from the pile in front of them while the tutor watched what they did, keeping himself at a slight distance. At least from this far away, she couldn't make out the prominent green color of his eyes. The overall handsomeness of his features, however, was still all too apparent.

She gently released Amelia's arm, taking a couple steps forward. "I didn't realize Mr. Clare had taken them from the schoolroom. I should go see them and ensure no plans are being devised to throw one another into the Serpentine."

Amelia flashed an indulgent grin in the direction of her nephews. "Yes, certainly, you go along. I'd accompany you, but it looks like Lady Rollins is still waiting for me. She recently wedded an earl, so I imagine she wishes to regale me with stories about married life. I'll join you as soon as I'm through."

With a nod of farewell, Theo continued down the path at a more rapid pace, veering sideways so she'd be closer to the lake. Ever since the morning four days prior when the boys had begun their instruction, she'd avoided interfering in the schoolroom, just as Lady Rockliffe commanded. Partly because she didn't need yet another point of contention between her and the dowager. And partly because ... well, the less she had cause to encounter tutors who stood too close to her, felt inclined to reach out and touch her, and defied all expectations while simultaneously being the exact sort of person she should never show interest in again, the better. However, that didn't mean she would let the potential for a chance encounter with her sons pass her by.

She rounded a bend in the path, drawing close enough to see that the pile in front of the boys contained an odd assortment of twigs, string, scraps of cloth, parchment, and nails. Rubbish, essentially, although it seemed to be causing them excitement.

"No, *I* need that." Alex's voice rang out as he reached into the pile for ... was that a wine cork?

"But *I* need it, too, and I saw it first," Ben snapped, attempting to pry it from his brother's fingers.

"Boys!" Mr. Clare stepped forward, crouching between them before their squabbling could lead to a mishap involving the lake. "There are more corks if you dig to the bottom of the pile, so you needn't fight over this one. An excellent choice of material, by the way."

Alex shoved the cork into his pocket as Ben began a hasty search of the items, both their faces filled with color from the pleasant springtime breeze. Their breeches were covered in grass stains, and their curly hair had taken on the appearance of disheveled mops. Yet they looked enthusiastic —maybe even happy.

Theo's lips twitched upward as she came up behind the trio, still unbeknownst to them. How much time had passed since they'd last spent a carefree day in the park? Back when Alex had been an infant, she would sometimes come to Hyde Park in the mornings to push him about in his perambulator as Samuel strolled alongside her with Ben on his shoulders. Once the boys had grown a little older, Samuel had often brought along a blanket and a book of poems or stories to read them, and Theo packed bags of breadcrumbs so they could feed the ducks.

That had been before all the debts piled up, the whisky consumption became excessive, and Samuel found a new friend in opium. A very long time ago.

"Mama!"

Theo realized her smile had vanished, and she'd been staring blankly into space, although it quickly reemerged at the sight of Alex turning around and gazing at her. He flung the twigs he'd been holding to the ground, leaping up and barreling toward her until they crashed into an embrace. "Mama, we're building sailboats, and we're going to have a race, and I'm going to win. But what are you doing here?"

He took a step backward as if suddenly wondering whether the fervent greeting he'd given her was excessive for a boy of nine. In response, she put a hand atop his head and did a quick sweep of unruly hair, so close in color to Samuel's russet brown. She knew from experience with Ben —two years his senior—that such gestures would soon cause scorn, so she best take advantage of them while she could.

"I was walking with Aunt Amelia," she said, wandering over to greet Ben, where he remained kneeling in the grass, with a light touch on the shoulder. "When I happened to spot my two favorite people off in the distance, I couldn't pass up the opportunity to come over and greet them."

Ben tried to appear reserved, although he couldn't hide the brightness in his eyes as he acknowledged her with a nod. "Good day. Alex is correct about what we're doing, although he did get one thing wrong. *I'm* going to build the best boat and win the race."

He snatched up another two corks from the pile,

causing Alex to dive back to his side and pilfer his own array of supplies.

"*Nicely*, boys," she warned. However, they'd each grown engrossed enough with their creation that they left one another alone.

She strode away from them a few paces, giving them space to work. And giving herself no choice but to confront what she'd thus far avoided.

She'd noticed him, of course. She'd spotted him turning around swiftly and widening his eyes when Alex first called her name. Pulling himself back up to his full height and lingering in the background as she greeted Ben. Now, there was nothing left but to acknowledge him.

"Good day, Mr. Clare." She inclined her head curtly, willing herself to look at him, as simple manners required, without truly noticing anything about his features.

"Good day, Mrs. Prescott. What a pleasant surprise." When he dipped his chin in response, the sunlight caught on the hair below his hat, making the brown look like it was layered with bronze, and—blast, she'd failed in her attempt at indifference already.

She squared her shoulders, keeping her tone quiet and clipped. "A surprise, to be sure. Do you not fear the Dowager Lady Rockliffe's wrath? For I seem to recall her giving you express instructions to keep the boys in the schoolroom, affixed to their books."

He tilted his head slightly, his face clouding over. "And do you agree with these instructions?"

"Of course not, but—"

"Good." He took another few steps away, far enough to be out of the boys' earshot, and blast if she didn't follow as if he led her on a string. "Firstly, I'd like to point out that not all education needs to come from books. What is this activity if not a study of buoyancy? Except when it's presented in this manner, the boys enjoy themselves so thoroughly that they forget to remark on what a dreary lesson it is. Secondly, I may answer to Lady Rockliffe, but I also assured you I would safeguard your sons' happiness. I hold the latter in the highest regard. Even if it earns me wrath from my employer."

Theo's heart gave a ridiculous lurch. She'd made so many uncomplimentary assumptions about Mr. Clare before even laying eyes on him, yet he was turning each and every one on its head.

He'll be sour-faced and stern. Except he was one of the handsomest men she'd ever seen, filled with a spark that drew her to him against her better judgment.

He'll submit to the dowager's will, just like his father. Except he very much had a mind of his own.

He'll not be the type of person you can rely on, for he neglected both his fellowship and church living in favor of a much lower, temporary position. Except none of that mattered when she saw him treat her sons with a rare sort of patience and kindness.

"It would be unreasonable," he continued in a low voice, "to suddenly expect Benedict and Alexander to sit in the schoolroom all day when they've never been made to do so thus far. I recognize that they've experienced a great deal of change lately, including a significant loss. Such things shouldn't merely be swept under the rug. Naturally, there will be an adjustment period, and we needn't try to rush through it. There will be plenty of time in the future for essays and exams."

Dear Lord, why were her eyes burning? She blinked, forcing away the moisture that tried to pool to the surface. She would *not* do anything so ridiculous—so useless—as cry. She'd long since realized that tears got her nowhere, so why waste her time? Yet this unexpected tutor had a strange power of unnerving her at every turn, making her feel the most unusual things at all the wrong moments.

She pivoted away from him, unlocking herself from his green-eyed gaze. "I'm sorry, boys, that I can't stay for your race," she called, taking measured footsteps back toward the walking path. She couldn't get too close, for if they pleaded with her—if Alex threw his arms around her again—the thread keeping her composure intact might snap. "I need to find Aunt Amelia, but I'll look forward to hearing more about your boat-building back at home."

Fortunately, Ben was so absorbed with tying a string around his wine corks and Alex with fashioning a sail from a twig and scrap of cloth that they barely looked up.

"Good day, Mama," Alex murmured, his small forehead creasing as he contemplated how to best attach the materials in his hands. "Too bad you won't be here to see me win."

"Is everything all right, Mrs. Prescott?" Blast, but the tutor had caught up to her, continuing to speak in that low, patient voice.

She swallowed heavily, pushing down the lump in her throat. "Good day, Mr. Clare. And ... thank you."

The last bit came out like a rasp, but at least she managed it before scurrying away with most of her pride still intact. Having him watch her flee like a timid little mouse would be unbearable. Luckily for her, the boys' renewed bickering over the projected winner of the race diverted his attention, leaving her with a clear, unobserved path away from the lake.

She could see Amelia in the distance, still standing by the barouche containing three vivacious, giggling young women. She made a point *not* to go that way. Instead, she crossed the walking path and trod across the grass, not stopping until she reached a large cluster of trees.

She pressed herself against a wide oak trunk on the side

opposite the walking path, letting her body droop as she caught her breath. Why was she behaving so strangely?

She supposed she had good reason to not act herself of late. Going through hardships, one after another, could change a person. The constant burdens of grief, uncertainty, and defeat could weigh heavy on a person's shoulders, leaving them to think and act in ways they normally would not.

However, today hadn't been made up of hardships. Rather, it had involved a carefree afternoon of sketching in the park. Of sunshine. Of piercing green eyes, and seeing her boys happy, and feeling like maybe, the whole world wasn't out to get them after all. It all combined to form a tight, prickling, unnamable sensation that spread across her chest.

Whatever the feeling was, it didn't have the pain of grief or defeat. But it was equally as frightening.

4

"This book is so dull that it makes my head hurt."
Benedict squinted at the page in front of him, his mouth turning down in a scowl.

Jeremy glanced up from Alexander's slate of Latin verb conjugations that he'd taken to his desk to assess, fighting back a sigh. This was growing to be a common theme with their time spent in the schoolroom together, and it was the oddest thing. When he set aside the books and slates and moved their lessons outdoors, such as with their boat-building excursion three days prior, they seemed to tolerate his presence relatively well. Why, he'd nearly dare to say they experienced moments of enjoyment, despite their frequent reluctance to show it. However, when rain confined them to the schoolroom, such as today, it was another matter entirely.

He'd given them the current book they perused, *A New History of the Grecian States*, thinking they might enjoy the battle descriptions. Except they didn't, and the subject matter he chose seemed to have no effect. Whether he presented texts on mathematics, history, geography, language, or a different obscure topic outside a normal course of study, Benedict would look at the pages only a short time before saying his head ached from the tedium. And Alexander, ever eager to keep up with his elder brother and follow his lead, would express his displeasure in turn.

Such as he was doing right now.

"Yes, *exceedingly* dull." Alexander slouched against his desk, pushing away the offending book—the one that had absorbed him in its pages before Benedict's plaintive comment. "It's too hot in here. Why won't the rain stop so we can open the windows? And I'm hungry. We haven't eaten anything in hours."

The temperature seemed nothing more than moderate, and the boys had eaten a hearty luncheon scarcely two hours ago. However, Jeremy knew to pick his battles. He rose to his feet, grateful Benedict and Alexander hadn't taken it upon themselves to grease the floor since the day of his arrival. Nor had he encountered any more rodents or amphibians. A few small incidents had transpired on occasion—like the salt in the sugar bowl with his tea service one afternoon—but they were nothing that surprised him. Nothing that made him march away from the schoolroom in defeat and disgust. Now that the boys seemed to recognize that, the incidents had all but stopped. Even if the complaining hadn't.

He sauntered over to the window, cracking it open as much as he dared without letting the deluge outside trickle in. "Why don't you go down to the kitchen and request a snack? We'll reconvene in half an hour, and perhaps the room will have cooled a little by then. Or better yet, the rain will have stopped, and we can go outdoors." Based on the current weather conditions, the latter appeared unlikely. Yet it was just as well to give them cause to hope, along with an incentive to return as he said.

If the Dowager Lady Rockliffe heard the clatter as they pushed their chairs away and raced out of the schoolroom or caught them as they ran down three flights of stairs to the kitchen in the middle of the afternoon, all three of them would experience no end of chastisement. Fortunately for him, the dowager's absorption with a soiree she was planning had led to a week much lighter in interference and scrutiny than he had imagined.

Hopefully, that trend would continue today, for he had a motive behind caving to the boys' complaints beyond just giving them a chance to stretch their legs. He had a suspicion he needed to address, and the sooner he could do so—without interference from the dowager—the better.

He stepped out into the corridor where, as luck would have it, a footman had just come up the stairs carrying a bucket of coal.

Jeremy hurried over to him before he could vanish behind one of the closed doors. "Could you tell me if Mrs. Prescott is at home?"

The footman's eyes narrowed as if Jeremy had just asked something odd, but ultimately, he nodded. "I believe she's in the library."

Well, that was convenient. The dowager had told him he was free to occupy the library as he pleased to obtain books for the schoolroom. Meaning he could see to this undertaking with much less caution than if Theo had been situated in, say, her bedchamber.

He uttered his thanks and started down the stairs, pushing the thought away at once. Although not before it caused a shock of sensation to rush through him. His reasons for seeking a private audience with her had nothing to do with that, and he would do well to remember it. Besides, what if she wasn't alone? He knew that she sometimes spent time in the afternoons with Lady Amelia. Or worse, she could be in the library with the dowager, discussing arrangements for the soiree.

By the time he reached the ground floor, his pace had slowed considerably as he pondered how he could request a private conversation with her without raising eyebrows. However, as he peeked around the library's heavy wooden door, open just a crack, a lone figure was visible. Theo sat before a large desk near the center of the room, its dark, polished top strewn with sheets of paper. She held a quill in one hand, tapping it against a sheet already partially covered with rows of tidy handwriting, her expression far away. Until suddenly, her quill flew to the inkpot, and she scrawled another couple of lines of evenly sloped letters across her page.

He froze on the spot, even his breathing now feeling too loud. He thought back to his ill-conceived admission of his writing endeavors and the look of distaste she'd given him. But was she a writer as well? He recognized her expression because it mirrored a feeling he'd often experienced himself. That flash of inspiration after a period of thought, when suddenly his quill couldn't move fast enough to get the words out.

It would be nearly an offense to interrupt her, but at the same time, he couldn't imagine her appreciating his observation from the shadows. Even if his reason for watching was that Theo leaning over the desk with a quill in her hand, her ruby lips pursed in concentration and several dark tendrils of hair escaping their pins to frame her face, was one of the most exquisite sights he'd ever witnessed. Moreover, he'd come here with a purpose, one he had a limited time to fulfill before he needed to return to the schoolroom or some other disruption came their way.

"Mrs. Prescott?" He pushed open the door just enough

so he could slide into the library, where he lingered near the threshold. "Forgive the intrusion, but might I have a word?"

Her head darted up at once, her quill halting against the page. "Mr. Clare. I didn't hear you come in." She took a long breath, her face a perfect display of indifference. "Very well."

He crossed the floor with surprisingly measured strides, given that his pulse had quickened beyond its normal rhythm. She made a haphazard attempt at straightening the papers scattered around her as he approached, although her efforts created only a moderate improvement. Immediately, his eyes wanted to travel downward to catch a better view of what she'd been working on, but he had too much confidence in her shrewdness to attempt sneaking a peek at the words. Instead, he stopped on the other side of the desk, fixing his gaze on her alone. His curiosity wouldn't allow him to forgo a subtle allusion to what he'd just witnessed, though. "Again, I apologize if I've interrupted anything."

"It's nothing," she bit out, her dark eyes boring into him. And the longer that happened, the more everything else—even the papers—seemed to melt away, and he could think of nothing but her.

"Well, what have you come to discuss?" She arched an eyebrow just a shade, making him hope he hadn't been standing in silence too long and overtly staring. "I assume this is regarding the boys?"

"Yes," he answered quickly before another awkward pause could crop up between them. However, with that one-word affirmation out of the way, he found himself at a loss regarding where to begin.

Without looking away from him, she crossed her arms over her chest, leaning forward until her elbows hit the edge of the desk. "I realize they aren't the sort of students you expected. Or perhaps they are, depending on what gossip reached your ears before you accepted the position. In any case, I'm sure it became clear to you on the first day that you would experience challenges, and truthfully, you and the boys have fared far better together than I imagined. However, as you may know, I've been warned away from the schoolroom, so if they've done something particularly egregious without my knowledge, you may as well tell me at once."

"Have you ever suspected that Benedict requires spectacles?" He blurted out the question more bluntly than he intended, yet he didn't want her to spend another second coming to erroneous conclusions or experiencing undue worry.

"What?" She jerked upright, a slight vee forming at the bridge of her nose.

"Yes, your boys are spirited, just as you told me, and yes, we've endured certain ... mishaps. That isn't what this is about." He offered a small smile of reassurance, but her face remained stony. "Although the boys might rather expire on the spot than have me recognize this, I find they display great curiosity and intelligence when they let their guard down. At first, I thought some of their more ... *creative* attempts at ridding themselves of a tutor came from a reluctance to accept their changed circumstances. However, I now wonder if the issue stems from something more. Benedict is unwilling to spend any length of time with his books or slate, and he frequently complains of headaches when doing so. He has no difficulties remarking on objects in the distance or responding to questions I ask aloud, when he's so inclined. Reading and written work, though, is another matter entirely. A classmate of mine at Oxford developed a similar issue, wherein he said the words on a page blurred before his face, despite how he was the sharpest-eyed partridge shooter on his estate. As it turned out, a pair of spectacles, designed for improving vision up close, was just what he needed to ameliorate the problem."

"Spectacles?" She turned the word over in her mouth as if it came from a foreign language. One she didn't understand but found offensive just the same.

"If my suspicions are correct, I'm sure you could obtain a pair without too much difficulty." Damn, but his assurances really weren't doing any good. He took an automatic step forward, his knees hitting the back of the desk. This was as far as he could go, then, even though he wanted to be much closer. As if proximity could get his point across and make her understand it wasn't that bad. "He likely wouldn't need to wear them all the time. Perhaps just for reading, or—"

"This isn't about an objection to spectacles!" Her hand lurched against the desk, sending several sheets of paper fluttering to the ground. For a split second, she froze, surveying the result of her clumsiness. Then, her arm swept across the desktop in one deliberate, violent motion, casting the remaining papers into the air before they floated down to form a scattered covering over the Aubusson rug.

Instinctively, he stepped to the side, about to bend down so he could help tidy the disarray. However, the warning glint in her eyes stopped him. Instead, he remained where he was, in the awkward position of towering over the desk as she sat at the other side, gazing up at him.

"Obviously, Ben should have spectacles if that's what he needs. I'll see that he visits an optician right away." Her voice was much quieter now, but the low tone held a note of unsettledness. "At least I can say, with certainty, that he didn't have this trouble when he was young and I first taught him his letters. As the boys grew older, though, Samuel insisted on seeing to their education himself. He didn't wish for my help, and I didn't push it upon him.

He'd received the finest education at Eton and then Cambridge—well, until he got sent down—and I trusted his abilities. An oversight on my part. For the trouble was, Samuel Prescott ... changed, and then he drank himself to an early death. Not, however, before saddling us with crippling debt."

Jeremy had learned as much from his father, although hearing the words come from her lips made them that much more poignant. He opened his mouth to utter ... condolences, perhaps? But a brief motion of her hand silenced him.

"His mother may now wish to erase that inconvenient truth as if it never happened, but I refuse to sweep it all away. For how else am I to explain my situation from the past year?" Her voice wavered just a shade, and she swallowed, preparing herself to keep going. "Do you have any idea what it's like to discover your life filled with trivial comforts and pretty things is actually a lie? Do you know how it feels to watch the person you married transform into someone you no longer recognize? It's a blow that hits you harder than any other could. At least, that's what you believe at first. Until suddenly, that person is gone forever, and you're left alone, except for the creditors who keep showing up at your door and the children who rely on you to provide for them. As it turns out, that hits even harder again, and you experience the blow over and over. You feel it when you watch the contents of your home be carted away, one item after another. When your children tell you they're hungry but there's nothing in the larder. When somewhere in the back of your mind, it occurs to you that they should be at a proper school now, but you have no means of paying the fee. When your one small hope for overcoming debt, the thing you held onto above all else, is snatched away, too, and you have no way of keeping your children off the street besides accepting help from the one source you swore you'd never turn to."

"Mrs. Prescott ..." Again, he tried to think of a suitable response, but no words sufficed. Her chin quivered from the quiet force of her speech, and he wished he could cup it in his palm and tell her, while gazing into her eyes, that all would become well again.

Her stony expression and rigid posture suggested he should still keep his distance. Yet as she took a breath, the severe lines vanished from her face, and when she spoke, the lowness of her tone no longer sounded hard but rather like a concession. "Regardless of any of those things, I still had a responsibility to recognize Ben was struggling. With an issue beyond those brought about by our circumstances, I mean. Because, to answer your question, no, I didn't suspect he needed spectacles. But I should have, as I'm his mother and the only parent he has left. In that, I failed him."

"No." Her last words brought Jeremy to his breaking point. He circled the desk in three brisk strides, coming to rest beside her chair. Because it didn't feel right to keep hovering over her, he sank to his knees, placing his eyes slightly below hers instead of high above. "I didn't tell you this to make you feel like you failed. You didn't."

At first, he thought she might jump from her chair, reclaim the distance between them, and tell him to be gone. Instead, his proximity barely seemed to register. The stiffness seeped from her shoulders, her body slumping against the chair back as if she'd gone numb. It was horrible seeing her like this as a result of something he'd told her. Yet if her current passiveness meant she would sit and listen to what else he had to say until she believed him, he couldn't consider it a total loss.

"You've faced a great many burdens lately, and I cannot begin to express how sorry I am for that. No one could fault you for letting the struggle against these hardships take precedence, and you shouldn't blame yourself, either. If my theory about Benedict needing spectacles is correct, he won't face any lasting effects from not having had them sooner. In the grand scheme of things, this is but a small matter, easily remedied."

She still didn't move from her slumped position in the chair, but the way she blinked as she gazed ahead while not quite looking at him suggested she at least took in what he said. Her hands, dotted with inky smudges, lay pressed across her lap, and his fingers twitched with the urge to reach out and clasp them. Not because she was the striking woman who had captured his attention from the moment he first saw her on the street, but simply because she was a person who deserved a comforting touch. For someone to share in the weight of her burdens.

He shoved his hands into his pockets before his actions could startle her away. He may wish to provide comfort, but that didn't mean she would welcome it. Perhaps she just needed a moment in silence to process all he'd said and recover from the heaviness of her own admission.

He turned to the rug below him, still littered with papers. And because it was as good a task as any, he scooped up the ones surrounding him, gathering them into a pile near her feet. At least that meant he was doing *something*. Certain words flashed before his eyes—*embrace, dissipated, inferno*—all begging to be put into context. Still, he held back, trying to pretend the papers that passed through his fingers were nothing more interesting than an account book.

"Did you know my husband was a writer? A poet, mainly."

Theo's sudden question, spoken in that low, restrained voice, caused his head to snap upward. She peered down at him, assessing him with a measured gaze. Perhaps he hadn't been as skillful at feigning disinterest as he imagined. The thought caused his neck to grow hot and his cravat to become too tight. Fortunately, she didn't appear displeased.

"He published several volumes of poetry with moderate success," she said before he could answer her question. Given that his father was the dowager's longtime man of business, yes, Jeremy did know a little about the reprobate, estranged poet second son. A fact of which Theo was likely aware. "Novel-writing didn't become an interest of his until later. Until ... close to the end. However, he approached it with such fervency that I believed his claims it would be our salvation. I should have realized he was already too far gone. But no matter. The publishers realized it for us. No one would accept his manuscript, despite the illustriousness of his name."

She gritted her teeth, her face contorting as if her mouth had filled with something bitter. "A prudent man would have taken that as a sign to reassess and revise his writing. Or if not that, to indulge his vanity by paying the publisher to print his work. Samuel, on the other hand, purchased a printing press." For the first time, he heard her laugh, though the sound rang hollow. "I'm not sure where the funds came from. I only know that he took me to the little shop on the Strand and said it was ours now, and that he needn't have anything to do with the publishers who rejected him because he would print the book himself. But very shortly thereafter, before he could see it through, he ..."

"I'm sorry," Jeremy choked out into the silence, his words sounding thick.

She dug her fingernails into her skirts, but it didn't mask the trembling of her fingers. "A prudent woman would have cut her losses and moved on. But I couldn't give up on the one thing we'd pinned our hopes on. Samuel had been unusually secretive about his manuscript. He even wrote out the fair copy himself. But after his death, I took the liberty of making another one. Perhaps he'd be very angry at me if he knew, but—well, I revised it. Not because I aspired to become an author myself, but because I thought, if I took my time, I could turn it into what Samuel would have created had he not been dealing with certain ... afflictions. I spent weeks pouring through it before I finally deemed it ready to bring to the printshop. All that remained was for me to restaff the shop, and Samuel's novel could be put out into the world. Its success would enable me to continue employing the printshop staff, which would allow me to take on other customers and, little by little, claw my way out of debt. At least, that's what I'd like to think. Unfortunately, I have yet to find out, as the night before printing was due to commence, a fire razed the shop with the manuscript inside."

Jeremy's breath caught in his throat. He could try to utter another apology, but the words *I'm sorry* felt woefully inadequate. While he may have previously known a little of her situation before she arrived in the dowager's household, the matter of the manuscript and printshop—and their subsequent destruction—came as an unexpected revelation. He stole another glance at the papers he'd collected for her, burning with the suspicion that they held far more significance than he could have imagined.

"Again, a prudent woman—or maybe even a woman with a single shred of sense—would have taken it as a sign that the venture wasn't meant to be. But I couldn't give up. I *cannot*." Her shoulders quivered and her voice along with them, but the fire in her eyes blazed more vehemently than ever. "I lost the first manuscript, so I'm creating another. I lost the printshop, too, but somehow, I'm going to find a way to get it back. Perhaps you think I'm wasting my time or that I'm foolish to entertain such fancies. But without that hope, I don't know how I would bear it."

Her wavering voice finally broke, and she drew in a sharp breath as if sucking back all the emotions that tried to clamber free.

Something in Jeremy broke as well. Something powerful enough to make him cast aside restraint and grasp her trembling hands. Her ink-stained fingers were icy to the touch, and he squeezed them, trying to communicate what he couldn't with words.

He should have known better than to reach out and touch her, this woman to whom he was little more than a servant. If he hadn't recognized that after their first meeting in the street, he should be well aware of it by now. Yet his body had other ideas; in fact, he found himself inching forward until his waistcoat brushed against her skirts. An overstepping of boundaries if ever there was one. Nonetheless, she squeezed back.

There were a great many things he should say to her as they remained hand in hand, in this position of closeness, as they both grappled with the weight of all she'd disclosed. He'd been set to become a vicar, after all. The person to whom parishioners turned when they needed either counsel or comfort.

Instead, a single word crossed his lips as a whisper. "Theo."

She made a barely audible sound in her throat, and her lips parted. But not to form an admonition for his unwarranted use of her given name. She didn't say anything; she merely looked at him. And did his imagination play tricks on him, or was she leaning forward? Drawing even closer to him ...

A rhythmic thump echoed through the corridor, the sound growing louder as it approached the library.

Footsteps, combined with a tap that could only be Lady Rockliffe's cane, an accessory she sometimes used as she moved about the house.

Theo shot out of her seat, wrenching her hands away from his as if his touch scorched her. The abruptness of the movement made his bended knees lurch, causing him to fling out an arm to steady himself. He was left feeling much like the green boy he'd been at seventeen, the time he and a few schoolmates had been caught sneaking back to Trinity College after visiting some of Oxford's more lurid establishments.

With resounding efficiency, Theo swept the papers he'd dropped on the desk into a pile, her ruby lips now pinched together so tightly they turned white, and—bollocks, why was he still on the floor staring at her?

He scrambled to his feet, damning the unsteadiness in his legs and the even worse tremulousness in his head. Why did this keep happening? Why did he put himself in a position to *allow* this to keep happening? At least this time, they'd detected the dowager's encroaching presence before she peered at them from the doorway. However, that minute victory brought but cold comfort.

He had the presence of mind to stride away from the desk and examine one of the floor-to-ceiling bookshelves. He could say that much for himself if nothing else. But by that time, Theo was already across the room with her stack of papers in hand, flinging open the door. She stopped only long enough to give a wordless curtsey to an undetectable figure in the corridor. Then, just as quickly, she was gone, replaced by a sight he'd known was coming but made him stiffen his spine nonetheless. The dowager.

Lady Rockliffe muttered something under her breath, her eyes narrowing as she gazed at the spot where Theo had just flown past her. He could see the reprimand on her lips, the inclination to call her back and demand an explanation for such abruptness. Ultimately, though, the dowager gave her hand a little flick, ignoring the flurry in the corridor and trudging into the room with slow, dignified footfalls.

He could nearly breathe a sigh of relief. *Nearly.* For having her attention turn to him instead was only a minimal improvement.

"Forgive my intrusion. I came to get a book for the schoolroom and will be heading back up directly." He grabbed the first volume he could reach, flipping open the leather-bound cover to glance at the title page. *A Copious Dictionary in Three Parts.* He promptly snapped it shut again, tucking it under his arm. Given he had no intention of actually reading it, one book was as good as another if it allowed him to make a hasty departure from the library and the dowager's scrutiny.

"A moment, if you please, Mr. Clare." The dowager shifted her cane outward, placing it in front of his path as he hurried toward the door, his eyes staying focused on the rug.

He should have expected as much. *Of course* he wouldn't escape the library without another lecture on his idleness and lack of effectiveness as a tutor. He tensed his muscles, preparing for a rebuke.

However, when he chanced to look upward, the dowager's narrow face had softened, making her appear almost placid. "As you may have heard already," she said, "we are holding a soiree here at Rockliffe House this Saturday evening."

He blinked, his nod coming slower than it should have. Anyone who had come within twenty feet of Rockliffe House over the past week would know a soiree was happening on Saturday for all the discussion and preparations that had gone into it. But what did that have to do with him?

"I've decided I would like Benedict and Alexander to come down for the first of it so they can receive an introduction to our guests. They're the grandsons and now nephews of a marquess, after all, and it's high time they be seen by the society to which they rightly belong." She gave a single nod as if assuring herself of the soundness of her plan. "As the boys have done well under your tutelage thus far, I would like you to stay and accompany them to ensure they behave in a manner that's fitting."

Well. That was a far cry different from the rebuttal he'd anticipated. Not that he was complaining. The subtle praise was just so ... unexpected.

The events from a few minutes prior may have turned his thoughts into a tangled heap, but regardless, he managed to answer quickly. "As you wish, my lady."

She was likely overestimating his ability to elicit the type of flawless behavior she'd expect from the boys on such an occasion. However, if she wished to believe he possessed a scrap of competence after all, he certainly wouldn't object. Besides, what if there was a chance his presence could make the introduction to a crowd of strangers easier on the boys? For though they may occasionally wish him bodily harm, he seemed to have developed a soft spot for them.

Not to mention, Theo would be there, also navigating through a society that was foreign to her. Perhaps also in need of a helping hand. He had no right to place himself in such a position with her, of course. That didn't mean he lacked the desire to.

"Well then, Mr. Clare, I see no further reason you should neglect your current duties in the schoolroom." The dowager turned pointedly toward the door, giving her cane a little tap against the floor to signal he'd been dismissed.

He almost laughed. *There* was the criticism, arriving just slightly later than estimated. It would have hardly felt like a proper conversation with the dowager without it. In any case, because it signaled an end to this encounter, he welcomed it gladly.

After bobbing his head and uttering a farewell, he burst through the doorway, taking in a breath of air from the corridor, which somehow felt lighter than the air he'd left behind. If he knew what was good for him, he would run all the way back to the empty schoolroom and prepare for the return to lessons. Instead, he found his feet moved slowly as he made his way to the staircase and up each step. He'd always made better sense of things while he was moving, and at present, he had quite a lot to sort.

His job was solely to provide an education to the dowager marchioness's two grandsons. Not to trouble himself with the circumstances that had brought them into her household. Certainly not to involve himself with their mother. He had no business wanting to share in her burdens. Or to get closer to her. Or to imagine more than just a stolen touch or some hushed, hurried words.

He shouldn't have wanted any of it. But he did all the same.

5

Theo stood in front of the full-length mirror in the back corner of her bedchamber, assessing the stranger who peered back. For nearly the past seven months, her wardrobe had consisted of black bombazine and crepe, occasionally mixed with muslin in either mauve or gray. All colors that made her look sallow and emphasized the gauntness that had overtaken her face.

Tonight, folds of scarlet satin draped across her body, and while the dress remained free of ornaments aside from some subtle lace detailing around the hem and sleeves, it clung to her in a way she could almost deem agreeable. Not to mention how the color provided a pleasing contrast with her dark hair—which had been meticulously subdued and then styled, with the help of a copious number of pins, by Amelia's lady's maid—and brightened her complexion. She could nearly imagine herself as the girl she'd been a decade prior, reclining in salons with her sketchbook or palette in hand, taking in poetry recitations and pretending she didn't feel gentlemen's eyes falling upon her.

She gave her head a shake, making the ringlets against

her neck and temples bob, and spun away from the mirror. That had all been a long time ago, and she certainly wasn't that girl anymore.

With a sigh, she ambled over to her bed and lowered herself to sit on the edge of the plush counterpane, careful not to wrinkle her skirts. She should really be down in the drawing room by now, for it was past eight, the soiree's commencement time. But perhaps she could take just one more moment alone first.

From across the room, the mirror gave her another glimpse of her reflection. Another reminder of the finery she'd received and the charade in which she took part. A familiar pang of guilt stabbed at her belly for what could rightly be considered her ungratefulness. She was in the enviable position of having all her debts—Samuel's debts— bought up as if they'd never existed. Not only that, but the dowager had then given her and the boys a home at one of the finest addresses in London and proceeded to bestow more clothing and fripperies on her than she could possibly need.

Anyone else would have jumped at such an opportunity rather than turn it away until there was no choice left but to accept. However, no number of material goods would make Theo forget what had transpired the first time she entered Rockliffe House as a girl of eighteen. The dowager had at least shown the grace to ask for a private word with Samuel, after the three of them had passed an uncomfortable quarter-hour sipping tea in the sitting room, before she'd started screaming. Although her admonitions had easily traveled into the corridor, where Theo lingered behind the closed door. *What could you possibly mean by bringing such a creature into this house? She said her deceased mother was an Italian opera singer? And her father is responsible for encouraging your ridiculous poet aspirations. It was bad enough for you to get sent down from Cambridge, but* this? *There are certain types of women the spare to a marquessate may seek out when he desires entertainment, provided he is discreet. There are other types of women suitable for him to bring home to his family when he has the intention of forming a union. You seem to have gotten the two confused.*

Theo's fingertips inadvertently brushed against her midsection, landing in the same place where her hand had shot on that long-ago day to cradle the tiny bump that wasn't yet visible through her gown. She could still taste the bitterness that had risen in her throat, could still feel the heaviness that had settled in her chest as she waited for Samuel to recoil from the admonition and admit he recognized the error of his ways.

But he hadn't. She'd been wrong to doubt him for even a second, for he'd yelled back just as heartily. *Theo and I are getting married, and I don't need your damned blessing. I don't need anything. If Nicholas deems me too disgraceful to receive an allowance, so be it. I'll make my own way. As a* poet. *None of you need worry about us darkening your door again.*

Theo shifted her arm, pressing her fingers into the counterpane to steady herself. Maybe the dowager's insults, and her subsequent shouting about how she wanted nothing more to do with him, shouldn't matter any longer. Time changed people. As did loss. Even if the dowager marchioness would never stoop so low as to apologize, it could be she regretted those long-ago words or had come to feel differently.

That still didn't make anything about what Theo did at present feel right. She was supposed to be a printshop owner, working hard to maintain the legacy Samuel had tried to build and might have succeeded at had circumstances been different. Instead, she'd gone crawling back to the one place he'd sworn they would never return, trying to pretend she belonged there, amongst people who would just as easily shun her should the dowager have another change of heart.

But doing so could help lead you away from this house. Back to where you belong. That little voice in the back of her head never missed the opportunity to try convincing her of the correctness of what she did. In fact, it didn't shy away from suggesting an uncomfortable but obvious way forward. *Be charming enough that your background won't matter. Catch a gentleman's eye. Remarry wisely, so you and the boys will want for nothing, and your time under this roof will come to an end*.

The plan sounded so easy, in theory. So sensible and direct, which was exactly what she needed. Yet her stomach knotted in protest, and though the little voice remained insistent, she never knew whether to believe it. Or whether she had it in her to go through with the plan.

A few gentle taps sounded against her doorframe. "Theo?"

She turned at once to see Amelia peeking into her bedchamber, her normally pale cheeks flushed pink. "Forgive my intrusion." Amelia took a tentative step into the room, her voice breathy as if she'd been running. "The guests are arriving with surprising promptness this evening, and Mother is wondering where you are. She's about to send a housemaid up to check, but I slipped away so I could see you myself first. I wanted to make sure you're all right."

Theo managed a small smile. Despite her many misgivings about living at Rockliffe House, she experienced, not for the first time, a pang of appreciativeness that her sister-in-law behaved so differently from the dowager that it was difficult to believe they were kin.

She got back to her feet, taking a moment to smooth her

skirts and ensure all her hairpins remained in place. Let no one have cause to fault her appearance. "I'm well, thank you." After one final glance across the room to the mirror, she joined Amelia by the doorway, ignoring how her beautiful but impractical beaded silk slippers pinched her feet. "Shall we go down together now?"

"Indeed. After a dreary winter, it's lovely to see the drawing room filled with people, and I'll be happy to introduce you." Amelia led her into the corridor, where light from the sconces brought out the copper color in her hair and made the beading against her pale green dress glimmer. "Lady Rollins, whom you saw at the park, has arrived, along with the earl. And Lord and Lady Stanton, and ..."

Theo really should have kept paying attention, but as she took small steps across the carpet and then down the stairs while continuing to gaze at Amelia, tall and resplendent beside her, she couldn't help the way her mind wandered.

Did Amelia show such enthusiasm for every party she attended? For some reason, Theo had imagined they would share a little of the same discomfort at such an event. Perhaps because she'd never heard Amelia speak of any of these esteemed members of society with particular affection, nor had Amelia deemed any of them suitable for marriage. Then again, maybe flitting about a drawing room as if one belonged there became easier with practice, and Amelia had been practicing her whole life.

Theo nearly asked her secret to appearing so serene, but her thoughts quickly took another turn. They'd reached the open double doors of the drawing room, revealing a crowd of elegantly dressed strangers mingling within. None of them made an impact on her, though. Not when in the far corner of the room stood Ben and Alex, both with their unruly hair combed flat to their heads and wearing a new pair of navy breeches. Accompanied by none other than Jeremy Clare, looking every bit the gentleman in a smart black coat and intricately knotted white cravat. Mild nerves had made her stomach flutter as she descended the stairs, but now it seemed to be doing full flips.

What were any of them doing here? She'd just assumed the boys would prefer keeping to their room for the evening and that she would go up and say goodnight to them later. As for Mr. Clare ... why was he not already back at his lodgings, where she wouldn't have to try ignoring the fact that only a few corridors and sets of stairs—or in this case, only a few people and pieces of furniture—separated them? She hadn't seen him for a few days, not since the afternoon when she'd broken down and revealed far more than was warranted. Their lack of contact had nothing to do with her avoiding him, for that would be cowardly. It was simply because ... well, it was just better that way.

"Amelia," she hissed close to her ear, just loud enough to be heard above the music that came from the pianoforte. "Did you know Ben and Alex were in attendance?"

Amelia followed her gaze to the opposite side of the room until she, too, caught sight of the trio. Except they were a trio no longer, for out of nowhere, the dowager emerged beside them, accompanied by another silver-haired lady and gentleman.

"I didn't see them when I was in the drawing room earlier, although Mother did mention something about bringing them down for an introduction," Amelia said as they both watched three brunette heads—Ben's, Alex's, and Mr. Clare's—bow in greeting. "Did she not say anything of it to you?"

"No." Theo was already stepping forward, trying to determine the least obstructed path to reach them. From this angle, she couldn't make out the expressions on the boys' faces and whether they contained scowls or stuck-out tongues. Nor could she detect if Alex had thought to stuff a frog, or something equally disagreeable, in the pocket of his dignified new coat. Perhaps it would be best for all three of them to flee upstairs and forget this business of a high-society soiree.

"Good evening, Lady Amelia."

Just like that, her opportunity to snatch up the boys and bolt vanished, for a dignified middle-aged gentleman stopped right in front of them to offer a greeting. He was tall and broad-shouldered enough to block her view of what transpired in the corner, even when he inclined his head. Would it be unthinkably rude to step around him?

But Amelia had clasped her arm, holding onto her even as she curtseyed, offering him a smile that appeared genuine. "Good evening, Lord Pembrook. Please allow me to present my dear sister, Mrs. Theodora Prescott. Theo, this is Viscount Pembrook, a neighbor of ours at Beaumont Manor in Kent."

Theo folded her legs into a curtsey, tilting her body to the side as she went so she could chance a look across the room. Fortunately, no one had jumped away in horror or let out an indignant shriek. In fact, the group appeared engaged in a perfectly ordinary conversation, and at worst, she could describe the boys' posture as signifying boredom.

She rose to find the viscount peering at her, not unkindly, with pale eyes that crinkled slightly at the corners. Amelia, whose added height meant she could better survey the situation across the room, shot her a glance. "I just remembered that Mother asked to see me," she murmured, her fingers pressing reassuringly into Theo's arm. "If you would both please excuse me."

"I—of course," Theo replied in time with the viscount's "certainly." While she'd been about to form a protest, she didn't even want to think about the consequences with the dowager should she behave impolitely enough to cause a scene. Besides, Mr. Clare appeared to have matters under control, and she had even more confidence that the boys would feel at ease and behave under the influence of their aunt's gentle presence. Furthermore, if Amelia thought to check on the boys on her behalf, thereby leaving her alone with this man, she must not consider him objectionable, for she wasn't the sort to do something deliberately unkind.

Theo spent a single moment watching Amelia's retreat —in the direction of the figure she could no longer see but knew all too well still stood there—before squaring her shoulders and turning to Lord Pembrook, trying to mimic Amelia's welcoming smile. If she was going to stay in the drawing room and socialize, this seemed as good a place as any to start.

"I'm very pleased to meet you, Mrs. Prescott." The viscount had a low, silky voice that matched well with the pleasantness of his features. "I'm an admirer of your late husband's work. And, if I'm correct as to your identity, your late father's as well."

She felt the smile slip from her face. She hadn't realized her father's poetry had made its way to members of the ton. Samuel's either, for that matter, although it made sense that the scandal of his deflection and estrangement would cause curious former acquaintances to purchase his work. She studied the viscount, looking for any trace of scorn behind the seemingly innocent compliment. But nothing in the way he looked at her in return suggested anything less than sincerity.

"Thank you," she managed, giving her arms a subtle shake to ward off the tension in them. The longer she peered at Lord Pembrook, the more it became apparent that he was really quite good-looking. The pale blue of his paisley waistcoat brought out the same color in his eyes, providing a striking contrast to his neatly clipped hair, nearly black except for where it grayed at his temples. Judging by the faint lines etched into his forehead and around his mouth, he had to be well into his forties, if not more. Yet any signs of age only served to give him a look of distinguished maturity. Contrasting with the face in the corner that his position concealed, the one that drew her in with its green eyes and youthful handsomeness.

"Given all these influences, do you write poetry as well?"

His question made her realize she was beginning to tilt sideways again, and she snapped herself upward, the flutters low in her belly becoming a sensation that contained far more weight. "You could be forgiven for thinking so, but I do not."

Best not tell him she was probably better off for it. For where had writing poetry gotten her father in the end? Sitting at his desk night after night with a quill in one hand and a whisky bottle in the other until his heart had given out, and he'd been found like that, on a morning five years prior, stone-cold dead. And as for Samuel ...

She blurted out the first thing she could think of; anything to steer away from this topic. "Actually, I far prefer drawing and painting."

"Do you?" Lord Pembrook's face lit up, suggesting she'd said just the right thing. "I must confess that while I appreciate poetry, I have an even greater fondness for art. Not that I have any talent for creating it, but I'm always looking to add to my collection of paintings at Rosemead—my estate in Kent—and I enjoy visiting the Royal Academy. Have you been to the new summer exhibition yet?"

"I fear I haven't had the time." In truth, doing something of that nature—attending an event for the sole purpose of enjoyment—hadn't crossed her mind with everything else going on.

"I was planning to go next week." The viscount gave her another of his earnest smiles. "Would you be interested in accompanying me?"

The stiffness she'd been trying to shake from her limbs seized them again. It was a perfectly congenial request made by a perfectly pleasant man. Why, then, did all her pent-up doubts hit her at once? No matter what the dowager deemed appropriate, or what her inner voice tried convincing her she needed to do to escape Rockliffe House, she'd been in mourning for less than a year. It was all happening so fast, and she didn't belong here, mingling amongst these people as if it were her birthright.

"I'm a widow," she mumbled, praying the heat in her face didn't show. "It's only been seven months ..."

"And I'm a widower." On another person, eyes that blue might have looked icy, but with him, they exuded pure warmth. "It's been eighteen months for me. A longer period of time, but still recent enough for me to mourn the loss. If you'll forgive my bluntness, Mrs. Prescott, I didn't ask you for a courtship or anything in that regard. I extended the invitation because we have a mutual interest, and I thought we might pass a pleasant afternoon in one another's company, getting to know one another a little better. If Lady Amelia has not yet attended the exhibition, perhaps she'd like to come as well."

Her skin burned hotter, and she let out a short, rueful laugh. The viscount must think her the worst kind of ninny. At least, he would if he were the type of person prone to malice, which seemed less and less likely with each second they spent together. She'd overreacted, of course. Going with him to the exhibition didn't have to mean anything beyond that. And so what if it turned out that it did? In the end, wouldn't that get her what she wanted—her freedom?

She reached up to push back a curl threatening to escape its pin, flashing a tiny grin that was no longer forced. "I don't know why I said that. I would be pleased to attend the exhibition with you."

Lord Pembrook's face brightened even further. "I'm glad to hear it. It will be a pleasure to attend the exhibition with someone who has a true appreciation for art. I'll look forward to seeing your own artwork at some point as well."

"I could fetch some to show you right now." Blast, but why did she keep blurting out the wrong thing? When she and Samuel had hosted soirees, the guests took great delight in the way she circulated through the room, choosing someone to sketch at random and then putting her work on display. But based on the viscount's slight pause, perhaps that wasn't done at ton parties.

The pause, though, quickly gave way to an encouraging nod. "I'd love to see your work, Mrs. Prescott."

"A moment, then. I'll return shortly." She dipped into a quick curtsey, forcing herself not to run. That brief encounter had gone ... well. Hadn't it? However, while the thought of returning to Lord Pembrook with her sketchbook, and having him appreciate her work, filled her with more anticipation than she would normally deem sensible, she had another, opposing, motive for suggesting such a thing. Namely, so she could have a short reprieve from the crowded drawing room as she fetched her book. So she could collect herself and go back to the scene without making another series of blunders.

And perhaps she even had a third motive. With Lord Pembrook no longer in front of her, she had an unobstructed view of the corner. But where Ben, Alex, and Mr. Clare had once stood, only strangers remained. Her eyes swept around the room, going from person to person. The dowager had moved to one of the green velvet settees, sitting atop it regally as she conversed with Amelia and an unknown gentleman. However, there was no sign of the boys. Or Jeremy Clare.

They must have all slipped out just moments ago. Had the dowager decided they'd received enough introductions? In any case, after their unexpected appearance here, their exit had come with no fanfare of the negative variety, which she should consider a very good thing.

And she did. Yet as she escaped the room, careful not to lock eyes with anyone in a manner that would necessitate her stopping to talk, she couldn't help the small stab of disappointment that pierced her between the ribs.

She could still go up to see the boys later and bid them goodnight, just as she'd previously planned. Ask them how they'd fared during their brief time in the drawing room. But despite the reassuring voice of reason that echoed through her head, the twinge in her abdomen wouldn't abate.

She stopped in the middle of the empty corridor, bending down to pull off her too-tight slippers. Relief came at once as she wriggled her cramped toes free. *There.* Maybe the problem actually stemmed from discomfort in her feet, and this little break would set her right again.

Why, then, had she begun glancing around the corridor as if looking for someone? As if maybe he still lingered nearby.

No. She was *not* going to entertain such thoughts right now. Or ever. Her sole undertaking needed to be going to the library to retrieve the sketchbook she'd left there, putting her slippers back on, and returning to the viscount who had showered her with affability.

Anything—any*one*—beyond that was excess she didn't need in a life already fraught with complications.

6

By the light of his candle, Jeremy scanned the shelves of Rockliffe House's impressive library—for real, this time—seeking out books he could add to the schoolroom. In truth, he was no better able to concentrate on the task than he'd been several days prior when Lady Rockliffe's sudden interruption had sent him dashing away from Theo and over to the bookshelves. Nonetheless, he wasn't quite ready to step out of Rockliffe House and into the drizzly dampness of an unusually chilly May night. Only to travel back to his solitary, equally chilly bachelor's lodgings with nothing for comfort but his quill and imagination.

With that said, a little cold might do him good. Might help dispel the uncomfortable heat that had settled in his chest. It was the solitariness he couldn't abide. The sitting alone in a dim room as he imagined Theo, magnificent in her scarlet gown, illuminated by numerous wall sconces as some titled gentleman made her laugh.

The door made a slight creaking sound as it slid open, accompanied by the rustle of skirts. Jeremy grabbed the copy of *Robinson Crusoe* he'd set aside at the front of a shelf and turned, ready to take his leave. The library's closed door and lack of illumination, aside from a low fire, had made him think it wouldn't be in use this evening. But perhaps a duo of guests had decided to partake in an illicit tryst.

He was already halfway across the room, prepared to bow his head in a gesture that was part polite acknowledgment, part apology, when his candle flashed across a fold of scarlet satin. His feet halted beneath him while his hand brought the candle upward, little by little, to determine what—whom—he'd encountered. Even though his pounding heart seemed to already know the answer to that question. His first glimpse of scarlet had given him cause to believe he'd imagined what he most wished to see into fruition.

The flickering flame revealed smooth, flawless skin, the generous swell of breasts where they emerged from the figure's bodice, and dark curls that rested against her neck and temples. Also, black eyes that flashed at him in the dimness. "What are you doing here?" Theo took in a quick breath before pursing her lips.

He motioned toward his book, trying to forget the encounter they'd had in this very room mere days ago. Trying to pretend that the fact she'd turned up here again when he hadn't laid eyes on her since, looking more achingly beautiful than he'd ever seen her, didn't affect him in the least. "Just fetching something for the schoolroom. For tomorrow." His voice came out *too* cheerily, to the point of sounding artificial. If he knew what was good for him, he'd follow through with his original plan of making a swift departure, like a member of the household staff ought to do. But how could he, when those eyes—that unfiltered loveliness—continued to hold him in?

"I see." She shifted, folding her arms across her chest. "I was unaware you'd stayed late this evening and that you and the boys would be attending the soiree. I assume that was at Lady Rockliffe's request?"

"Yes." He held the candle up a little farther again, watching as the light bounced off her features. Was she angry? "I didn't know Lady Rockliffe neglected to apprise you of the arrangement. I assure you, I would have said something to you otherwise. Would you have preferred Benedict and Alexander didn't attend?"

For a moment, she simply looked at him with an unreadable expression, the candlelight casting shadows across her arched eyebrows and high, defined cheekbones. But then, she let out a quiet sigh, allowing her arms to drop back to her sides. "I suppose it's just as well. Like me, they need to be introduced to the society of which their grandmother now insists they are a part. If it was bound to happen sooner or later, then why not get started tonight? I merely thought the dowager would consider them unprepared for such an undertaking just yet, although far be it from me to understand her whims. I trust the necessary introductions took place without incident?"

He made a low sound that was nearly a laugh, his mind flashing back to the schoolroom's slippery floor and assorted vermin that had accompanied his introduction to his new pupils. That had taken place a mere fortnight ago, but for all that had happened since then, it seemed much longer. Almost long enough to make him see humor in the pranks. Definitely long enough to make him appreciate the progress they'd made together. "I'm pleased to report that no amphibians, rodents, or any other type of objectionable creatures or objects made an appearance this evening. The boys bowed when required, were remarkably patient as Lady Rockliffe and her peers exclaimed over them, and Alexander signaled his desire to leave with nothing more dramatic than a yawn. They eagerly retreated to their bedchamber, and while I cannot confidently say they enjoyed their time in the drawing room, they passed it without complaint. Lady Rockliffe was pleased, I think. I hope you are as well."

"Yes. Indeed." Her voice came out thin and tight, lacking all its usual power. Was it possible for a person to express both joy and sorrow at the same time? For on one hand, her slight smile from hearing him speak about her sons couldn't mask her pride. But on the other, a crease formed between her eyebrows as if she'd just solved a riddle to which she didn't like the answer.

His fingers twitched against the candle holder. There it was again, that powerful urge to reach out and touch her, to offer comfort despite what the rules of propriety allowed.

She spun away from him before he had the chance, heading toward the center of the room. "I should let you get back to your task, Mr. Clare. I'll just fetch my sketchbook and be on my way."

For the first time, it occurred to him that she clasped her slippers in one hand while her feet were clad only in stockings. That's why she glided so noiselessly across the floor, and somehow, that added intimacy made his fingers burn to touch her even more.

But more importantly ... her sketchbook? She'd reached the vast desk that stood as a midpoint between two opposite walls of bookshelves. The same place he'd come across her before, hard at work with her paper and quill. He'd been mistaken about her pursuits as a writer—as she'd revealed herself to be more of a copyist—but he hadn't stopped to consider if she had other hobbies instead. Ones that belonged to her alone, not shared with her late husband.

"Are you an artist?" It wasn't his place to ask about her favorite pastimes or talents as if they were old acquaintances. He had no cause to stay in the library now that his duty was done for the night. No cause to turn back from the door, to tread across the floor in her direction. But he did anyway, unable to take his eyes from the leather-bound sketchbook she retrieved from a drawer. Curiosity bubbled within him, demanding a closer look. Why was it that when he discovered an unknown facet of her, it only fueled his desire to learn more? Perhaps it was due to his suspicion that when Theodora Prescott put her heart into something, she did it extraordinarily well.

"I suppose you could say that. I may not be a gently born lady, but drawing is one skill I possess that could be deemed acceptable by the ton." She clasped the book tightly beneath her arm, eliminating his hopes that he'd catch a glimpse of its contents. "Or deemed acceptable by at least one viscount, in any case."

His free hand clenched into a fist at his side as the heated feeling in his chest returned with fresh vehemence. Her declaration—specifically, her reference to the viscount, who'd stood before her and chatted with stars in his eyes—should have had no more effect on him than if she'd commented on the weather. But it did. Oh, it did.

"Theo ..."

He didn't mean to breathe out her name. Nor did he intend to step forward as she crossed the room so their paths intersected. His feet moved across the rug and the name escaped his lips just the same.

She halted abruptly so they didn't collide, sucking in a quick breath of air. Her stockinged feet—her whole scarlet-clad body—were just inches away as she peered up at him, waiting. Which left him with a difficult conundrum. What the hell was he going to say next? *Don't go. Don't return to the viscount. Stay here instead, with me. I want to learn everything about you.* No, those would hardly make for suitable topics of conversation. Even though they were the only words that pounded through his head.

"Why do you do that?" Her sharp tone cut through the silence, sparing him the need to form a proper sentence. Just as well, given how their proximity seemed to have eradicated that ability. As if his composure weren't already dangling by a thin enough thread, she stabbed a black-gloved finger into his chest, creating a sensation fiery enough to burn straight through to his skin. "Why do you always stand so close to me? Why do you feel the need to reach for me? Why do you use my given name when you have no right to it? Why do you consider yourself free to partake of such intimacies?"

She glared at him, her eyes flashing in the dimness like two glittering pieces of onyx. Her anger should have made him jump backward, apologize, flee. Yet it was as if the finger in his chest had locked him in place. As for intimacies ... it was fortunate she couldn't see the type that began running through his mind.

For the first time, he noticed that her hard, searing finger had begun trembling against him. Her other hand, the one clutching her slippers and sketchbook tightly against her side, wavered, too. Until, with the faintest rustle, a lone piece of paper slipped free, floating to the floor.

It was enough to undo the magnetic effect of her finger against his chest. As if by reflex, he bent down to retrieve it for her, just as he'd done with the scattered pages of her manuscript when they'd shared those moments of closeness, when she'd granted him her trust. Moments he desperately wanted to get back.

He had no intention of staring at something she'd never meant to show him. However, the light of his candle flashed over the paper he picked up, and suddenly, he couldn't look away.

The page displayed a lifelike sketch of a person. A man. *Him.* Crouched down beside the Serpentine, a slight smile on his face as he gazed over his shoulder at an unknown something or someone. Her sons, if she'd drawn the sketch from the memory of their boatbuilding in the park. Yet the sketch featured him and him alone.

Her hand darted out, snatching the paper from his grasp and shoving it back into her book. Far too soon, for he could have gazed at her creation, dumbfounded, for countless minutes longer. But although the sketch had vanished from sight, he knew what he'd seen. And she knew it, too.

Even the dimness couldn't conceal the flush that spread across her cheeks, traveling down to her neck and chest, disappearing below the neckline of her bodice. Were he to touch her, would her skin feel hot beneath his fingertips? Much like his own, which burned beneath too many layers of clothing.

It would; of course it would. In fact, she stood so close he could practically feel the heat radiating from her each time she exhaled. Her eyes widened, her lips parting to form a small o. No longer a look of ire. No, this was something else. But something equally as fierce, as captivating ...

Did he move forward? Did she? In any case, their lips connected, sending a shower of sparks coursing through his body. Her mouth was every bit as soft and full as he'd imagined, the pressure of it against his every bit as intense.

The copy of *Robinson Crusoe* slid from beneath his arm, hitting the floor with a thud, as he reached out to encircle her waist. Not that the book mattered. Nothing mattered beyond her body pressed against his, covering him with an intoxicating blend of pliability and warmth, filling his nose with the scent of something sweet and floral—lilacs?—but also enticing. With his lips still molded to hers, he fumbled sightlessly behind him until his candle holder connected with the desktop and he could release it from his grip. His jerky movement snuffed the flame, but that didn't matter, either. He had no need for extra light when he now had a second hand free to explore her. He brought it to her neck, to one of the inky curls that hadn't been confined by pins. His fingers itched with the yearning to pull the rest free, to run through the thick tresses as they spilled over her back. Instead, he trailed his fingertips down her throat and to the bare skin above her bodice. All while her lips parted wider, and the tip of her tongue brushed against his, giving him his first true taste of her.

He responded to the invitation emphatically, plunging into her mouth so his tongue could circle over hers, desperate for more. There was another low thump as something else hit the carpet. Her sketchbook, it vaguely registered within his mind. Followed by her slippers. She brought her hands to his shoulders, her nails digging in as they established a rhythm—an alternation between light, teasing flicks and ardent strokes that allowed him to truly drink her in.

Flames licked through his limbs while insistent bursts of yearning shot straight to his groin. Her breasts were crushed tight to his chest, a fact that made his cock strain against his breeches in response. There was no way she could remain unaware of how badly he wanted her, and perhaps that was his sign to pull away now before they kissed each other into oblivion and crossed a line from which there was no going back. He would just take one more moment, one more taste—

She shifted, dragging herself along his hardness with a husky sigh that vibrated through him. A moan tore from his throat before getting swallowed up in their kiss, and any brief musings he had about releasing her from his grasp evaporated along with it. He dragged his hand downward, inserting it into the tight space between where their chests connected so he could trace over her nipples, taut beneath the thin, smooth fabric of her bodice.

She whimpered into his mouth again, thrusting her

breasts upward as if presenting him, insistently, with the best sort of gift. One that would take his pleasure higher and higher the longer he spent unwrapping it.

He cupped the soft weight in his palm, continuing to thumb the hardened peak in the center. Her low cries—and the way she kept rocking against him—brought him to a point beyond rationality. He only knew that the more he had of her, the more he craved, for there was still so much of her for him to discover.

He could let his lips follow the pathway of his fingers until he connected with her nipples through her bodice and grazed them with his teeth. Better yet, he could rip the bodice away and savor her without a barrier, all while his fingers continued their journey downward. Far enough to slide under her skirts, to travel up her thighs, to feel the slickness and heat at the center of her. He could grip her hips, lift her onto the desk behind them, position himself between her parted legs—

A clatter, followed by the high, tinkling sound of shattering glass against floorboards, echoed from the corridor.

"What on earth?" The appalled baritone voice, though distant, was clear enough that Jeremy could recognize it as coming from Flynt, the house's stern-faced butler. "How could you be so clumsy?"

"I'm so sorry, sir." The shaky male voice that answered could only belong to an unfortunate footman. "My foot slipped, which caused the tray to waver, and I really did try to right it, but—"

"Never mind." Flynt's voice grew more distant again as his footsteps carried him away, presumably in the direction of the servant's stairs. "Just start cleaning this up at once before any of the guests have a chance to tread in it. I'll call for some housemaids to assist you."

In another moment, the sound of Flynt's hurried footfalls vanished entirely, leaving only a quiet rustle, barely discernible above the pianoforte solo that had just commenced in the drawing room as the footman remedied the damage he'd done. The commotion had nothing to do with the library; in fact, he and Theo remained as secluded as ever. Yet whatever spell had come over them, twisting them up in an uncontrollable haze of yearning, shattered as thoroughly as the glass from the footman's tray.

Theo's gaze shifted to the array of objects deposited upon the library floor, little more than shadows in the darkened room. He and Theo, too, had been clumsy. She wriggled beneath his grasp, and he released his hold on her waist at once, even though his body screamed in protest from the loss of contact.

"I shouldn't keep Lord Pembrook waiting any longer." She crouched down, hastily reinserting a few loose sheets that had come free of the sketchbook before springing back to her feet.

When they'd been absorbed in one another, a tangle of limbs and lips and tongues, time ceased to exist, but now, those lost seconds came rushing back, making this moment speed by far too quickly. The mixture of envy, disbelief, and unfulfilled longing made it difficult for him to think straight.

Theo. He almost called to her again, although the name died on his lips. Despite any lack of clearheadedness on his part, he knew she wouldn't thank him for it. Not when she was already using her feet to feel around for her slippers and then wiggling her toes inside, clearly intent on making a swift exit.

"Goodnight, Mr. Clare." She spoke without meeting his eye, her words filled with a stiff formality. Only the unsteadiness of her breath suggested that, maybe, he wasn't the only one to have his composure rattled.

However, before he could determine what to do with that knowledge—and before he could figure out how to make time slow down—she rushed out of the library, closing the door quietly behind her so he stood alone in the darkness.

And while he may have trouble keeping his desires in check, and he may be a fool, he wasn't idiotic enough to go after her.

The only thing left was to follow her example and retrieve his book from the floor. As if the intensity of his passion hadn't caused him to drop it in the first place.

He turned the book over in his hands, although he'd abandoned any plans to bring it up to the schoolroom this evening. Instead, he placed it back on the edge of the shelf where it would await him tomorrow. For now, it was best he face the damp, the cold, and his stark bachelor's lodgings. If he'd just done that in the first place, none of this would have happened.

He had to assume that's what Theo wanted. To pretend this encounter didn't exist. Why else would she have rushed away—back to a lord—with only a terse farewell?

Something hot and invasive clawed at his gut. Something that intensified as he let himself into the corridor, where the thrum of cheerful voices from the drawing room became louder and stayed with him even when he made his way out to the relative quiet of the street.

It would be to everyone's benefit if he forgot the encounter as well. If he remembered that he was a tutor and nothing more. If, for once, he could be content with his place in life and not find a way to muddle it up.

Yet his ability to do that was doubtful at best.

7

For the second time that night, Theo found herself treading through the corridor in only her stockinged feet, trying to shake feeling back into her numb toes. At least now the house was quiet, for most of the guests had departed, plus she traversed one of the upper floors, far from the former bustle of the drawing room. Just as well, given there was more than enough noise in her head as she replayed the evening's events over and over.

She reached the last door on the right, the one next to the schoolroom, and carefully eased it open. It was past midnight, far later than she'd intended to come up. But although the boys would have long since gone to sleep, she still needed to lay eyes on them, just for a moment. To assure herself of their well-being.

The light from her candle flickered over a lump in each of the beds against the opposite wall, causing a little of the tension she'd been carrying to melt away. The boys were no worse for wear. Not that she had reason to believe otherwise, but seeing them herself made it all a little easier.

"Goodnight, my darlings," she whispered into the dark, moving to close the door again and tiptoe away.

However, no sooner did she take a step than there was a rustle from beneath the bedclothes and Alex's curly head shot upward. "Mama?"

She paused in the doorway, taking care to keep her voice low. "I'm sorry to have woken you. Go back to sleep now, for it's very late."

"But I'm not tired." Alex peered at her intently, his eyes bright beneath the glow of candlelight. Indeed, very little in his face suggested he'd just been roused from a deep sleep.

She breathed out a sigh that quickly became a grin in spite of herself. From the time he'd been little more than an infant, Alex had tended to stay awake late into the evening, often emitting protests if told he needed to go to bed before a gathering at their home took place. The fact that some little things like that never changed was oddly reassuring.

"Very well." She tiptoed into the room, mindful of the still-sleeping Ben, and settled herself on the edge of Alex's bed. "You may stay awake for *one* minute longer. Tell me about your evening. I'm sorry I missed speaking to you in the drawing room. I didn't know that your grandmother wished for you and Ben to be there."

Now it was Alex's turn to sigh, although it wasn't a sound of true distress. "It was fine, I suppose. Grandmother's friends aren't nearly as exciting as yours and Papa's. And they do no end of talking. But Mr. Clare said that if we could endure it, he would pilfer the largest cake he could find on the buffet table for us to eat in our room afterward."

"Did he, now?" She tried making her whisper sound stern, but with the way the mention of that name made her pulse suddenly quicken, it came out more like a squeak.

His mouth drooped. "You're not angry about the cake, are you? Because if you ask me, it was only right."

The lump in the next bed shifted until another curly head slid out from beneath the counterpane. But unlike Alex, who appeared alert enough to run laps around Grosvenor Square, Ben lay nestled against his pillow, rubbing his eyes with a slow yawn. "Stop talking about cake, Alex, and go to sleep."

Alex stuck out his tongue, although, in his state of partial wakefulness, Ben didn't seem to notice. "I'm only making sure Mama isn't cross with us. Or with Mr. Clare. You wouldn't want us to get punished, would you? Or for him to get in trouble and be sent away?"

"Of course not," Ben grumbled, pulling his pillow out from under him and shoving it atop his head. "Which is why you shouldn't say another word about it and go. To. Sleep."

"I'm not cross." Theo hurriedly reached for Alex's small hand, giving it a squeeze. "If cake made the evening tolerable, then, by all means, I'm glad you had it. This once, anyway, for I'm not sure you should make a habit of eating desserts in bed. Shall I take that to mean you've come to appreciate Mr. Clare's tutorship?"

Her heart pounded with fresh vigor as she posed the question, then gave a small lurch at his emphatic nod.

"Yes, I—" He broke off, his gaze darting over to Ben's bed as if he sought approval. But with Ben still underneath his pillow, possibly back to sleep, Alex gave a firm nod. "I would far prefer him over someone else if we must have a tutor. He doesn't have a strap or yell the way Ben said he would. He's really quite agreeable. Well, I suppose."

She bit back her grin at that last part, which he seemed to have included for Ben's benefit. It wouldn't do to voice excess enthusiasm in the presence of his more skeptical older brother, in the event he happened to still be awake. Yet even Ben had just expressed a willingness to have Mr. Clare stay on with them.

And really, why shouldn't the boys feel that way? He'd done exactly as he'd told her that first day: shown them patience and understanding, even when they made it difficult. Put their happiness first; the dowager's complaints and orders be hanged. Whatever respect or feelings of affability he garnered from the boys, he'd earned them heartily.

Again, her heart pounded at a rhythm that didn't seem quite regular.

"Did you have a nice evening, Mama?" Alex, ready to move on from the topic of cake and Mr. Clare's merits, pulled her out of her thoughts with his question.

However, it quickly sent her mind spinning in countless different directions. "I ..."

She tried to respond fast, but the words wouldn't come. It was a simple enough question. However, the answer had more layers than she could currently comprehend.

The evening had been a success, had it not? Despite her worries going into the soiree, the event had gone as well as could be expected. Better. Perhaps it was only from fear of displeasing the dowager marchioness, but everyone she met had spoken to her cordially. No cuts direct. No scorning looks due to her lack of full mourning attire or, more significantly, her position as a rebellious second son's lowborn widow.

Not only that, but she'd caught the attention of a viscount. Not that she wished to get ahead of herself, but if she desired a life independent of Rockliffe House, where she could get back a little of what she'd lost, this seemed a promising start. And what's more, she genuinely liked him.

Lord Pembrook was gentle and courteous, and he'd said and done all the right things. Like flipping through her sketchbook and praising her talent as an artist. Or calling over several other acquaintances to admire her work. Or finalizing their conversation by setting a date of next Monday to visit the Royal Academy with her and Amelia.

The thought of the excursion to a place she had a sincere interest in visiting brought her a tiny spark of anticipation. But at the same time ... the image of Jeremy Clare wouldn't leave her mind.

Specifically, the sight of him standing too close to her in the darkened library, his face covered in shadows but still clear enough to make the intensity of his expression visible. And the sound of him uttering her name, low and wanting. And the feel of his lips against hers, the strokes of his tongue, the skilled caresses of his fingers ...

"I did," she managed to say before her thoughts spiraled out of control altogether. That was the safest answer. And it was even true, in a way.

She smiled at his eager face, letting it anchor her to the present. "I know life at Rockliffe House isn't what any of us envisioned for ourselves, but as long as we're here, maybe we'll find ways to enjoy it after all. Well, I suppose."

"I suppose." Alex flashed her a grin that showed the small gap between his bottom front teeth, and she ruffled his hair before pushing herself back to her feet.

"Try to sleep now, all right?"

"Oh, all right." He flopped backward onto his pillow, giving a tiny yawn. "But I'm really not tired."

She brought her fingers to her lips, blowing him a kiss as she crept back across the room. "Pleasant dreams. I'll see you in the morning."

She slipped back into the corridor, making silent footsteps along the rug and then down the stairs to her bedchamber. At least the memory of Alex's smile—and Ben's subtle words of approval, which, coming from him, meant the same as a dozen smiles—brought a sort of calm to the chaos raging within her. For as long as she knew the boys were happy and provided for, she would endure whatever else came her way.

However, that led her to consider something she hadn't before. What if it were possible for her, too, to obtain happiness—rather than just survival—in this new life?

Of course, that brought about an even more puzzling question. In what direction should she turn to find it?

She let herself into her bedchamber, where a fire burned high in the grate and the bed linens were folded down, awaiting her arrival. This room, with its plush carpeting, delicately painted wallpaper, and gilded furniture, was by far the finest she'd ever occupied. Furthermore, if she wished for help in removing the scarlet gown and preparing to retire, she had only to ring, and Amelia's lady's maid would attend her without delay. An enviable position in which to find herself. At least, it should be.

After dropping her errant slippers to the floor, though, she stretched her arms around to the back of her dress and began pulling at the tapes herself. Just like she'd done for all her life up until this point. Besides, she needed the time alone. To think. To make sense of all that had transpired over the past few hours.

As her dress came loose at the shoulders, she tried to conjure up the image of Lord Pembrook, with his trim, elegant figure, slightly graying dark hair, and pleasing smile. Developing a friendship with the viscount could only help her. And if it became more than that … She swallowed, kicking her dress to the floor so she could work on her stays. The thought didn't cause any anticipatory flutters to take hold low in her belly. Then again, it was still so early, and these things could take time. And even if the flutters never came, did it matter?

She'd experienced that tingling, burning ache with Samuel when, as a girl of eighteen, she'd first encountered him in her father's study, reciting sonnets. She was too world-weary to need that now. A relationship built on cordiality and respect, and even a degree of distance, would serve her far better. As long as she and the boys could live in comfort and she had the means to pursue her printing endeavor, she required nothing else.

At least, that's what she would assert to herself, and wholeheartedly believe, were she a woman of good sense. Yet as she draped her discarded garments across a chair and sank onto the crisp linen sheets adorning her bed, Lord Pembrook's face had been replaced by something—someone —else.

She leaned toward her nightstand, taking hold of the brass handle to pull open the drawer. After this evening's ... *incident* in the library, she'd rushed away as quickly as she could, not wanting Lord Pembrook to think she'd neglected him. However, out of necessity, she'd made a rapid detour before returning to the drawing room, flying up the stairs to her bedchamber and back down again as fast as her pinched feet would carry her.

She lifted out the sketch, now crumpled at one corner from how carelessly she'd shoved it in the drawer, and traced her finger over the shadows and lines she'd created. It was the image that had stayed in her mind like a brand and made her fingers itch until, after that day by the Serpentine, she'd picked up her drawing pencil and let it pour onto the paper.

Had she left the sketch tucked into her book for Lord Pembrook's perusal, it was unlikely he would have taken notice of it above any of the others or remarked upon the subject's identity. The problem lay with how she'd doubted her ability to gaze upon it in the middle of the drawing room without her skin turning crimson and her heart beating out of her chest.

Much like what was happening at present. How could she help it, given the events that sketch had set in motion back in the library? After that most inopportune page of her sketchbook went floating to the carpet, everything transpired so fast, to the point she'd led with emotion, not thought. She'd been hit with a weighty mixture of disbelief, humiliation, frustration, anger ... and, most of all, yearning so strong it made what happened next inevitable.

The remainder of the evening had become an exercise in *not* letting memories of the library consume her, especially when she already had so much to consider to ensure she didn't commit any egregious social blunders. In the end, she must have succeeded in ignoring the storm raging within her, for she'd conducted a pleasant conversation with Lord Pembrook and received other introductions without incident.

But now that she was alone in her bed, dressed in only a thin shift, the rapidness of her pulse became more noticeable while the ache between her legs grew more insistent. It was fortunate indeed that the footman had shattered his trayful of glasses in the corridor when he did, before desire swallowed her whole and the situation in the library reached a point from which there was no turning back. However, that didn't stop her nerve endings from continuing to throb with yearning for something that nearly could have been. Something passionate and blissful and wicked in the best way imaginable.

It was all futile, of course. Mr. Clare was her boys' *tutor*. Someone Lady Rockliffe considered little more than a household servant. She would never condone such a pairing. Not that Theo wanted to place herself in the position of constantly striving for the dowager's approval. But if she didn't—and if she displeased Lady Rockliffe enough to find herself cast out again—she would lose what small steps forward she'd made.

Any hopes of forming high-up connections would disintegrate before they truly had a chance to take hold. Her printshop would remain burned to the ground, its recovery an impossible dream. Worst of all, she could once more find herself struggling to put a roof over her boys' heads. Or even worse again: Lady Rockliffe, wielding her power and influence, could use Theo's shortcomings as an excuse to banish her while taking guardianship of the boys herself.

Theo could *not* risk allowing that to happen. No, it was far better for her to continue on her path with Lord Pembrook, wherever it may lead. A path she would traverse using her head and not her delinquent heart.

She shoved the sketch back in the nightstand drawer and slammed it closed, blowing out the bedside candle. *There.* In the dark, she would have no use for sketches.

Too bad the dimness didn't extinguish memories as well.

She burrowed under the bedclothes, *not* thinking of green eyes and a finger brushing against her cheek. Or of a sturdy, comforting figure kneeling at her feet. Definitely not thinking of hardness pushing into her, and hands upon her bodice, and what it would feel like if, instead of lying alone, she had all those things in her bed, ready to continue the pleasure.

Not thinking of how on one hand lay what was sensible and right. And on the other lay what she wanted.

8

"I'm still not certain about this." With his brow furrowed, Alexander pushed himself up from the picnic blanket where he'd been reclining in the back garden, letting his copy of *Robinson Crusoe* fall to the grass.

Jeremy quickly dropped the paper he'd been writing upon into the satchel at his side, not taking the time to blot it. He wasn't in the habit of pursuing his *silly hobby*, as his father liked to call it, while in the boys' presence, even if they were otherwise occupied. However, as Benedict and Alexander had lain reading quietly beneath the afternoon sun, and he found himself with nothing in particular to attend to, an idea for the final scene of his latest novel suddenly sprang up, and he thought it best to jot it down before it had a chance to slip away.

Now that Alexander had set aside his book and was looking at him questioningly, though, he snapped back to attention, every inch the focused tutor. "Certain about what?"

Had one of the boys made such a comment during their

first week together, Jeremy would have expected it to be followed by complaints of the drudgery he made them endure. But now that he'd been with them at Rockliffe House for nearly a month, they'd progressed enough for him to have faith the boys would meet him with something beyond pure pessimism. Indeed, he had to bite back a smile at the sight of Benedict, a small pair of wire-rimmed spectacles perched atop his nose, still sprawled out on the picnic blanket, engrossed in his book. He'd finished *Robinson Crusoe* the day before and had since moved on to *Gulliver's Travels*. As a result, they'd fallen a little behind with their mathematics and Latin lessons, but for now, Jeremy was more than happy to permit the lapse.

"I'm not certain about the story." Alexander glanced at the book he'd just discarded, his brows knit. "It's exciting enough, what with the pirates and shipwrecks and all, but there's something missing. I think what it really needs is a dragon."

"Ah." Again, Jeremy found himself fighting not to grin. "If you read on, you'll be rewarded with a pack of ravenous wolves, but sadly, there are no mythical creatures to be had."

He drummed his fingers against his satchel, racking his brain for mythology books he could suggest in its place—ones that would meet with approval this time, hopefully. His other hand still clutched his quill, which he just needed to return to its case, along with the tiny inkwell, so he could fully concentrate—

"If the story lacks some of the elements you seek, have you considered creating your own?" he asked before he could think better of it. He doubted very much that the Dowager Lady Rockliffe would appreciate him encouraging her grandsons to develop an interest in novel-writing, especially because she'd hired him to help the boys assimilate with high society and *not* develop rebellious, unconventional tendencies like their father. But Alexander was already peering at him, clearly intrigued.

"No, I haven't. But I could, couldn't I?" He popped up from the blanket, shuffling his feet over the lush springtime grass. "I could invent a story with pirates *and* a dragon. Or perhaps something even more terrible, like the Minotaur or even Typhon. I could write it down, so someday hundreds of people could read it, just like Papa wanted for his novel. Oh, and maybe I'll ask Mama to do some illustrations. Did you know that she's a very good artist?"

A sharp pang hit Jeremy between the ribs. He spent his days trying not to think about the person in question, but it was a losing battle. His mind flashed back to the sketchbook tucked under her arm, which she hadn't opened for him but he knew nonetheless would be filled with proof of her talent. And to the sketch that had tumbled to the floor, displaying how she'd captured his features perfectly.

Displaying how he wasn't alone in his desire.

"Don't be silly." For the first time, Benedict spoke from behind the pages of his book. "We no longer have the printshop, and I doubt Mother has an interest in illustrating dragons. Even if she did, where would she find the time? These days, she's always out with Lord Pembrook."

Again, a hot, heavy feeling twisted Jeremy's insides. He hadn't crossed paths with Theo for nearly two weeks now, since the night of the soiree, and had he stopped to think, he could have easily discerned that her engagements with that other gentleman were the reason why.

Except he hadn't stopped to think. It was easier to imagine that she remained preoccupied with her writing and revising project, or that Lady Rockliffe had warned her away from the schoolroom again, or that she'd decided herself to keep her distance until the heat of what happened between them had a chance to cool and they could determine, with level heads, what came next.

But with the truth spelled out so plainly—that Theo stayed away because of her burgeoning association with the viscount—he could avoid it no longer.

He swallowed away the thickness in his throat, giving himself a silent reminder, for the thousandth time, that he was here to be a children's tutor. Nothing more. "You don't need a printshop to craft a story for your own enjoyment. And while illustrations would be a nice addition, they aren't wholly necessary." He offered a reassuring smile to Alexander, who still paced along the grass, before turning his attention to Benedict. "What do you think, Benedict? Would you like to try your hand at creating a story as well?"

Benedict shrugged, but his dark eyes turned bright behind his spectacles. "Maybe. Although I'm not sure I want any dragons in mine. I'm going to have something better, like—"

"A dog!" Alexander cried, sprinting across the back garden.

"That's ridiculous." Benedict flung his book aside, sitting up in indignation. "A dog isn't better than a dragon. Unless it's a fearsome, monstrous dog, like Cerberus, but even so—"

"No, I mean, there's a dog. Here." Alexander stopped beside the low stone wall bordering the back of the garden, where, sure enough, a bulldog's broad white and brown head peeked over, its front paws resting against the stone.

"You don't say! What's he doing, standing there like that?" Benedict scrambled to his feet, running to join his brother at the back of the garden, while Alexander rushed over to the gate, motioning for the dog to follow.

"Alexander, not so fast—" Jeremy tried to warn, but it

was too late. Alexander swung the gate open, and the dog came skulking into the garden, its skinny tail swishing behind it.

Hell and damnation. Jeremy lurched forward, desperate to put space between the boys and the dog. In his excitement, Alexander must not have noticed that the animal didn't have the appearance of a docile family pet. On the contrary, the dog's thick body seemed designed for combat while an angry-looking scar ran along his muzzle.

Pushing himself in front of the boys, Jeremy peered into the animal's bulging eyes, preparing to be met with bared teeth or a threatening growl. Wondering what in God's name he would do after that so this whole situation didn't end badly.

But the dog merely stood there, eyeing him in return, his tail swinging back and forth.

"Really, Mr. Clare." Impatient, Alexander ducked under his arm so he, too, stood before the dog. "He may look dangerous, but he's not. See? His tail is wagging. He must be lost, and I'll bet he's hungry. We should feed him."

As if proving Alexander's point, the dog took a tentative step forward to sniff the air around them, then dropped to his haunches with a whine. Despite his outward appearance of a fighting dog, he showed no signs of aggression. Rather, he looked worn out. And, like Alexander said, hungry.

Now, it was Jeremy's turn to sigh. "I suppose we should." If anyone saw them all rambling about the garden with a stray bulldog, they'd think he had both neglected his duty and taken leave of his senses. But he could hardly ignore an animal in need of aid, either, especially if it meant so much to the boys. "Why don't you go to the kitchen door and ask for a few scraps?"

"I'll go." Benedict bolted across the grass, turning his

head backward just long enough to give a high-pitched whistle. "Come along, Achilles."

The dog needed no further invitation to go trotting after him until they'd rounded the corner of the house and were out of sight, while Alexander stayed beside Jeremy, his face creased in thought.

"Achilles ..." He let the name roll off his tongue as he shifted his weight from one foot to the other. "Yes, I suppose that's a proper name for this dog. And he must like it, for he followed Ben without a second thought."

Alexander bent his arms at his sides, looking on the verge of running after them, when the sound of light footsteps began tapping against the stairs that led from the terrace and into the garden. There, swooping across the grass to approach them, was Theo.

With every day that passed without him seeing her, Jeremy had tried to convince himself that he built her up in his mind to something that exceeded reality. Yet it turned out the opposite was true. She wore another colored dress—this one a deep green—that accentuated every curve and gave a generous view of the skin above her neckline. Skin even more flawless than he remembered, containing a subtle golden glow that begged him to stroke it. Her hair, though contained by pins, appeared even thicker, even readier to tumble down her back, while her eyes shone even more intensely with their dark beauty. As for her face ... she smiled.

He'd seen her smile before, of course, when conversing with her sons. Not like this, though. Not with an air of pure, carefree joy that made her features light up and his heart thrum more rapidly within his chest.

"Alex," she called, welcoming her younger son's embrace as he crashed into her, a wide grin brightening his face as well. "I'm glad you're out enjoying this lovely spring day. And good day, Mr. Clare."

Jeremy had been anticipating this moment when, at last, they'd encounter one another once more. Wondering, after what had transpired last time, how they would act, what he would say. He hadn't imagined her standing beside him with an eager smile as if matters between them weren't complicated in the least.

He bowed with all the nonchalance he could muster, pondering what this meant. But before he could come to any conclusions, Alexander launched into an animated discourse, his cheerful voice filling the air.

"You won't believe what's happened, Mama! Ben and I were reading in the garden when a dog, of all things, poked his head right over the fence. Mr. Clare seemed concerned when I opened the gate to let him in, for the dog looked a bit fearsome, but he's really quite friendly, and we think he's lost and hungry. Ben just took him to the kitchen to get something to eat, but you'll get to meet him as soon as they come back. Oh, and we've named him Achilles."

Theo's eyes widened as she tried to keep up with Alexander's animated storytelling. "That's quite something—"

"And guess what else?" Alexander was nearly bouncing out of his shoes. "I've decided to write a book about pirates and dragons. Mr. Clare said that if I don't care for the stories I'm reading, I should create one myself, so that's exactly what I'll do. And because I want everyone to enjoy my story and find it especially exciting, I thought it would be just the thing if you could illustrate it. Although Ben says that maybe you don't like illustrating dragons."

Jeremy's gaze darted from Alexander to Theo, a tremor of doubt pulling at his insides. Lady Rockliffe's feelings on the matter aside, maybe Theo wouldn't appreciate him encouraging her boys' novelist tendencies either. Not after everything that had happened with their father.

But she merely gave a little laugh, clasping Alexander's hand just as his mouth began to turn down. "I can't say I have much experience with illustrating dragons, but I certainly have no objection to attempting it."

"Brilliant! Thank you. I plan to get started as soon as we've seen to Achilles." Alexander peered back toward the side of the house as if again contemplating if he should go after his brother and their new companion.

However, Theo kept hold of his hand, crouching down so they were closer to the same level. "As it turns out, I've had a pleasantly eventful day as well. Would you like to know why?"

He nodded, finally stilling his body as he peered into his mother's face.

"You recall that I attended Lord Pembrook's garden party this afternoon?" The airiness in her voice as she uttered the name caused another jab between Jeremy's ribs, which he promptly tried to dismiss. "Well, he asked me to bring along my sketchbook and a few of my small paintings, and then, as it turns out, he invited a number of friends who also have an interest in art. Some are even involved with the Royal Academy. And do you know what? They admired my work. So much that one gentleman insisted on purchasing —*purchasing*—one of my landscape paintings. And another guest—a rather eccentric baroness, if you can imagine—has offered to provide compensation if I sketch her portrait when she returns to London in the winter. She said she has yet to see anyone do her justice with a pencil and paper, but she's certain I'm equal to the task. I always thought my art could be nothing more than a hobby, but Lord Pembrook has helped to make it otherwise."

"Well done, Mama." Alexander gave a hearty nod of

approval. "But I already knew you could draw and paint better than anyone I've ever met."

"Do you realize what this means?" She reached into her gold-tasseled reticule, pulling out a handful of coins to display in her palm. "This money belongs to us and no one else. I *earned* it. And if I can only keep doing so, just think of the possibilities. We could have our own home again. We could get back the printshop. Wouldn't that be wonderful?"

"Yes," Alexander answered her quickly, but again, he seemed deep in thought. "Although ... well, never mind. I suppose that would be all right. Our own home. You, me, Ben, and Achilles. Oh, and Mr. Clare, when it's time for our lessons."

A flicker of ... *something* swept across Theo's face while Jeremy's own face twitched in return. But there was no time to reflect on what any of this meant—and how it should or shouldn't make him feel—before the garden erupted into chaos.

"Good day, Mother," Benedict called cheerily as he rounded the corner of the house to rejoin them, with the dog licking his lips and trotting at his side.

However, the last syllable of his greeting was drowned out by a horrified shriek. The exterior doors leading from the drawing room had been flung open, and Lady Rockliffe marched across the terrace, her face pink with indignation.

"What in the name of all that's holy?" The dowager carried her cane with her today, but instead of leaning on it in her frenzied stomps down the stairs and into the garden, she waved it wildly in the air, charging toward the dog. "Be gone! Be gone at once, I say, you wretched animal!"

"Grandmother!" Benedict and Alexander cried in unison, their eyes widening in dismay.

But it was too late. With an affronted whine, the dog

had bolted through the open gate and was already halfway to the mews.

"Grandmother," Alexander repeated, his small fists trembling at his sides, "how could you? That was our new friend, Achilles, who was lost and in need of food. There was no reason to drive him away. You didn't even give Mama a chance to meet him."

He peered into the distance, his feet beginning to shuffle like he intended to bolt after Achilles and retrieve him, even though the dog must have darted behind a building, as he was no longer in sight. Any such plan, though, was hastily snuffed by Lady Rockliffe, who traveled the remaining distance to the back of the garden and slammed the gate closed.

"Enough of your impudence." She glowered at both boys in a manner that invited no protest. "You couldn't possibly mean to feed such a creature. If it has been left to run loose, that would only encourage it to come back."

Jeremy inched his arm to the side, giving Alexander a subtle nudge. They would accomplish nothing by letting Lady Rockliffe know that the damage in that regard had already been done. Fortunately, Alexander must have interpreted the meaning behind the gesture, for he opened his mouth but then snapped it closed.

Just as well, for the dowager hadn't finished her diatribe and didn't take kindly to interruptions. "A dog like that is no cherished companion and certainly doesn't belong in Mayfair." She thumped her cane against the ground, her mouth curled in repulsion. "Really, one would think you had all gone mad, trying to befriend that savage thing. It's fortunate that such foolishness didn't cause anyone to lose a limb."

Her frosty glare traveled from the boys to Theo and then Jeremy, and he retreated to the picnic blanket to retrieve his satchel and the discarded books. "Boys," he said quietly, as if tiptoeing around a fire-breathing dragon, "perhaps we should go back to the schoolroom to finish the remainder of our lessons for the day."

After granting himself that seconds-long reprieve, he straightened up again and squared his shoulders, prepared to face the dowager marchioness. More specifically, her reproach for the numerous ways in which he'd erred. He'd failed to keep the boys in the schoolroom. He'd neglected to maintain a rigid schedule of lessons. He'd permitted a dangerous dog to enter the garden. The examples of his incompetence were so prolific, it was difficult to say where Lady Rockliffe would start.

However, after another moment of fixing her icy blue gaze on him, she merely gave an impatient sigh, unable to fully conceal how her weight now rested against her cane. "I think returning to the schoolroom would be a very wise idea. I'm sure that, as an accomplished scholar, you can come up with something better to do than traipse about the garden all afternoon."

Still relying on the cane's support, she pivoted toward Theo, making a curt motion with her head. "You come inside, too, Theodora, so you can tell me how you fared at Lord Pembrook's garden party."

Theo shot the boys an apologetic glance, mouthing the words *we'll talk later* before beginning a slow jaunt toward the house, lest she give the dowager another reason for displeasure. She decidedly did *not* look at him as she departed.

Once again, Jeremy stood stiffly, lamenting the fact that an interruption had ended their time together far too soon. Not to mention left Ben and Alex solemn-faced after what previously had been an afternoon of excitement.

Without a word, the three of them headed across the

garden as well, the boys going at a far slower pace than usual. Perhaps in part due to wanting to avoid another confrontation with their grandmother and in part due to dejection. Leaving Jeremy to ponder how to turn things around so the remainder of the day wouldn't be a total loss.

"At least I can still work on my story," Alexander said eventually, once his mother and grandmother had disappeared through the terrace doors.

Jeremy gave an encouraging nod, although Benedict still appeared less than enthused. Maybe it would help if he promised to keep an eye out for Achilles on his way back to his lodgings in Barton Street that evening.

For now, though, he supposed it wouldn't hurt any of them to have a few minutes of silence. While they walked, he needed a moment—just a moment—to set himself straight.

So what if another period of days that stretched into weeks passed before he saw Theo again? It shouldn't matter to him. And if she raised herself up with the help of Lord Pembrook? He should be glad for her. For *them*, if that was the way things were to be.

And he was. How could the uninhibited joy of her smile make him anything less? After everything she'd been through, she deserved happiness, success, and everything that was good and right in the world.

Only, he couldn't stop the hollow feeling from swelling in his chest at the thought of never seeing her—for that matter, never seeing any of them—again. Contrary to Alexander's belief, he wasn't under any illusions that he would be asked to continue with his position if she gained her independence. He'd been hired by the Dowager Marchioness of Rockliffe and remained in the house on her whim and hers alone. Whether Theodora Prescott achieved greatness as an artist or a viscountess, or some unlikely combination of the two, he couldn't imagine her feeling inclined to take on the tutor forced upon her boys. The tutor who had the unfortunate distinction of being the son of the dowager's man of business.

The tutor who forgot his place and wished he could be so much more.

Jeremy threw open the terrace door, letting the boys trudge back into the sunlit drawing room ahead of him. He didn't need a mirror to realize he appeared just as somber as they did.

9

Theo's heart shouldn't have fluttered each time she climbed the stairs leading to the schoolroom. It did anyway. Perhaps this time even more than usual, given the several weeks that had passed since her last visit, allowing anticipation a chance to build. She was becoming a coward, a designation she'd long fought to avoid. Yet it was so much easier to spend time with the boys at the end of the day when their lessons were through. When a certain instructor had already hailed a hackney to take him back to his lodgings until the next morning.

However, the task at hand involved Alex, and while she could have waited until evening to bring it to his attention, it also involved his studies, so it was just as well to address it now. Especially given how pleased she hoped he'd be. In any case, she would only stay for a quick visit, for it was nearing the time when the boys typically vacated the schoolroom and Mr. Clare took his leave. Likewise, she'd been coerced into paying an hour's worth of calls with Lady Rockliffe and Amelia before dinner, and the carriage would be brought around for them shortly. She would merely pop in, give Alex the surprise she had for him, and pop back out again. Before she became caught up in Mr. Clare's green gaze and any feelings of awkwardness—or worse, feelings of lust—had a chance to arise.

Coward.

She approached the schoolroom quietly, keeping her footfalls light in the silent corridor in case the boys were in the middle of an assignment requiring concentration. But as soon as she drew near enough to see in through the open door, she was met with only an empty room. Her heart gave a little lurch. Of relief, surely. Not disappointment.

She crept inside, glancing around as if the boys ... or their tutor ... might suddenly materialize. But perhaps they'd finished early for the day or opted to take their lessons outside again, although it seemed a bit rainy and gray for that.

Oh, well. As she didn't have time to track Alex down, she could always leave her offering here for him as a surprise for tomorrow.

For the past few evenings, he'd been eager to tell her about the story—an epic tale of a band of pirates who encounter three-headed dragons in the Aegean Sea—he'd begun working on each afternoon after his other lessons were finished for the day. If she could just find his work in progress, she could slip in the drawings she'd sketched late last night, and he would hopefully think she'd done his dragons justice. However, his desktop was clear of everything but a slate pencil, as was Ben's.

She peered around again, at bookshelves and chairs—and at Mr. Clare's large weathered oak desk at the front of the room, upon which rested his satchel. So, he hadn't left for the day yet after all. Again, her heart seemed to shudder, almost like it had skipped a beat. But while he may not have left, he wasn't here, either.

She tiptoed forward, which was ridiculous, as she seemed to have this floor of the house to herself. Also, there was no reason for her *not* to be here. She tiptoed nonetheless, approaching the desk like a covert bandit. The satchel, of course, was none of her business. But before she searched the desk drawers, if she could just shift it a little, in case Alex had left his writing on the desktop—

Blast, but why did her arm have to jerk at the worst possible moment? The satchel went crashing to the floor, creating a noise profound enough to alert the entire household. Well, maybe not that loud. In truth, the sound was probably less noticeable than those the boys made as they cavorted around the house. Still, she bent down quickly, because if she could only return the satchel to its original position fast enough, it would be like this mishap had never happened.

A few papers had spilled out, creating a disordered pile on the floorboards. *Damn, damn*, damn.

But never mind. Again, if she just cleaned up her mess quickly, she could forget the whole incident, and besides, maybe these were the pages of Alex's manuscript, which was what she'd been looking for all along.

Except this wasn't Alex's manuscript. A single glance at the markedly adult handwriting made that much plain. She grabbed the papers and shuffled them into a neat stack, trying to ignore the thudding in her chest.

It was like the library incident—incidents—all over again. Her revised pages of Samuel's manuscript, and then her secret sketch, scattered across the floor, putting pieces of her heart on display. In an unexpected turn of events, though, she was the intruder this time.

She hadn't set out to pry, yet the words of a title page were beneath her fingertips, staring her in the face. *The*

Peculiar Exploits of Peregrine Plumtree. A novel by Jeremy Clare.

She nearly smiled until, just as quickly, the pages of Samuel's manuscript flashed in her mind instead. *A Descent to the Underworld.* The gothic tome contained pages upon pages of vengeance and hauntings, which she worked through tirelessly, trying to turn them into what they needed to be. However, what she held now had nothing to do with that at all. This manuscript belonged to *Jeremy*. It was a different creation entirely. Dare she believe it even had some humor in it?

She should stand up, return the pages to the satchel, and leave the schoolroom at once. Yet here she remained, crouched on the floor, her fingers unwilling to release the pages within their grasp.

He'd seen her writing—Samuel's writing. Her sketch. It was only fair if she saw something of his in return. At least, that's what the nagging voice inside her head whispered, although she struggled with whether to believe it. Really, the content of this manuscript should hold no interest for her whatsoever.

Yet her arm trembled again, causing the title page to slip down partway, and a new series of words revealed themselves. *Chapter 1: In Which Peregrine Plumtree Leaves Oxford.* She could feel her lips rise in a true smile as she envisioned Mr. Clare bent over a desk, scribbling away with a quill as the products of his imagination broke free. Had he possibly penned this while still at Oxford himself, preparing to become a vicar but perhaps dreaming of something different?

Her eyes automatically scrolled downward, seeking out the first line. *Peregrine Plumtree had occasionally found himself on the wrong side of Oxford's rules, but the May Day pig incident could lead to nothing but his certain expulsion.*

A giggle broke free from her throat. An actual, ridiculous giggle! She was supposed to be striving for silence and speed. To be downstairs with the dowager and Amelia, forgetting her clumsiness and what she'd seen as a result. Still, her eyes kept traveling over the page before her. Just one more line. And one more after that. Perhaps she could sit on the floor for just one minute and look at one more page—

"Mrs. Prescott?"

She leaped to her feet at once, the manuscript still clasped tight within her hands, putting her guilt on full display. However, the voice that had called to her was high and female, and the person peering at her from the doorway was merely a chambermaid.

"Is everything all right, ma'am?" The maid took a step into the room, eyeing Mr. Clare's satchel where it still rested on the floor. "Lady Rockliffe and Lady Amelia are waiting in the carriage. When you didn't join them, Lady Rockliffe said I was to search the house for you."

"Yes, quite all right." Why did her voice come out so breathlessly? She grabbed the satchel off the floor, cramming the papers back inside as quickly as she could without crumpling them. Then, she returned it to the desk, trying to replicate its original position as if she'd never touched a thing in the first place. "I was looking for my boys, but as they're not here, I'll have to seek them out later. I'll go down to join Lady Rockliffe and Amelia immediately. Thank you."

If the maid looked at her strangely, she had no time to dwell on it. She paused only long enough to drop Alex's drawings onto his desk. Not how she'd intended to present them, but it was the best she could do at the moment. Every extra minute she delayed the carriage would add to the dowager's wrath. As it was, she needed to come up with an acceptable excuse for her lateness. All while the opening lines of *Peregrine Plumtree*—and the author who'd created them—spun through her head.

Oh, Lord, what had she been thinking? As she ran, a few curls from her chignon sprang free, and her face grew hot from exertion, making her more disheveled by the second. At this point, it was probably best to claim she'd been overtaken by a headache and needed to stay home. That way, she could have some time alone in her bedchamber while she waited for her mind to stop racing and her body to cool.

But as she got to the bottom of the final set of stairs, it became apparent that the dowager no longer awaited her in the carriage. Instead, her voice—a loudened, irate bark—traveled through the front door, which remained open just a crack, guarded by Flynt, who seemed to be debating if he was needed to intervene. For the dowager wasn't yelling at nothing. Shooting back at her, in tones equally as infuriated, came the unmistakable voices of Ben and Alex, followed by a plaintive cry from Amelia.

Footsteps came pounding down the corridor, causing Theo's focus to break from the commotion for a split second. Just long enough to see Mr. Clare bounding from the direction of the library and toward the front door, his face etched with alarm.

For once, her heart didn't take the opportunity to grow fluttery. Her focus was solely on getting outside, and it seemed Mr. Clare was of a similar mind, for they pushed past Flynt in unison, bursting onto the stone steps.

It was as if a volcano of voices erupted around her, each one fighting to be heard amidst the chaos.

Ben's hands were planted on his hips as he glared at his grandmother. "You had no right—"

"We already discussed the matter," the dowager barked over him, "and I will not accept this kind of insolence—"

"Mother, I don't feel right about letting this happen,"

Amelia interjected, barely audible above the yelling, "and I really don't see why we couldn't have allowed the boys to—"

"Benedict, Alexander," Mr. Clare said in the voice he must have used to lecture to a large room at Oxford, "you said you were going to the kitchen to fetch a snack. Why, then, are you—"

"Enough!" Theo bolted down to the pavement, placing herself between Lady Rockliffe and the boys. She may not have the loudest voice of the group or experience as an Oxford lecturer, but she'd parented two spirited children long enough to know how to speak so her audience would listen. "Boys, could you please explain what's going on? And I expect the truth."

Alex's chin trembled, and he couldn't hide how he was on the verge of tears. "We *did* go to the kitchen, just like we told Mr. Clare. Except the Chelsea buns needed another minute to cool, so we decided to take a turn about the garden, and he'd come back! Achilles, that is. Standing alongside the gate waiting for us, just like we hoped he might do someday, except—"

"Except Grandmother drove him away again," Ben bit out, his eyes like flint.

"Yes, but that's not the whole story." Alex took a shivering breath, then rushed to keep going. "First, the gentleman came and tried to grab Achilles, and we had to chase—"

"Gentleman? Ha!" The dowager's abrupt laugh cut through the air, and she glared at Theo as if her errant daughter-in-law had somehow played a part in the misfortune. "The man was a ruffian of the worst kind. Imagine my horror when, after being forced to sit *waiting* in the carriage for an ungodly amount of time, I peered out the window to see the likes of him running after that same ragged dog who had the nerve to show up here before, who was, in turn, being chased by *my grandsons.*"

"Of course we were chasing him!" Ben snapped. "Couldn't you see that Achilles didn't want to go with that man? If instead of coming out of the carriage and yelling at them to be gone, you could have just let us—"

"Be that as it may, that vagabond claimed the dog as his, and the sooner they both go back to wherever they came from, the better. I doubt you would see two more sorry-looking creatures in the depths of the Westminster Pit. We will have no further association with them, and that's final."

Ben threw his arms up, letting out an aggrieved groan as he stalked back toward the front steps with Alex at his heels.

"Now," the dowager continued, giving her cane a characteristic thump against the ground before taking hold of Amelia's arm, "we shall return to the carriage, and I suggest, Theodora, that you join us without delay. This incident will cause no end of talk as it is, and every moment we remain standing here is another moment we're putting ourselves on display."

They *were* getting strange looks from passersby— servants and gentry alike—who happened down the street. If she looked up, maybe Theo would even notice faces peeking through curtains of the surrounding houses. However, her head spun too much from the commotion to make it signify. Where to even begin ...

"I'm so sorry!" In an abnormal gesture of defiance, Amelia shook off her mother's grip, rushing forward to place her arm on Theo's instead. Her chin trembled just like Alex's, while her cheeks had gone flushed. "I wish we could have resolved the situation in a way that wouldn't have upset the boys. It all happened so fast, and when the man came, I didn't know what to say, and—"

"It's all right." Finally, a calm voice of reason interceded.

That of Jeremy Clare. "I'll speak with the boys and see if we can't—"

The boys. It suddenly occurred to Theo that the boys were no longer on the pavement or the front steps. But neither had she heard the front door open. "Where did they go?" She whipped her head around, surveying the street from both directions—well, what she could see of it through the patchy covering of fog that hung in the air— but only strangers revealed themselves. "I'm certain I didn't hear them return inside."

"I'll check with Flynt, just to be sure." Amelia, eager to have a task, bolted forward, her long legs nearly flying up the steps.

"And I'll check around back in case they returned to the garden or kitchen." Mr. Clare knew better than to touch her in front of their current audience. However, the way he looked at her as he spoke, so close and intent, made it feel almost like his fingers ran over her skin. Reassuring her.

She nodded, watching him disappear around the side of the house until a creak drew her attention to the front door. Amelia reemerged, giving a single shake of her head.

Only then did Theo's heart begin to beat faster while simultaneously dropping into her stomach. The boys had probably just slipped into the garden while no one was looking and would be brought back by Mr. Clare any minute. Still, she couldn't stop her sense of unease. "Benedict, Alexander!" she called into the fog. "If you're hiding somewhere, I'd thank you to come out at once."

"Stop that this instant," the dowager hissed, taking Theo's sleeve in a pincer-like grasp and trying to steer her toward the steps. "As if the spectacle we already caused weren't bad enough, you're now drawing more attention to us. I've changed my mind about paying calls today. We'll have tea in the drawing room instead, and once the boys are found, let it be known to them that they had best modify their behavior unless they wish to go to bed without dessert tonight."

"I'm not going to the drawing room!" Theo jumped away, clutching her arms tightly against her chest. From the day when she'd first shown up on the doorstep of Rockliffe House, finally conceding defeat, she'd made a sort of unspoken bargain. In exchange for all the dowager could offer her and the boys, she would do her best to comply with whatever was expected of her. No matter how distasteful. However, her obedience had limits, and absolutely *nothing* would entice her to sit quietly by if there was even a chance something was amiss with her children.

She scanned the street again, out of the dowager's reach and oblivious to her spluttered words of affront, before turning back to the house's towering brick facade, just in case she'd missed something. Which she hadn't, of course. Children didn't materialize from thin air. Which meant there was nothing left to do but wait for Mr. Clare's return. Or better yet, she could join him in the back garden and find out firsthand what had become of the boys.

Except the opportunity never came. No sooner did she take a step toward the side of the house than Mr. Clare, with his gray wool coat, emerged from a patch of fog that was equally as gray. Running. And alone.

"What is it?" Theo's legs scrambled into motion, reaching him in several long strides. "Where are they?"

He stopped where they were, with some distance between their position and that of Lady Rockliffe and Amelia. But his gaze didn't fall on her. It traveled up and down the street. "I spoke to several scullery maids and the cook, and they all swear that no one came in through the kitchen. The terrace doors were locked, so the boys couldn't have entered that way either."

Amelia might have gasped, but Theo's heartbeat pounded so loudly in her ears that she couldn't be sure. The Mayfair street, leading to so many others, stretched out before her like a foggy labyrinth. Giving no clues whatsoever as to where Ben and Alex might have gone. "We must start looking at once. I'll alert the footmen that they need to come out and help. Or perhaps it would be best if I take the carriage right away and begin covering ground before the boys get too far. Or I might get a better view if I go on foot." She shivered against the gust of icy wind that came up. That, and the terrifying helplessness of knowing her boys were gone and having no idea how best to locate them.

"Nonsense." The dowager stomped toward them with a scowl. Whatever else may ail her, there was certainly nothing wrong with her hearing. "I don't know what you hope to accomplish by traipsing about London. More likely than not, Benedict and Alexander slipped back inside without detection and have hidden away somewhere to sulk. Should we not at least search the house before jumping to erroneous conclusions?"

The misty drizzle creating a chill in the air suddenly turned to a steady stream of rain, and the dowager gave an affronted cry, scurrying over to the steps while shooting Theo a pointed look. *Follow me. Now.* As much as it pained Theo to admit it, the dowager's scornful words had merit. Yet something stopped her from running into the house and dashing through each room on a search for the boys. Intuition? Whatever it was, she found herself unmoving, raindrops splashing against her face, as she surveyed the street once more. The boys were out here somewhere. Not inside. *Here.* But the city was so impossibly big, and the clutch of fear in her chest was making it increasingly difficult to breathe.

For the briefest moment, a hand brushed against her

sleeve, and a voice spoke low enough as to be for her ears only. "I'll search the streets."

Jeremy. Mr. Clare. With all the uproar, her mind whirled in dizzying circles, her attention flitting from one place to the next. But throughout it all, Mr. Clare was still here beside her, calm despite the crease that had formed between his eyebrows. Not dismissing her or telling her she overreacted. Even if he couldn't take hold of both her arms in a gesture of support, and even if she couldn't fling herself against his chest as if doing so would guard her from everything that was wrong, she knew he understood. That he would help.

"I'll come with you," she said, already starting toward the street. London remained impossibly big, offering her no hints of what way to turn, but at least the task would be made that much easier with an extra set of eyes. Especially because they belonged to someone who'd proven how much he cared for her sons' well-being.

"No." Again, his fingers hit her sleeve, giving just the faintest touch before slipping to his side. It was already more than could be deemed suitable, given they remained in plain sight, but she couldn't find it within her to care about propriety. The touch was what she needed to keep her from crumbling. To draw her gaze back to his and feel that, somehow, everything was going to be all right. "I think you should stay here. Perhaps search around the stable area or ask a few neighbors if they've seen any sign. If you remain nearby and it turns out the boys did get into the house undetected, or they decide to return of their own volition, you'll be the first to know."

"And where will you go?" She stared into green eyes and a sharply angled face dripping with rain. Neither of them had dared voice the suspicion aloud, but it clearly ran through his mind just as it did hers. Ben and Alex could have run off in pursuit of the dog. And if Lady Rockliffe's conjectures about the unsavoriness of his owner were correct, Lord only knew where the chase would take them. Certainly not anywhere safe for unaccompanied children.

He glanced around as if trying to see through the fog, and her stomach dropped even lower. He didn't know any more than she did. How could he?

But then, he squared his shoulders, pulling his coat against him in a poor defense from the rain. "I'll head south. I suggest you send footmen to search the parks. As for me … I believe it warrants looking in the direction of the Westminster Pit."

Theo swallowed back the wave of bitterness that rose in her throat. She'd only heard tell of the infamous blood sport arena in passing, but that was enough to let her imagine its horrors. The thought of the boys wandering that far, to such a place, alone … she couldn't allow herself to stand here and dwell on it or she would go mad. As soon as they returned home safely—and they *would* return home safely—she was going to strangle them for their recklessness. Either that or hug them and never let go.

She nodded and then watched him go without another word. Well, unless she counted the way she opened her mouth and a sound little more than a whisper rushed out. *Please be careful.*

He probably didn't hear her, but she had no occasion to remedy that. It was time to begin her own search. In the mews, or across the street, or … somewhere, as she simultaneously trusted that Mr. Clare would search just as thoroughly in places she didn't even want to think of.

In a world that spun before her in a foggy haze, filling her with terror, therein lay the single speck of brightness. Trust him she did.

10

Darkness wouldn't fall for another few hours, but it may as well have for all Jeremy could see in front of him. The thick fog and driving rain had followed him on his walk from Mayfair, persisting as the buildings around him became less stately, and the murmured snippets of speech from passersby grew less refined.

His voice had gone raspy from persistently calling the boys' names—in the hopes that if they chanced to hear him, they would then deign to reveal themselves—but thus far, his efforts had earned him nothing but sideways glances from strangers. Yet given the obscuring fog, the muddy streets, and the fact that he was partially responsible for allowing two children to slip out from under the noses of four supposedly able-minded adults, what else was he to do?

He had only his voice. That, and an inference based on the last words spoken to the boys by the irate Dowager Lady Rockliffe before they'd disappeared. *I doubt you would see two more sorry-looking creatures in the depths of the Westminster Pit.*

Perhaps it was a long shot and he roamed London in the

rain for nothing. Indeed, Lady Rockliffe had seemed certain the boys had returned to the house and the rest of them overreacted. However, Jeremy had come to know Benedict and Alexander well enough to realize they weren't the sort to sit idly by in the face of perceived injustice. They were intelligent. The sort who wouldn't let a passing comment go by undetected. A fact their mother clearly believed as well, and she should know better than anyone. The terror she felt upon discovering her sons were missing had been plastered across her face, and if there was even a chance he had it in his power to remedy the situation, he didn't need to think twice before acting.

"Benedict! Alexander!" He was coming upon what had to be his destination, although presently, the arena—which looked innocuous enough, despite the revolting activities that took place within—was deserted. Whether he should be glad of that or not, he had no idea.

He approached the front entrance, giving the door a tug, but it was locked. He let out a quick exhale. At least that meant the boys hadn't gone inside to witness God knows what. But at the same time, that also meant he'd been wrong. And if Benedict and Alexander weren't here, where should he look next? As vile as the idea was, he might benefit from procuring the addresses of other lesser-known dog-fighting establishments. Unless that wasn't where Achilles had been taken, or Benedict and Alexander hadn't tried following the dog after all—

A high keening sound shot through the air, just audible above the pounding rain. An animal sound, coming from the back of the building. He'd heard something so similar the day Lady Rockliffe had first chased Achilles from the garden.

He bolted into the misty alleyway alongside the arena, relying on his ears alone for guidance. Probably not the wisest idea, but in a situation where every second counted, he had no time for caution. Fortunately, nothing—no *one*—impeded his path, leaving him free to run to the opposite side of the arena.

And there, standing only feet away from him, close enough to be visible through the rain and fog, was a bulldog tethered to the building with a chain.

He hadn't spent as much time with Achilles as the boys. Yet it had been enough for him to remember the one brown hind leg that stood out against a white body and the brown patch around one eye. The scar beside his nose. It was him: the dog he'd rushed through the streets of London to find, hoping Benedict and Alexander would follow.

He burst forward, trying to shield his eyes from the rain as he whipped his head around, searching for any sign he wasn't alone, that they could possibly be near.

"Psst, Mr. Clare. Mr. Clare!" A quiet voice that could be considered something of a shouted whisper called to him, echoing through the fog. Suddenly, there was a flash of motion as a small head peeked out from behind a crate propped next to the other end of the building, and a trembling hand beckoned to him. Alexander.

Jeremy nearly flew across the wet gravel, diving behind the crate and crouching low to the ground. Benedict was there, too, shaking beneath his sodden clothes just as Alexander did, his hair plastered against his head like a wet mop. At least the angle of the crate provided a semi-shield against the rain. Most importantly of all, Jeremy had found them. He'd really, truly found them.

A torrent of conflicting sentiments washed over him, fighting to dictate what he'd do next. Ask the boys if they were well and unharmed? Ask them what the bloody hell they'd been thinking, and did they have any idea of the uproar they'd caused? Tell them how unequivocally relieved he was to see them?

They would have time for chatter—whether he chose exclamations of gratitude or censure—later. Rainwater ran down the back of his neck and into his collar, and for now, he clamped his hands into fists to keep from shivering himself, opting for two simple words. "Let's go."

"We found him." Benedict peered around the side of the crate, eyeing the dog as if Jeremy hadn't spoken. "We caught up with the man and Achilles and followed them all the way here. The man went inside, through that back door there, not five minutes ago. Now that he's gone, we just need to determine how to free Achilles and get him away from this place as quickly as possible.

"The chain has a lock," Alexander supplied, shoving his hands into his coat pockets. Not that it would do him much good in the way of warmth, given how wet the garment was.

"Boys ..." Jeremy took a quick glance at the dog before turning back to their rain-streaked faces. He'd been about to launch into a tirade about how they needed to get home before their grandmother turned the house upside down and their mother grew sick with worry. Before they caught lung fever from lingering outdoors in the chilly dampness. However, one look at them told him such protestations would be futile. And really, he should have known that all along. Of course they wouldn't leave the dog they'd taken such trouble to find. Not when the animal had proven to be so hell-bent on escape and had befriended them as a result. Nor could Jeremy, in good conscience, abandon a creature who would likely suffer unspeakable cruelty if they didn't intervene.

With a sigh, he mimicked Alexander's gesture of stuffing his hands in his pockets, although, just as he suspected, the soaked wool did nothing to warm him. Not that it mattered.

If he did this right, it would only take a matter of minutes and they could be on their way. "I want you to stay here, behind this crate, and not move a muscle until I reappear and say you can come out. Is that understood?"

Benedict's dark eyes and Alexander's pale ones widened in unison before the meaning behind his command set in, and they both gave enthusiastic nods.

"Oh, thank you, Mr. Clare. I know you can help Achilles." Alexander pulled a hand from his pocket to squeeze Jeremy's shoulder just as the dog emitted another high-pitched whine.

Something in Jeremy's chest clenched, and with an abrupt nod in return, he scrambled to his feet and toward the unassuming back entrance of the arena before the sensation had a chance to intensify. A sensible man would be sitting in a hackney with his pupils by now, on their way back to Mayfair. Whether this undertaking made him noble or a great fool, he would have to determine later.

Unlike the locked front door, the latch of the back door came open easily, and he found himself stumbling into a room lit only by a single high, narrow window and a lone candle resting atop a desk. The first thing that hit him was the smell. The odor of unwashed bodies, and the metallic tang of blood, and ... God, he didn't even want to think of what else. When he returned home, he may have to take a short hiatus from novel-writing to compose a strongly worded essay on the barbarism of such places.

But that was a task for another day. Right now, he needed to focus.

He righted himself, giving his eyes a moment to adjust to the dimness. Not that there was much to see. The room was little more than a dank closet, big enough only for a shelf containing a few books, a couple wooden chairs, and the desk he'd already observed. But behind it sat a man, his head of stringy, shoulder-length dark hair bent down over a ledger.

Jeremy's sudden intrusion caused him to raise his eyes for merely a second before turning back to his work. "Yer too early, guv. Fight's not 'til eight."

Jeremy paused, trying not to gag from the stench. He'd burst in here with plenty of foolhardiness but no plan. Low candlelight flickered across the desk, illuminating the ledger, inkpot, and quill, but nothing resembling a key. But maybe …

He slumped his body again, staggering forward a few steps until he came to an inelegant halt at the edge of the desk. "I want to make a way-zher. A way-dger," he repeated thickly, flopping his hand onto the desktop. Some years had passed since he'd been an undergraduate at Oxford, partaking in all manner of revelry and the alcohol that went along with it. Still, the memories were fresh enough that he should be able to emulate a man in his cups.

"You can come back at seven—" the man started to say when Jeremy abruptly flung his arm out, pointing an unsteady finger toward the door.

"I wanna make a wager *now*," he slurred, "on that dog out there. He's a lucky one; I can feel it." He leaned in close to the man, hoping the smell of the building would mask the fact that Jeremy *didn't* reek of ale. No sign of a key around the man's neck either, or on the shelf behind him.

"That one?" the man scoffed, his lips curling in a sneer that revealed a row of jagged teeth. "'E's more blasted trouble than—" He stopped, his eyes glinting as he caught sight of the handful of coins Jeremy pulled from his pocket. Whatever else Jeremy could say about today, he'd had the good fortune of receiving his monthly salary that morning. Not that he could have anticipated needing to use it in such a manner.

The man rose from his seat, his gaze never straying from the coins as he opened the desk's top drawer and pulled out a book. "Very good, then. I'll mark you down. What's yer name?"

"Tom," Jeremy spit through his teeth, stumbling around to the other side of the desk so it no longer stood between them. "Plumtree." He collapsed forward, aiming his hands for the man's tattered coat pockets. Right away, his knuckles connected with a piece of grooved metal, and he released his fistfuls of coins, snatching the object into his palm in their place.

"Oh. Sorry about that. But look how quick I got you the money." He staggered backward quickly at the man's yelp of indignation, flashing him a doltish grin and then laughing as if he'd just said something exceptionally witty. "I'll be back at eight to shee it doubled. No, tripled. No, quad-rippled."

He took plodding footsteps back to the door, yanking it open and then slamming it closed behind him. For a moment, he stood frozen on the other side, back in the pouring rain, scarcely daring to breathe. That asinine performance hadn't actually worked ... had it? No sounds emerged from inside the arena's back room. No footsteps thundering toward him. No shouts from the man that he'd been robbed. Coins, Jeremy supposed, provided a sufficient distraction. At least temporarily.

He bolted toward the dog, crouching low to the ground as soon as he reached him in an effort not to appear threatening. Achilles—just as soaked through as the rest of them —merely looked at him, his eyes dark and mournful. Jeremy pried open his wet fingers to reveal the key, as his other hand traveled along the dog's chain until it connected with the lock. Despite his drenched body, his mouth suddenly turned dry. If it turned out he'd grabbed the wrong key, this would all have been for naught, and then what would they do? They were all becoming more sodden by the minute, and he had no other plan. He'd become accustomed enough to his own failings. However, knowing he failed Benedict and Alexander—and yes, even the dog—would be another matter entirely.

But he hadn't grabbed the wrong key. It turned in the lock as smoothly as if it were slicked with oil, allowing the chain to fall free. The dog took a hesitant step forward, not removing his eyes from Jeremy's. The creature was understandably wary, but at the same time, he seemed to regard Jeremy with a fragile sort of trust.

Which meant there was just one thing left to do.

He raised himself off the ground, turning toward the other end of the building where, just as he suspected, two heads peeked out from behind the crate. They squirmed, much like two additional chained animals waiting to break free, yet they were taking his instructions to not move from their hiding spot with surprising gravity. He waited until he was certain they watched him and not just the newly freed Achilles. And then mouthed a single word.

Run.

The boys slid out from behind the crate without making a sound, their footfalls quietly hitting the wet ground as they sprinted over to him. He waited just until they were at his back, Achilles excitedly wagging his tail beside them, before dashing into the alleyway with a brisk hand motion for them to follow.

The sooner they escaped the vicinity of the Westminster Pit with their stolen dog, the better. Besides, running down a street or two might help them warm up. At least until they encountered a hackney to take them the rest of the way back to Mayfair. Assuming they could find a coachman who wouldn't object to having Achilles as a passenger. And then there was the question of what would happen when the dog stepped through the front door of Rockliffe House—

"G'day. Why the 'urry?"

Jeremy collided with something hard, and in an instant, all his other concerns became trivial. He'd sprung into the narrow, fog-enshrouded alleyway on his way here and discovered it empty. Now, clearly, it was not. The smell of rot and stale gin assailed his nose as he took a step backward, nudging the boys firmly behind him while assessing the hulking figure before them.

Not the same man from the back of the arena, if that were any consolation. Yet this one had a grin, adorned by nothing but a few decaying teeth, that flashed even more menacingly.

"Apologies. We're anxious to seek shelter from the rain," Jeremy uttered, moving to traverse the remainder of the alleyway as if danger didn't stare them in the face.

The man took a step to the side, creating an effective barricade. "Empty yer pockets."

His demand didn't come as a surprise. Unfortunately for the footpad, Jeremy had already emptied his pockets. To another man who would also soon be after them if he possessed any bit of astuteness.

Jeremy fished around in his coat, coming up with a single shilling he hadn't grabbed earlier. "This is all I have. Now, if you'll let us pass—"

"Can't say as I believe ye." Still displaying his wide, threatening sneer, the footpad lunged forward so their bodies nearly touched, and Achilles let out a low growl. His hand went in and out of his ragged coat pocket like a flash, revealing the glint of a silver knife blade that he held precariously close to Jeremy's chest. "Let me tell ye again. Empty. Yer. Pockets. Or should I do it for ye?"

Jeremy's head pounded with a thousand different ideas

about what should come next. Technically, he *should* be sitting in a parsonage right now, a vicar with his lovely, sedate wife. But he hadn't chosen that path, or maybe it hadn't chosen him. Whatever the case, he was instead standing in the middle of a wet, foggy alleyway outside a notorious blood sport arena, treading alarmingly near to life-threatening peril, accompanied by the children he'd been charged to tutor. Despite anything else that happened, he needed to ensure they returned home unharmed.

The man had the advantage of a blade. However, Jeremy had the advantage of speed, unimpaired by drink. There could be no more time for stopping to think. Only action.

His left hand crept back toward his pocket until suddenly, it was lunging for the knife while his right hand delivered a swift punch to the footpad's meaty jaw. Pain sliced through his left palm as the man stumbled sideways. Still gripping the blade, but momentarily incapacitated, and off to the side enough to leave an open path back to the street.

"Run!" he commanded the boys again, this time shouting with all the force he could muster. This was what he'd been waiting for, the opportunity for them to get away, and he hadn't failed. Yes, he'd still be faced with an irate footpad a good three stones heavier than him, and his hand hurt like hell, and he knew the wetness in his palm was no longer just rainwater. But there would be enough time for the boys to escape ... He hadn't failed ...

The stars in his vision made it difficult to process the great many things that happened at once. There was a growl. A low, canine growl from behind him, just like the one he'd heard a few minutes prior. Then came a flash of motion, not from the boys bolting down the alleyway but from a stocky, fur-covered body leaping through the air, coming to land on the footpad's leg.

There was an enraged, throaty scream, and small hands clutching his coat, and the clatter of hooves and screeching of wheels.

And a coach coming through the fog and rain to reveal an elaborate crest on the door, which vanished from his sight when the door flew open and a figure wearing a heavy gray cloak jumped to the ground.

An angel. A dark-haired, dark-eyed angel with the most inviting, kissable lips he'd ever seen. Theo.

There was more screaming. High-pitched this time, with frenzied words about getting in the carriage *immediately*. There were youthful exclamations, and a whistle, and hands tugging him. And then, somehow, they were all in the coach, out of the rain and fog and clutches of footpads, rattling down the street at a breakneck pace. Jeremy, Theo, Benedict, and Alexander, with Achilles lying at their feet.

Blood poured from Jeremy's hand, dripping onto the legs of his breeches and down to the plush carpeted floor. And yet, he felt surprisingly content.

11

Theo jumped into Jeremy's lap, tugging fervently at his cravat. Either that, or he'd fallen into a delirious dream.

His eyes, which he'd closed while he waited for his head to stop pounding and his hand to stop smarting, flew open, revealing that he still sat within the coach's dim interior, barreling down the road in the driving rain. With Theo truly in his lap, all lilac-scented softness and curves, and heat detectable even through her bulky cloak. Working intently to rid him of an article of clothing.

Judging by the way his palm bled, the knife must have cut deep. That still didn't make him immune to a woman's warmth—*Theo's* warmth—pressing into him. Maybe he really had gone delirious, for this was the worst time and place, and a sharp ache shot through his hand, but even so, a faint stirring of longing tugged at his gut. And lower. How could he help it when the object of his desires straddled him, her fingers trailing over his skin?

Except then she was gone, her warm weight shifting

onto the seat beside him, and a fresh jolt of pain radiated through his hand and up his arm as she grabbed hold of him, wrapping his cravat securely around his palm.

"Sorry," she mumbled when he flinched, not looking up from the knot she tied in the makeshift bandage. "We need to stop the bleeding."

Yes. Bleeding. It suddenly occurred to him that Benedict and Alexander sat on the opposite side of the coach, watching him with pale, stricken faces.

At least the bandage had the issue under control, for the moment, anyway. He rested his head against the window, attempting a weak smile. "I'm sure it will be fine in no time. However, I think we'll have to put off lessons for the rest of the day. We're not far from my lodgings, so if it's not too much of an inconvenience, would you mind letting me out at Barton Street on your way?"

Theo's mouth fell open, her arched brows rising high. She sucked in a breath as if about to speak but then turned to the boys and Achilles before finally turning back to him. "Are your lodgings equipped with clean linens and some sort of spirits?"

Jeremy felt his own brows rise, his mind whirling with questions, but instead, he just nodded. He *thought* he had those items. But in truth, the constant lurching of the carriage amplified the way his head spun, making it difficult for him to focus on any one thought for more than a moment.

His response must have satisfied Theo, though, for she banged on the coach's ceiling, opening the door to call instructions to the coachman as soon as they slowed.

At last, a reprieve from the lurching. But just as quickly, they were on their way again, the coach taking an abrupt turn. The lingering fog made it impossible to tell their precise location, but they must be close enough that he could endure the journey a few minutes longer, especially knowing his reward would be dry clothing and a bed where he could sleep off the day's events. Likewise, the boys would soon arrive home to do the same, and by tomorrow, the biggest problem any of them had would be getting Lady Rockliffe to accept Achilles as the new household pet.

The carriage jerked to a stop, and sure enough, the muted red brick of the building containing his bachelor's apartments appeared like a beacon through the mist.

Not that he particularly relished leaving any of the coach's occupants. With each day he returned home, his rooms felt a little emptier. And now that he'd just experienced Theo's heated caresses—even if only in the name of wound treatment—the space would seem especially cold. Yet what good could he do them in his current state? Better he take a brief period to recover and deal with the aftermath of the situation in the morning, he told himself as he stumbled out of the coach, uttering what hopefully passed for a coherent farewell.

He crossed the pavement toward the front door, half cursing the return of the rain and half grateful for the solid ground. As he walked, he waited for the sound of the coach creaking back into motion and speeding away to come from behind him, reassuring him that Theo and the boys were on their way home to safety. Instead, the coach remained where it was, a hint of Theo's faint but insistent murmur traveling through the door he'd neglected to close.

It was only a moment, though, before there came a soft thump, followed by hooves pounding away and the carriage rattling along behind them, just as he'd anticipated. Good.

But then, there were more sounds—hurried footsteps against wet pavement and the swishing of skirts. And Theo, grabbing hold of his good hand as he fumbled with getting the key in the lock. "Allow me."

He gaped at her, again questioning the state of his mental faculties. "Wh-what are you doing here?"

She let out a quick puff of breath from between pursed lips. "You really thought I would leave you alone in your condition?" She plucked the key from his grip, turning it in the lock in one fluid motion and pushing him through the door.

"I'm well," he muttered, treading toward the darkened stairway, steeling himself for the climb. "At least, I will be. You needn't have troubled yourself. Especially when the boys—"

"The boys," she snapped, "are being taken back to Rockliffe House in all haste to alert the dowager of your urgent need for a doctor. I haven't even begun to *think* of what comes after that, as, at this point, it's all secondary. I only know that your face in the carriage was turning alarmingly gray, and the constant jostling certainly didn't help in impeding the blood loss. If I can just take a look at your hand outside the moving carriage, I can better assist you until more skilled help arrives."

He opened his mouth to argue but ultimately decided against it. Better he save his breath for keeping up with her on her steady march to the top of the stairs. On a positive note, he didn't seem to be trailing blood through the barrier of his cravat bandage. Nor did his head pound nearly as intensely, despite the exertion.

However, he couldn't help the shiver that racked his body as they reached his sparsely furnished, unheated sitting room. His maid of all work came in the mornings only to tidy, leaving him to light the fires himself when he returned home each day. An arrangement that suited him well when he hadn't just spent an extensive period of time out in the rain. And been stabbed.

"We'll need a fire." Theo quickly echoed his thoughts, glancing around at the sorry state of the room they occupied. An under-stuffed armchair. A lopsided sofa. A single end table. The only piece of furniture with redeeming qualities was his bookshelf, although that did them little good at present. "Where are the spirits and linens?"

"My bedroom." He nudged his head toward the door at the far side of the room, feeling almost as if he'd made an indecent proposition. Yet he told the truth, for the linens lay in his chest of drawers while a bottle of brandy rested atop the desk by the south window, where he got the best light.

"Come along, then." She was so matter-of-fact about the way she marched toward his bedroom door that he could nearly believe this was a normal, appropriate occurrence. Nearly. Perhaps he would have been better convinced had they not tumbled into his room in unison, putting him in view of his bed. The place where he so often lay with a stiff cock as dreams of her flooded his head, regardless of any efforts he made to push them away.

"Now, let me see." She took hold of his arm gently this time and lifted it up, squinting as she examined his bandage in the dimness. "The bleeding seems to have slowed. That being the case, I suggest you prioritize changing into dry clothing while I light the fire. Then, I'll take a closer look."

Light the fire ... She must mean in his sorry sitting room, where he would afterward try to push the furniture close together to give her an appropriate workspace. But no, she was kneeling at his bedroom hearth, reaching for the tinderbox, her intention unmistakably clear.

Which made him pause. First, he'd directed Theo to his bedroom. Then, she'd asked him to undress while she lingered mere feet away. Sad to say, it all happened in a context quite the opposite of that from his dreams. Yet his addled brain was having a hard time distinguishing between the two.

"I'm not peeking, Mr. Clare." Theo spoke without turning her head, her matter-of-fact voice bringing a sharp bite of reality. "Although I must say, I never took you for the modest sort."

Goddamn. He slunk to his chest of drawers and hauled everything open at once, snatching up the first shirt and pair of breeches he could find. Heat crept into his face and neck, and even as chilled as he was, he wished to hell he could make it vanish.

Very well, then. If Theo wanted him to strip naked behind her and could remain unaffected enough to address him as *Mr. Clare*, that's exactly what he'd do. He tugged at buttons and fabric, letting his wet, blood-stained garments fall to the floor. Trying to view the process as simply a necessary act that didn't have to mean anything to him, either. Although, truth be told, the lingering pain in his hand was likely the only thing preventing him from developing a rampant erection.

For someone with a hand injury, he dressed with impressive speed, acutely aware of Theo's every movement at the fireside. He didn't know if he could handle having her turn around before he'd finished and look at him with disinterest as if their stolen moments in the library had never happened.

He turned to his writing desk, retrieving the brandy bottle that had proven his companion on nights when both sleep and words wouldn't come, and knowledge of his failings pressed too close to the surface. "Drink?"

Theo whipped her head around, taking stock of him with the help of light from the fire she'd just created. She seemed almost ... surprised to find him standing there already in clean clothing, even if he'd forgone the formality of a waistcoat, cravat, and footwear. But maybe he just imagined the glint in her eyes.

"No, thank you." She turned back around to focus on some undetectable task at the hearth. "But you can bring me the bottle, if you please. Perhaps you should have a drink yourself first."

She didn't need to tell him twice. He filled the tumbler that kept a permanent place next to the brandy bottle—currently the only other thing to adorn his desk, given the satchel containing his manuscript and writing implements remained at Rockliffe House—and tipped it to his lips. The liquid created a comforting burn as it slid down his throat and seemed to make the remaining pounding in his head lessen. Too much brandy, of course, could make a man lose his wits and turn him into a blithering idiot, which was definitely not something he needed at present. In moderation, though, it could bring about a sense of carefree calmness. And that, he needed very much.

"I hope that helps." Finally, she rose from her place by the crackling fire with a candle in hand, assessing his empty tumbler. She hurried over to his desk, giving him a whiff of lilacs as she opted to fetch the brandy bottle herself. After giving a quick scan of the room, she approached his bed, on the side closest to the fire, laying both the bottle and candle on the bedside table. She drew back the counterpane with a swift flick of her hand, then patted a spot near his pillow. "If you could sit here, on the edge of the bed, I think that would give us the best light."

He blinked, feeling his throat go dry. He'd parted with the brandy too soon, it would seem. But didn't her request flow with the natural progression of things? First, enter his bedroom. Second, get undressed. Then, get into bed beside her.

All under the worst possible circumstances.

He obeyed, helping himself to a second small tumbler of brandy once seated upon his sheets. He drank it while watching her continue scurrying about his room, fetching the basin and towel from his washstand.

Another mellow burn flooded his throat, combined with heat flickering from the flames in the grate. That was better. If he could just focus his attention on getting warm and seeing his hand set right, perhaps they could both come out of this unscathed.

Theo made one final stop at his chest of drawers, plucking a white linen cravat from a drawer he'd carelessly left open, before returning to his bedside table to set down the rest of her load. And to sit down beside him, creating a light dip in the edge of the mattress. He'd prepared himself for this moment, enough to keep his face neutral and his posture unaffected. But then, her body leaned into him, and her hands were upon him, tucking the counterpane around his shoulders. He hadn't prepared himself for this at all.

"You need to warm up," she murmured, her breath tickling his neck as she drew her body away from him again. Her touch didn't leave him, though, for she rested his bandaged palm in hers. Unlike in the carriage, when her movements had been rough and frantic, she ran her fingers over him now in the softest caress. "I'm relieved that the bleeding seems to have slowed, although I'd like to examine your hand more closely, just to be certain."

He nodded. At least, he thought he did, although he was having a hard time turning his attention away from their joined hands, and from the way she cradled his palm, unwinding the cravat with such slow, precise gentleness.

Whether due to the effects of brandy or time, the aching had dulled considerably. Likewise, he'd acclimated—well, as much as possible—to the concept of having her in his room, in his bed. And with his head no longer overtaken by a confusing swirl of pain, shock, and lust, another thought pushed its way to the forefront.

"You came after us. You were supposed to be at home." At home, where he didn't have to worry about her, too. For what if something had happened? What if she'd been the one to encounter footpads or sustain an injury?

"Yes. Well." She unwound the final layer of his cravat, leaving his palm bared. Notwithstanding the angry-looking gash, the blood loss had slowed to a trickle. The tightness around her mouth slackened, and she glanced up at him with something he could nearly call a smile. "I don't always do what I'm supposed to."

Her dark, glittering gaze lasted only a moment before she turned to the end table, picking up the towel and brandy. Even though he knew what would come next, he could almost smile as well.

Because, no, he supposed she didn't. But he wouldn't want her any other way. After all, she'd shown up at just the right time. Had saved them.

There was only one thing left to say. "Thank you. For listening to your instincts. For coming when you did."

The brandy spilled over his palm, and he tensed, sucking in a breath as the liquid seared so deep it felt like it would hit bone.

Stay still. It's for your own good, she would no doubt tell him if he dared complain. So he said nothing, merely studied her as he waited for the stinging to abate. The dark curls at her nape. The lush lips. The skilled, slender fingers.

She dipped one end of the towel into the basin, wringing it out and pressing it carefully to his palm, bringing the tiniest scrap of relief. He closed his eyes a moment, preparing himself in case this was a precursor to another dose of brandy. But when he opened them, she was dabbing the towel against his skin, washing away the dark red smears that had begun to dry there.

"Actually," she said in her low, even voice, not looking up from his palm, "it is I who needs to thank you. You didn't question me when I said the boys had run off somewhere. Furthermore, you knew where to find them, and the dog besides. I don't know how you accomplished it. Only that you *did*, while putting yourself in danger. It was beyond what anyone could have expected of you. I'm truly in your debt."

"No." A muscle squeezed tight in his chest, perhaps because she'd done away with the towel and now applied pressure to his hand, causing a shock of discomfort as she wrapped it in a clean cravat. Although truthfully, he didn't think that was the reason. He cleared his throat, willing her to look at him. "I told you from the beginning that I care for the boys' well-being, and that has only become truer with each passing day. I would never want to see them hurt. I would never want to see you hurt as a result."

He trailed his fingertip over her thigh, where her dress peeked out from beneath her cloak, and she gave his hand a jolt, tying the cravat in a hurried knot before scooting farther up the bed.

"I apologize." He placed his hands firmly in his lap before they could lead to more trouble. As had been the case on numerous occasions past, the pull he felt toward her overtook everything else without him even thinking about it. Yet the last thing he wanted was to step over a boundary she didn't wish to cross.

With that said ... what *did* she wish for? Thanks to the effects of pain and confusion, he'd done a satisfactory job of sitting next to her on his bed without letting yearning place itself at the center of his thoughts. However, her words—

that hint of vulnerability and trust—had ignited something inside him.

He craved every facet of her. The woman with fire in her eyes who stared adversity in the face and found a way to overcome it. The woman who needed a shoulder to cry on during those brief moments when she lowered her guard. And the woman who burned with passion, clinging to him, pressing against him, driving his desire higher than he'd ever known it could go. She'd sketched him, shared an embrace with him, and felt that desire in return. Hadn't she? Or somewhere along the way, had she experienced a change of heart?

The easiest—perhaps the *right*—thing to do would be to forget it all. But how could he go on indefinitely without ever truly knowing what was in her heart?

"Theo ..." He took a breath, then let the words pour out. "I'm half out of my head with longing for you."

There, he'd done it. However things turned out, the admission felt satisfyingly freeing. Yet he couldn't stop until he uttered the next part. "That being said, I understand if you don't feel ready to return the sentiment."

There was a slight shift in the mattress as her body stiffened beneath her cloak. But she didn't say a word, didn't move. Merely looked at him, her face unreadable.

Which meant ... what? A deep pit formed in his stomach as a new realization began to take hold. Well, perhaps not a new realization, but an old one he could no longer avoid. He'd seen so little of her lately. Because, as Benedict had tersely explained that afternoon in the garden, *These days, she's always out with Lord Pembrook.*

Maybe he didn't wish to know the truth after all. Nor did he want to say anything else. Yet, after coming this far, he couldn't back down now. Even if the words burned his throat and were far from genuine. "I also understand if … your affections are engaged elsewhere."

Her expressionless mask vanished, and color flashed across her cheeks. "You don't understand! I'm not in a position to be guided solely by my *affections*. As you should well know, I have other things to consider. I *cannot* live at Rockliffe House indefinitely. I need to find a way to regain some independence. To get back the printshop."

The sensation of being stabbed hit him again, but this time, it was from an imaginary blade to the chest. However, he may as well blame his own hand for putting it there. She didn't believe he could provide what she needed, and she wasn't the first woman to think this. The failing lay with him.

That didn't stop spite from bubbling to the surface and overflowing. "I may not be privy to all the inner workings of the peerage, but it's my understanding that viscounts don't typically allow their wives to own printshops."

"Maybe some do!" she hissed through her teeth. She glowered at him, her eyes black with ire, her hands that had been so steady as she worked now quivering in her lap. When he'd unthinkingly traced over her thigh, she'd shuffled away from him, but throughout the course of their conversation, they must have inched together again, for the edge of her cloak lay against his breeches. Her heat nearly close enough to warm him.

Until suddenly, she sprang to her feet, glaring down at him like a beautifully tempting but dangerous siren. "Damn it! Do you think I don't long for you, too? That you don't twist my heart each time you show compassion like it's something to be taken for granted, and you don't fill my thoughts when I lie aching in bed at night? Even though you're my sons' tutor. Even though I'm widowed less than a year, and everything about my life is complicated, and I'm too old for you besides."

He may have shaken her with his declarations, but she returned the favor tenfold. Because she'd actually said— she'd admitted that ... that she felt ... that he ...

"None of that matters." He shook his head with a passion to rival her own. He may need another moment to process the fact that her words had just made his dreams come true, but he could at least speak coherently enough to tell her this much. "I wouldn't want you to be any different. I desire you exactly as you are."

"I'm *thirty*, Jeremy."

He cocked an eyebrow. Out of all the things they'd discussed, was this really the one troubling her the most? "And I'm seven and twenty. What of it? My longing for you cares nothing for numbers."

She still peered down at him, but her countenance no longer radiated anger. That wasn't to say she'd let down her defenses, though. Her eyes continued to blaze, her face animated, alert. "Perhaps you should learn to be more discerning with your longing, Mr. Clare."

It hadn't escaped his notice that she'd finally used his first name, only to revert to the more formal address directly afterward. Grasping for distance to wedge between them. Yet she stood so close, her position such that the outline of her leg became faintly detectable against his through all their layers of clothing.

"Why do you still call me that?" His voice was husky. He raised his uninjured hand toward her, and when she didn't move, he let a finger brush over her hand. This was the moment it all came down to. The pivotal choice between embrace and retreat. For whatever her decision, he would take it as final from this point forward.

His heart pounded. Her fingers uncurled. Carefully, he

pressed his palm against hers, and with the faint return of pressure, he slid his fingers into the spaces between her own so their hands were twined. Hers slender, his large. Both of them dotted with ink stains. Fitting together like a lock and key.

He breathed out her name as a ragged whisper. *Theodora*. Squeezed her fingers, gently tugged.

And then, her body was atop him, and they were tumbling sideways, heads colliding with his pillow, bodies pressed against the sheets in a tangle of limbs.

12

Theo crushed her lips against Jeremy's, opening to allow his tongue to sweep in and claim her. To allow her to circle over his in return. He tasted of brandy. Intoxicating.

They lay side by side on his bed, her hand fisted in his damp hair, his hand cupping her jaw, firm but gentle all at the same time. Had she planned this when she gave in to the subtle tug of his fingers? To crash onto the bed that had begun taunting her, to align their bodies so they connected in all the right spots, to surrender herself to a shower of bliss?

She couldn't say. She only knew she didn't regret it.

For most of the afternoon, desire had been the last thing on her mind. Instead, terror had clutched her within its grip as she scoured rainy streets around Rockliffe House and then screamed for the carriage to come and take her farther, desperate for things to be set right. She may be no stranger to loss, but she didn't think she had it in her to lose again. Not her boys. Above all else, that pain would break her.

But not Jeremy, either. The fierce torrent of relief she'd

experienced upon spotting Ben and Alex in the street had vanished with the sight of Jeremy Clare appearing from behind them, his face ashen and his hand gushing blood. From there, her mind had focused on a single task. *Fix this*.

That's what had allowed her to burst into his bachelor's lodgings, into his bedroom, without a second thought. Because she'd needed him to stop shaking. To stop bleeding. In a situation that could have fatal consequences, propriety hadn't intervened in the least.

But then, his hand had ceased pouring blood. He changed his clothing, and his body began to warm by the fire. His face regained color.

Relief had flooded her once more. And suddenly, the desire that had been pushed down by fear broke free, crashing into her like the pounding rain outdoors. She'd held herself stiffly, trying to forget it. To ignore the intimacy of sitting on his bed, and his bare feet, and his shirt that gaped open at the neck. Until little by little, her resolve had crumbled away. His words—his caresses—had been her undoing. Maybe she still *should* have said no. But she *needed* to say yes.

She dragged her fingers down the back of his neck, absorbing the warmth from his skin, holding him close. This moment was for pleasure and pleasure alone. Any other details they needed to sort out would come later. Except ...

"Your hand," she murmured, finding the strength to pull away just enough so her lips hovered above his. She forced her eyelids open, glancing down at the bandaged palm he kept pressed to his side. An abrupt reminder of what existed beyond their desire, pulling her back to reality before the flames burning within her turned all-consuming. "You need to rest; you're injured."

His mouth traveled downward, pressing kisses along her

jawline. Back up to her earlobe. Into the shell of her ear, where his words came out as a heated whisper. "How fortunate that I have another hand to compensate."

He turned his attention to her neck, covering her with fiery caresses, and she became vaguely aware that he tugged at the fastening of her cloak. *Yes.* She ached with the need to be free of it, to be free of every layer of clothing until all that remained was skin against skin. But amidst the haze of pleasure, another galling speck of common sense pushed its way through.

"The doctor," she rasped. She could barely speak, barely think, for his fingers found her nipple, tracing over it through her thin muslin bodice with a featherlight touch that would drive her mad. Until abruptly, the touch became a pinch, and a burst of sensation shot through her. Her body jerked forward, into him, where the evidence of his arousal hit her in exactly the right spot.

Oh, Lord, how she needed to cast off her skirts, to free him of his breeches, to feel that motion again and again. To have him fill her, to bring them both over the edge.

But there was still common sense to contend with. Reality.

"The doctor." She tried again, although speech had become only more difficult. But she had to keep going. To use her last scrap of reason. "We cannot. The doctor ... could arrive any moment. Cannot ... be caught like this."

"No." He mimicked her movement, dragging his body against hers in one brisk, purposeful motion. His hardness brushed her again, causing the pleasure at her core to build. Creating his own pleasure, if his sharp exhale was any indication. "No, we cannot."

She *would* get out of bed. Put her cloak back on. Tidy her hair. Wait by the window for the first sign of the doctor, for surely ample time had passed to summon one by now.

She *would*. But maybe she could allow herself just one more moment of pleasure first. One more moment in Jeremy's embrace.

She moved again, because now that they'd started the rhythm, she didn't know how to stop it. She craved it like air, that hint of his rigid length against her sex, bringing her as close as was presently possible to what she really wanted.

He palmed her woefully overclothed breast while keeping his movements in time with hers, just as she needed. Driving her ever higher but also ensnaring her in an agonizing state of frustration. For they were so close, yet her skin burned and ached for his touch, free from barriers, and yes, the doctor was coming, but she was about to go out of her head.

"Jeremy," she cried, thrusting toward him with marked force. A plea. Because any moment, the interruption could come, sending this crashing down around them. But still, she needed. She *needed*—

"Shh." He returned to her ear, grazing the lobe with his teeth. "Let me make it better for you."

His hand released her breast, traveling downward to bunch up her skirts. The very thing the rational part of her said they had no time to do. Yet the fire at the center of her raged so frantically that she couldn't have said no if she tried.

And she didn't want to try.

He slid his hand into the small gap between her thighs, causing her legs to splay without hesitation, leaving her open, ready. For he was so close to where she needed him, working his way upward along her prickling skin into the wetness that had accumulated at her entrance.

A sturdy finger stroked inside her, followed by another, and she let out a low moan. A sound of relief for the aching emptiness he'd helped fill. But also a cry for more.

"Do you like that, Theodora?" He stroked her again, and she plunged down onto his fingers, trying to absorb every fragment of the sensation. It was the only answer she was currently capable of giving.

"Or perhaps you like it when I do this." He locked eyes with her, his green gaze glittering with unfiltered lust. His thumb rubbed against the swollen bud at the top of her sex, circling over her as his fingers continued to press inside.

"Yes," she managed to choke out on a breath and a cry. "Don't stop."

"Never." The muttered word heated her neck while the wicked skillfulness of his fingers made the pleasure build until her body quivered, and she didn't know how much more she could bear. "Not until I've watched you come."

His declaration shattered her, sending her intimate muscles pulsing around his fingers as she was racked by potent waves of bliss. She clutched him tight, grasping his shoulders as if that could anchor her from floating away. She needed to stay next to him, grounded. For despite her release, a tingling still pulled low in her belly. A need to tear open his fall, feel his hardness in her palm, and make him shatter with as much force as she had—

A knock pounded against the front door, the noise of it shooting up the stairs and into Jeremy's bedroom. Then silence, followed by another three brisk raps against the door, more insistent this time.

The blood drained from Theo's face all at once, the delicious heat that engulfed her skin replaced by sudden coldness. They lay pressed together in a tangle of sheets, the counterpane having been pushed to the floor at some point and her cloak along with it. All this evidence had to be erased as if nothing had ever happened. *Now.*

She forced her still-shaky limbs to launch her out of bed and staggered to the front window, peering around the curtain. A man carrying a black leather bag—the doctor, most certainly—stood on the doorstep, impatiently awaiting entry so he could escape the rain. And behind him, on the muddy street, was the coach that proudly displayed the Rockliffe crest, the gold detailing glinting through the fog. The coach that would carry her away from here and back to Mayfair, for she'd fulfilled her duty in seeing to his hand until help arrived. She had no further excuse to stay.

She pivoted away from the window and scurried back to the bed, snatching up the discarded counterpane on her way. Her body had turned so heavy that the motions took considerable effort.

She sat down on the edge of the mattress, near where Jeremy now sat up as well, trying to straighten the sheets. Tentatively, she ran her fingers through his hair. Touched his shoulder. In truth, she didn't know what to do with herself. It was like she'd been promised an elaborate gift, only to have it snatched away before she could finish opening it. No doubt he shared the sentiment.

"It's all right, angel." His voice came out quiet and unaffected, despite the way his chest heaved up and down. Much like her own. He grasped her hand, guiding it upward so she cupped his jaw. Leaned in, pressed a light kiss to the bridge of her nose. And released her. "But if you don't mind, perhaps you could be the one to answer the door."

THEO'S HEART rate still hadn't slowed to normal when Flynt admitted her through the front door of Rockliffe House. Her body tingled; her mind whirled. Yet now she had another undertaking of the utmost importance to deal with. One that required her full attention.

"Where are my boys, Flynt?" She handed off her cloak

and boots in a hurry, ready to dash toward whatever location he named. To say she, Ben, and Alex had a few things to discuss would be an understatement.

"Theodora." The voice cut through the air just as Flynt opened his mouth to speak, causing the dour-faced butler to remain silent. None of the household staff would dare do anything else when the dowager approached from the top of the stairs, her cane thumping resolutely against each carpeted step.

"Good evening, my lady." Theo managed the barest of curtsies, already eyeing the pathway up the stairs. Her hair drooped from its pins and her skirts were wrinkled, circumstances for which she had no ready excuse. Nor did she have an interest in inventing one.

But although the dowager took a quick scan of her from head to toe, her nose developing the slightest wrinkle, she merely turned with a curt flick of her hand, starting down the corridor. "I would like you to accompany me to the library. There's something I must discuss with you."

It was a command, not a request. Yet given the circumstances, Theo had no time for blind obedience. "I'm sorry, but I must see to the boys—"

"The boys," the dowager cut in, "can wait. Amelia went up to their bedchamber a short time ago, only to find them already asleep."

"Asleep? But it's not even dinnertime."

"Nonetheless." The dowager arched an eyebrow. Being questioned clearly didn't agree with her. "I suppose they were weary after the day's events and needed a repose by the fire. They will be up looking for dinner soon enough, I'm sure, and whatever you need to discuss, you can do so then. I cannot imagine you being heartless enough to wake them in the meantime."

Theo took a steadying inhale, fighting the urge to

bound upstairs without looking back. Yet the idea, while tempting, would hardly be worth the aftermath. And if the boys really were sleeping ...

"Very well." She moved stiffly, falling in line behind the dowager. In her experience, when Lady Rockliffe summoned a person for a discussion, it was rarely for the purposes of something agreeable. And indeed, at the moment, the dowager had a lengthy list of things to cause her displeasure.

The dowager strode into the library, crossing over to the large desk at the center. The same desk where Theo and Jeremy had—

Oh, Lord. She could *not* let memories of that evening distract her. Or worse, let them lead to more memories of what had transpired between her and Jeremy in his bedroom only a short time ago.

"How is Mr. Clare?" The dowager stopped beside the desk chair, not seating herself but resting her hand atop the leather. The glow from the blazing fire and lit sconces illuminated her face, revealing the sharpness in her eyes as she peered at Theo. As if Theo, too, were illuminated enough for the dowager to see everything about her. Including all she'd just done.

Which was impossible, of course; she was merely being overly anxious. Wasn't she?

She swallowed, the back of her throat feeling like it had been coated in dust. "He's as well as could be expected given the circumstances. The doctor planned to stitch his hand. Said it was nothing that couldn't be mended."

"Good." The dowager glanced down a moment toward the inkpot and quill resting against the polished desktop. "I'll see that a message is sent to his father."

Yes. Mr. Adolphus Clare, the dowager's longtime man of business. Yet another complication Theo and Jeremy would have to overcome. However, that was a problem for another time and not something she could afford to focus on at present.

She folded her hands in front of her and pressed them against her skirts, thinking it wisest to say nothing. At the same time, waiting in silence, with the dowager's astute gaze upon her, was agony. Why had the house become quiet enough to hear a pin drop? Why did each second that slipped by feel more like an hour? Why—

"After all that transpired today, I've had quite enough of London. Therefore, I wanted to inform you that we'll be leaving for the country on the morrow."

The dowager's declaration cut through the stillness, hitting Theo all at once. She didn't mean to gasp, to show any reaction whatsoever, but a sound escaped her lips nonetheless. Receiving an incensed reprimand for her disobedience would have come as no surprise, but this? *Leaving for the country. Enough of London.* The world began spinning far too quickly for her to keep pace.

"Ah." The dowager tilted her chin, looking as if she'd just solved a complex puzzle and now had the answers to everything. Yet she didn't appear displeased. "You needn't trouble yourself over leaving before the Season is through. At any rate, it will soon be drawing to a close, and I have it on good authority that several notable people also plan to take their leave for their country seats within the week. Including, as it turns out, Lord Pembrook. Our *neighbor* at Beaumont Manor."

Lord Pembrook. The ton. The handful of people who'd expressed interest in paying money for her artwork. That's where her mind should have immediately turned.

Except it didn't. She thought only of Jeremy Clare. Jeremy, who lived in London. Who was injured and may not be able to travel. Who may not be asked to travel ...

"I'm pleased to hear it." Theo managed to speak, although her jaw felt brittle. She couldn't afford to give Lady Rockliffe any cause for suspicion. At the same time, she couldn't let everything she'd just gained slip away, either. "It's only ... I wonder about Ben and Alex. They've done remarkably well here under Mr. Clare's instruction, and I'm concerned about the consequences of disrupting that—"

"You said Mr. Clare had suffered no grievous injuries and was already on the road to recovery, did you not? That being the case, I see nothing that would impede him from joining us at Beaumont and continuing the boys' lessons there. If anything, he should be glad for the change of scene, for there are far fewer sources of mischief for impish youths to discover away from London."

Theo had already betrayed herself once with her gasp, so under no circumstances could she do so again by breathing an audible sigh of relief. However, a crushing weight suddenly lifted from her chest, leaving her with a sense of unhindered lightness. Yes, they would retreat to the country, but Jeremy would accompany them, should he choose to accept. And he would accept. They would live under the same roof while dealing with none of the distractions brought about by the London Season. And at night, nothing would separate them but a few corridors and stairs.

She held her body still, fighting against the pleasurable shiver that tried to shoot down her spine. Perhaps this arrangement would only lead to trouble. But after the day's events—Jeremy's rescue attempt and injury, and tumbling with him onto his bed—she couldn't feel anything but gladness. Anticipation. Whatever needed to come beyond that, she would figure out later.

Which left just one more matter to deal with, for Ben and Alex would never forgive her if she didn't bring it up. "And what of the dog?"

The dowager's eyes narrowed, her mouth twisting into a scowl. Theo had been so close to coming out of this meeting unscathed, and now she was playing with fire. But she couldn't regret it. In fact, she refused to do anything but stand there with her head held high, returning the dowager's shrewd gaze. Because for the first time in a long time, she had a feeling her luck was going to change.

"The *dog*," the dowager spat, looking like she'd just swallowed something vile, "will fare better in the country, too, I daresay. That is, assuming he can be trusted to behave himself in the servants' coach for the duration of the journey. Heaven knows why I agreed to permit such a thing in the first place. Frayed nerves, I suppose, are interfering with my good judgment. It's best we say no more on the subject, or I may begin to see reason and change my mind."

Giving her cane a sound rap against the floor, the dowager spun away from the desk and started toward the door, clearly finished with the conversation. Theo had been dismissed, her orders clear. But for once, she wasn't left with an overwhelming sense of defeat.

Thank you, she nearly said before stopping herself. Lady Rockliffe wouldn't welcome the attention drawn to anything that could be considered a concession on her part.

Theo would stay as she was, then, in silence. But also in gratitude. Not just for the unexpected compassion toward Achilles, but because the dowager had granted her a gift. Perhaps unintentionally—or at least, far from the one the dowager thought she gave—but a gift nonetheless.

The country. *Jeremy*.

Not the goal toward which Theo was supposed to be striving. But something new, which, against all reason, had soundly worked its way into her heart.

13

"A lovely evening for a stroll. Is the temperature agreeable to you, Mrs. Prescott?" Lord Pembrook slowed his pace as they left the back steps of Rosemead House and approached the garden path, turning to Theo with his usual warm regard.

She nodded, taking in a breath of the fragrant country air before continuing to the pathway. "It *is* lovely. Thank you."

She'd brought only a thin shawl with her, but although darkness had already fallen, the night was balmy enough that she required nothing more. A good thing, because when Lord Pembrook had suggested a walk following the dinner he'd hosted for his neighbors at Beaumont Manor, she had a feeling Lady Rockliffe would have quickly agreed regardless of the weather. Especially as the dowager had then determined that her legs pained her too much for a walk after all, and she needed Amelia to stay behind and keep her company, but that Lord Pembrook and Theo should carry on as planned.

The dowager certainly wasn't subtle with her feelings on

a match between Theo and the viscount. But really, was that a problem? Hadn't Theo entertained the exact same thoughts herself? And wasn't this the perfect time to continue doing so?

She stepped onto the path, keeping her hand resting atop the arm Lord Pembrook had proffered the moment they'd walked through the terrace doors. The same pose they'd adopted many times over the past weeks, during excursions and soirees, days in the park, and nights in ballrooms. All the occasions they'd had to get better acquainted.

Yet his attentions never strayed beyond that politely proffered arm. No leaning in so his lips hovered near hers. No letting his fingers slip so they brushed against her waist. Everything he did was the picture of propriety. Whatever she could make of that. Perhaps under different circumstances, she would have felt disappointment or fear that she'd misjudged. But how could she rightly feel those things when she didn't *want* his arm—his body—to stray?

"I must confess, I was pleased to learn of your departure for Beaumont so soon after my own for Rosemead, and I'm glad Lady Rockliffe was amenable to accepting my dinner invitation though it came only three days after your arrival. After all the events we've had the pleasure of attending together of late, I'd have considered it a hardship to go too long without seeing you." He didn't break stride as he delivered the compliment—didn't adjust his posture so much as an inch—but flashed her one of his pleasant smiles.

For that matter, everything about him, and his whole estate, was pleasant.

Rosemead. How aptly named, for although their surroundings were shadowed, lit only by sparse torchlight, she could make out the carefully pruned rosebushes lining the path, each one bursting with blooms. Their sweet perfume scented the air, and they were no doubt a sight to behold in the daylight. Beautiful. *Pleasant*.

Just like the house itself, with its spotless interior and inviting decor. Just like the perfectly polished dining table laden with perfectly cooked food, brought in by efficient servants who appeared perfectly happy to serve such a genial master.

It would be a *perfectly* good place of which to find oneself the mistress. A place to live in carefree luxury until memories of past difficulties faded to nothing.

If that's what the viscount wanted. If her mind—her heart—hadn't traveled elsewhere ...

"Mrs. Prescott? Or Theodora, if I may. As we've been granted a moment alone, I was hoping I might speak with you on a private matter."

Now, he did halt in the middle of the path, and she along with him. He spoke just as smoothly as always, his pale eyes shining just as clear in the torchlight. Yet new lines appeared around his mouth as he tensed his jaw. A rare crack in his facade, as if he were anxious about something.

"Yes, please call me Theo. And by all means, you may speak to me on whatever subject you wish." She dropped her hand back gently to her side, hoping she appeared convivial. In truth, nervous energy flowed through her as well.

Was this the moment she'd been anticipating? Or perhaps she'd secretly hoped it would never come.

Was this the time when he made a declaration? A proposal? The time when she forced herself to listen and think logically and not remember that Mr. Jeremy Clare had finally been deemed well enough to travel and had arrived at Beaumont just that afternoon.

"Theo, then. And I hope you'll feel comfortable addressing me as Percy." The tension around Lord

Pembrook's—Percy's—mouth vanished as he gave her a brief, appreciative smile. Suddenly, his hand was in hers, holding her close in a way that rendered her unable to look away from him. It wasn't disagreeable, exactly. Merely unexpected, for she'd never seen him look at her—at anyone—that intently. "I've come to you because ... well ... if I understand correctly, your husband was a man of unconventional ideas. Is this true?"

She blinked, steadying her feet so she didn't stagger. Out of all the words that could have left his mouth, these were the last ones she expected to hear. He wanted her alone so they could speak about her late husband?

At least the mention of Samuel no longer stung as deeply as it had in the early days. And if this was the viscount's subject of choice, she may as well address it without delay, even if she didn't know the exact answer he sought or why he sought it. "I think that's a fair assessment, yes."

"I see." Percy's fingers curled more tightly around hers while he gazed at her as though he tried to see right through to her soul. "And would you say you shared his propensity toward free thinking?"

"I ... yes, in a manner of speaking." This was growing more perplexing by the second. If only she could stare at him the same way he did to her until she could see what lay at the center of him. "Although I admit, I'm not entirely sure to what you're referring. Perhaps you could explain—"

"Forgive me." He abruptly released her hand, taking a step back. "I'll stop speaking in riddles and just come out with it. I have a proposition for you. An arrangement I believe could benefit us both. A proposal of marriage."

She pinched her lips together before her jaw had an opportunity to fall open. So, she hadn't merely imagined his intentions toward her. But at the same time, this proposal felt more like something to be discussed in a solicitor's office than a declaration between future spouses.

"I hope I haven't offended you by speaking so bluntly." He continued to assess her as she stared right back. No longer within his grasp but too perplexed to look away. "While we live in a world that sometimes necessitates dishonesty, I've come to esteem you too much to be anything less than truthful with you. Therefore, I'm going to explain matters exactly as they are, so I can feel confident you're not making a decision under false pretenses. The arrangement I propose is a marriage in name only. You're recently widowed, and I wouldn't expect you to make free with your affections so quickly. Likewise ... I confess, my affections are already engaged elsewhere. Unfortunately, they are not considered the marriageable kind."

"Oh." For the first time since they'd stopped in the middle of the rose garden path, something began to make sense. A memory of the wide array of people with whom she and Samuel used to attend soirees. Sometimes the couples were made up of two women. Sometimes two men ... "I think I understand."

"I wish it didn't have to be this way." He gave a barely audible sigh, his face once again looking strained despite his best efforts at pleasantness. "However, I've found marriage to be the best means to keep rumors at bay. After the birth of our son, Amy—my first wife—and I came to an arrangement, and I hope we might do the same. If you wished to seek companionship elsewhere, I would hold no objection. As for our own union, the matter of an heir is now irrelevant, so we need never stray beyond friendship."

"I ... see," she muttered thickly, surprised she'd managed to speak at all with the way her thoughts pounded through her head. A little farther down the path, a stone bench beckoned. If only she could sit there for a moment to sort through her thoughts, to determine what she should do.

"Again, I apologize if I misjudged and my proposition has caused offense." He tilted his head, his boot making a faint scuffing noise against the ground. "I merely thought ... well, I suppose I thought you could understand better than most the challenges of living in a society that requires you to become someone other than who you truly are."

"I do." Her heart gave a small tug, and she shot a hand out to rest on his shoulder, her need to sit currently forgotten. "Please understand, this isn't a matter of causing me offense. It's only—"

"I want to make you happy, Theo." He placed his hand atop hers, still on the soft wool of his coat, giving it an appreciative squeeze. A gesture that would never cause sparks for either of them. But perhaps it could evoke feelings of comfort. "I know you've struggled, and I want that to end. Become Lady Pembrook, and you would lack for nothing. Rosemead would be yours to do with as you please. My town house, too. We could convert a room into an artist's studio if you wish. And your sons, of course, would join you until you deemed them ready to head off to Eton. Anything else you desired, you'd need only to ask for it. I would do everything in my power to help you. Just as you would be helping me."

Theo froze. Fool that she was, she stood mutely in place, not so much as blinking.

Yes. Yes. It would be so easy for her to utter that one simple word, and then, as if by magic, her troubles would melt away. Everything she'd dreamed about the day she sat shivering, hungry, and utterly broken in the burned-out shell of the printshop would be granted to her. A home of her own, away from the family that had once shunned her and Samuel both. A home for her boys, where *she* would have control of what they did and where they went. The freedom—perhaps even the encouragement—she needed to pursue her artwork if she so chose. And the time and funds to see Samuel's manuscript revised and published, because after all the ways in which Percy had been accommodating, surely he wouldn't deny her that, either.

If anything, his business-like proposal was better than one that came with expectations of love. After all, where had following her heart ever gotten her? Widowed, alone, and struggling beneath a mountain of debt.

This arrangement was based in practicality, which was far more likely to serve her well. It even had the added advantage of allowing her to feel that, in a small way, she helped Percy as well.

Besides, it wasn't as though she'd have to forgo intimacy altogether should her heart—or whatever part caused her to ache and burn—get the better of her. If she really wanted, she could request Jeremy's continued services as a tutor, and maybe nothing between them needed to change.

But even the promise of a carefree future didn't blind her enough to think that particular arrangement could successfully come to fruition.

"I don't know!" Her free hand flew to her temple, so for just a moment, she could close her eyes and let her head rest against her fingertips. When she opened her eyes and straightened her neck again, Percy was still in front of her, looking more inquisitive than ever. Awaiting an answer.

"I'm sorry." She took a long breath, willing her head to stop spinning. "Please don't conclude I'm not grateful for your offer because I am. Only, I cannot give you an answer right now. I need time to think."

Oh, she was the greatest sort of ninny. She may very well have let her best opportunity for salvation slip through her fingers. However, when she chanced another thorough look at Percy, his expression showed nothing but kindness.

"Of course." Giving her hand one final squeeze, he brought his arm back to his side, extending it toward her so they could carry on with their walk. "I plan to be away from Rosemead for a few days, paying a call. Perhaps we could revisit the subject when I return?"

She nodded, coaxing her legs back into action. Back down the flawlessly groomed pathway on a perfect spring-time evening, surrounded by the delicate fragrance of roses. If anyone happened upon them now, they would be hard-pressed to see anything but an amiable-looking couple enjoying an evening stroll. The fact that said couple had stopped to discuss a matter with life-altering consequences, where the outcome still hung in the balance, wouldn't be detectable at all.

Theo, of course, didn't forget the matter so easily, despite what outward appearances might suggest. True to her word, she thought about it.

She thought about it when they walked back to the house, and when they rejoined with Lady Rockliffe and Amelia in Rosemead's drawing room, and when they all uttered their thanks and farewells to Lord Pembrook. She thought about it during the carriage ride home, and when the butler admitted them through the front door of Beaumont Manor, and when she bid everyone goodnight.

She thought about it when, instead of stopping at her own bedchamber, she crept through corridors like a thief in the night. Trailing after servants, listening to hushed words, until she was able to determine the location of the room— one of the more basic guest chambers at the opposite side of the house—she sought.

She thought about it when, with her heart pounding, she gave three quiet taps against the door. Until it silently swung open and Jeremy appeared, his brown hair disheveled, his green eyes wide. Wearing a banyan that gave her a glimpse of his bare chest, of taut skin, of a sprinkling of golden-brown hair. A suggestion of what she'd find if she could explore even lower without the hindrance of clothing.

Wordlessly, she stumbled into his arms, her hands clutching the back of his neck, running through his hair. Her lips crashed into his, drinking him in, her body desperate, needy.

And then, she thought about it no more.

14

Jeremy had little experience with life in the country. Aside from a brief stint he'd spent at the seaside with his mother in an ill-fated attempt to restore her health —an event that happened so long ago he possessed only vague memories of it—he'd lived all his years in either London or Oxford.

The country, as it turned out, agreed with him quite well. Not because he held partiality toward grandiose manor houses, woods replete with gamebirds, or sprawling fields; to those things, he was indifferent.

But because Theo was here. In this airy bedchamber, in this vacant wing of the house, she stood in the doorway like an illusion brought to life. The crush of her lips upon his, though, was real. As was the heat of her body. The frantic pull of her fingers.

And suddenly, the country—specifically, Beaumont Manor in Kent—became the most wonderful place on earth.

His arms shot out to encircle her waist, holding her

close. With one swift step, he pulled her into his room, taking care to swing the door shut, without slamming it, behind them. That may well be the one time this evening he'd have the presence of mind for caution, for she pushed against him like her body had ignited, and he burned along with her.

He thrust the tip of his tongue against hers, letting out a low groan as she teased it with a rhythm suggestive of his every desire. Ever since the day he had her in his bed—half out of his head with the need to pleasure her, only to have her ripped away from him just as they were getting started— he'd thought of her with the attentions of an over-lustful schoolboy. It was as if she'd entered his bloodstream, filling him with a need that his hand alone could never satisfy. But now, it didn't have to, for she was here, embracing him, reaching for the buttons of his banyan.

Which led to the issue that she was also far too over-dressed for his liking. Giving her lips one last caress, he pulled back to better evaluate the construction of her evening gown. It was an elaborate affair, perhaps intended to suggest the demure mauve of half-mourning, but with a bodice more the color of ripe plums, adorned with flowers and lace and little silver threads that glimmered in the candlelight. The gown she'd selected for an evening in a certain viscount's company.

A fiery tightness gripped his chest, swirling with his desire and causing it to flare. He fumbled with the tapes at her back, the stiff material, infuriatingly, showing no signs of giving way. Damn his left hand, still covered in a thick white bandage that allowed for little motion in his fingers. Maybe he'd be better off using his good hand to tear the bodice in two, letting silk and lace fall to the floor until she was bared to him. Except that would leave her without clothing when the time came to return to her room. Not that he could stand giving that moment even a second's thought.

"Undress for me." There, that was a better solution. He ran a finger across her skin, following the curve of her breasts displayed above the embellished neckline of her gown. "I want to see you. All of you."

Her chest rose and fell beneath his touch, and she drew in a quick breath as he pulled his hand away, taking a step backward toward the bed. All the while watching her.

She didn't hesitate. She stepped with him, keeping their proximity, as her hands reached around to her back. Tugging until the gown grew slack around her shoulders, she eyed him with a look of pure temptation.

He took another step backward, feeling as though his blood had been set on fire. After all their stolen moments that unfailingly had ended with an interruption, it took great effort not to carry her to the bed at once and slake their desires before such a thing happened again. Yet tonight was different. Not a hurried moment but a series of hours in a secluded wing of the house, with no other demands on their time. And now that they'd started this little game, seeing it through would make the pleasure that much sweeter.

She stepped as well, the motion causing her gown to fall in a puddle at her feet. Already, her hands were at her back again, making quick work of the laces of her stays. That garment, too, dropped to the floor, leaving her only in stockings and a thin white shift that hinted at every curve about to be revealed to him.

He stepped backward again, and she followed, bending to remove the stocking as she lifted her right foot. Another step, and she repeated the action with the left. Under no circumstances would he turn to glance behind him, or anywhere in the room but directly at Theo, yet even without looking, he knew they had to be approaching the bed. They had to, because his footsteps were growing quicker, less measured, and she followed him with the same speed, her hands ripping away feathers and pins from her hair.

His own hand traveled to the buttons of his banyan, shakily managing to slip the first one free of its buttonhole. Then the next one, and the next, and mercifully, the backs of his legs collided with a bedframe and mattress, because waiting had turned to agony, and there was a growing danger they'd give in to pleasure in the middle of the floor.

But now, they'd both reached the bed, as for every step he'd taken backward, Theo had made an equal move forward. Her body rested so close to his, not touching but near enough for him to feel its heat. Her hair spilled across her shoulders, down her back in thick, untamed curls while her fingers toyed with the ribbon at her shift's neckline. The one thing holding it closed, keeping her from being completely free.

Finally, something he could manage. His fingers raced from the final button near his waist to her ribbon, giving it a firm tug. He shrugged his shoulders backward, causing his banyan to fall away, as meanwhile, her shift gaped and dropped, leaving her standing before him in the candlelight in all her curved, golden beauty.

Her hands grasped the back of his neck at the same time his took hold of her hips, and abruptly, he spun them so that her legs now pressed against the edge of the bed. He kissed her again, getting another taste of the lips he couldn't get enough of, easing her down until her back rested against the mattress while her legs dangled over the side. This time, though, he didn't have to stop with just her lips. He had all of her now, and he intended to explore every part.

He kissed her neck. The depression at the base of her throat. The generous curve of her breast and the hardened pink nipple in the center, swirling his tongue so he could taste this new part of her, first on one side and then the other. All the while, she cried out her pleasure, her nails digging into his shoulders to hold him close, causing his erection to strain impatiently against her thigh. The moment he sunk into her would bring bliss beyond words. But at the same time, he wasn't finished with his exploration yet. And for once, they had all night.

He kissed beneath the rounded weight of her breast. Her belly. Her navel. Her skin was smooth and warm beneath his lips, filling his nose with the faint scent of lilacs and something else that was uniquely Theo. Something invigorating.

He sank to his knees, anchoring his hands against her thighs, easing them farther apart. From this angle, he had a perfect view of the most intimate part of her—the nest of curls, the delicate folds. And she was, indeed, perfect.

He kissed along her thigh, working his way inward, loving the way she stared down at him, her eyes nearly black. Then, he kissed the very center of her, the bundle of nerves that made her whimper a distorted version of his name. He kissed all her secret flesh, down to her entrance and back up to her peak, sweeping his tongue over every part. This was what it truly meant to taste her. To feel her heat and wetness, to have her arousal coat his lips.

Her cries drove his yearning higher, if that were possible. Yet as badly as he wanted to be inside her, there was something about watching her *watch him* give her pleasure that was equally as gratifying.

They had all night.

"Jeremy." She moaned his name again, with more purpose this time. Her body began wriggling, her fingers clawing at his shoulders.

All at once, he knew. It was time for what he'd been awaiting since they'd tumbled onto his lumpy mattress in his sparse lodgings back on Barton Street. Since before that day, too, if he were being honest with himself.

She scrambled backward into a sitting position, drawing her legs onto the bed. Giving her chin the slightest nudge toward the mattress. An invitation.

He dropped onto the bed beside her, taking her into his arms and giving her a deep kiss that would allow her to taste her own arousal on his lips. Without breaking the contact, he began lowering them both toward his pillow, ready to have her stretched out beneath him, to have their bodies joined—

But suddenly, he felt a firm push against his chest, her hands insisting that he be the one to fall to the bed instead, and he had no will to resist. She peered down at him with her face partially obscured by thick strands of hair, although they didn't conceal the desire that flashed in her eyes.

"Your hand," she murmured, gently raising his injured palm and brushing her lips against the bandage.

Yes, his hand. That same old conundrum. Maybe the injury would make supporting his weight while he continued putting his other hand to good use somewhat difficult. However, he'd scarcely paid heed to such thoughts, for any discomfort would be secondary to the unthinkable pleasure he'd derive from the act.

Yet now, it no longer mattered, for in a flash of dark hair and candlelit skin, she moved to straddle him, her entrance resting temptingly close to the tip of his cock.

"Theo," he hissed, his hips making a reflexive motion upward. Yet, with every remaining ounce of strength he possessed, he stopped just short of connecting with her. With this change in position, he would leave that final step for her alone.

She sank down on him in one fluid motion, sending a flash of light shooting across his vision as they both groaned out their desire. He may have dreamed of her countless times, but nothing his mind could invent compared to the real sensation of being buried inside her. Of watching her sit atop him like a goddess in all her naked beauty, beginning to move in the rhythm that most pleased her. A rhythm that sent sensation jolting through him each time she retreated only to come crashing back down.

Having had yearning simmer inside him for days, he couldn't imagine himself lasting long with this torrent of ecstasy pouring over him. However, he was determined to make every moment count.

His hand went everywhere, desperate to take hold of her and drive her higher. Her taut nipples. The curve of her hip. Her damp thigh. And then the bud at the apex of her sex.

He circled her with his finger while she continued to move, more frantically now, watching as she threw her head back, parting her ruby lips. Her thighs trembled around him, the muscles in her neck growing tight. A precursor to her final downward plunge, her final cry, before release tore through her body.

The feel of her intimate muscles pulsing around him—the sight of her face awash with satisfaction, the sound of her once more uttering his name—was the definition of bliss. His own climax had drawn close, *so* close, and he gave a couple brisk thrusts before urging her upward, jerking his body away. She took him in hand, and his seed spilled over her fingers and onto the bed as surges of pleasure vibrated through him.

Not the pleasure of being nestled deep inside her. But still, the pleasure that came from having her near, embracing him. The pleasure of having finally—*finally*—gotten what they desired. No interruptions.

The best part was, at this time of night, in a house all abed, they had no cause to expect interruptions for hours yet. After his breathing slowed enough for him to retrieve a towel from the washstand and clean them, and he lay beneath the sheets with her huddled against him, he traced lazy patterns over her belly, imagining how, exactly, they would fill the rest of those hours. However, when he peered down at her face, it was clear by her drooping eyelids that she fought sleep.

"It's all right," he whispered, leaning close to her ear. "You can rest now, angel. I'll wake you before dawn."

Her lips moved, almost as if about to form a protest. But instead, she pressed her cheek to his chest, her eyes fluttering closed.

He continued the soothing motion of his fingers until her breaths slowed and he felt certain she'd truly fallen asleep. *They had hours.* His mouth twitched into a smile as he gazed at the woman in his bed. Sleep had softened her features, giving her a whole new type of beauty. She was peaceful. Content. Showing him unhindered trust and vulnerability, which, thus far, he'd only caught quick glimpses of. It wasn't the fiery allure that had drawn him to her right from the start, but this opposite side of her was equally as exquisite.

If much of the night consisted of him watching her sleep instead of additional bed sport, that was all right, too. What was the hurry? After all, couldn't this be the first night of many? A whole summer stretched before them, in which he had a bedchamber in a secluded wing of the house, and these dark, silent hours belonged to no one but them.

Of course, it would be shortsighted of him to think this arrangement could continue indefinitely without complications. Even through his haze of gratification, lust, and whatever else tugged at his heart, that much was plain to him. Despite her humble origins, Theo was the daughter-in-law of a dowager marchioness. She had other expectations of her.

Yet why did he have to ruin an extraordinary evening by thinking of such things now? He closed his eyes, trying to drown out the heavy sensation that spread through him. When he did, though, an unexpected face flashed in his mind.

Blue eyes, the color of the summer sky. Delicate blond brows. Pale pink lips that smiled at him so readily, at least in the beginning. It was the face once intended to represent his future. A future that, despite the frequent writhing in his gut, he'd chosen because it seemed sensible and expected and *right*. That was, until the wrongness of the arrangement caught up with him, and everything fell apart.

His eyes flew open, his gaze falling on Theo's sleeping face. He continued peering at her, letting the warmth of her body draw him back to the present. And letting a realization hit him with full force.

With Theo, things were the opposite. Everything about their relationship was outwardly wrong. Their social stations weren't equal. Their families would never approve. And furthermore ... could he truly provide her with what she needed? For who was he beyond a failed vicar with sad bachelor's lodgings and a trunk full of ridiculous manuscripts? A tutor who would find himself without employment and references should he choose to make his affections public.

But even so ... even so, something about this felt right. As irrational as it was, he'd never known this type of contentment before.

He ran a finger over one of Theo's stray curls where it stretched across his pillow. It was all because of her. Her determination. Her strength. Her devotion as a mother. Her passion. All these qualities worked to fulfill him in more ways than he could have imagined. And in turn, he wanted nothing more than to support and fulfill her, too.

Somehow, he needed to take this relationship that felt right but was all wrong and find a way to make it work. For as he leaned down to press the gentlest kiss against her forehead, something else became abundantly clear. The sensation gripping his heart went far beyond lust.

15

"Must I say it again?" Theo peered over her drawing pad toward where Jeremy reclined at the base of an oak tree, shooting him a look of mock exasperation. "Keep *still*."

He'd been shifting against the tree trunk, appearing almost like he planned to leap to his feet, but her words stilled him, his eyebrows drawing together in an exaggerated look of contrition. "As you wish. I would never want to displease the artist. Only, it's difficult to sit here at a distance when said artist is so lusciously enticing."

She giggled, no different from if she were some inexperienced young miss at her first soiree. Jeremy seemed to have that effect on her. Yet somehow, it didn't bother her in the least.

"You may find," she said, using her pencil to shade a section of his boot, "that the artist will reward you for your patience." And as tempting as it was to look up again to see his reaction, she bit her lip, forcing her eyes to stay on the paper. She would never see this to completion otherwise.

The day had shaped up with the perfect series of events

to lead them to this moment. First, the early light of dawn had given way to brilliant sunshine and a cloudless sky. Then, a message had come to the breakfast table from the dowager's bedchamber, saying her joints troubled her and she didn't wish to be disturbed. Then, Amelia had asked if the boys might have a reprieve from their lessons and accompany her to the village to meet some of the local children.

Theo had decided to forgo the trip to the village, thinking the few hours of quiet in the house would give her a good opportunity to continue her revisions of Samuel's manuscript—a task she'd been neglecting lately far more than she should. However, the sun had beckoned so invitingly. At that time of morning, the light would be perfect in Beaumont's east wood, filtering down through the trees. If she ventured there, she would be alone. Just like Jeremy was alone, having found himself in the unusual situation of not having pupils to instruct.

The rest of the arrangements had been surprisingly easy. A hastily scrawled note, slipped under a door. An announcement to the housekeeper that she was going outdoors to draw. A later announcement by Jeremy that he planned to take a walk until Ben and Alex's return. They hadn't even been required to utter anything untrue.

The difficult part, when Jeremy had happened upon her in the wood in the place where she'd selected the perfect backdrop, was not tumbling to the ground with him then and there. For a week now, she'd knocked on his bedchamber door around the time the clock struck midnight, giving them a stretch of predawn hours in which they could succumb entirely to one another. To pleasure. However, that didn't mean she ceased wanting him in the daylight.

Today, though, she'd set out, pencils and drawing pad in hand, with a different purpose. She'd already sketched him once, from memory, when she'd been fighting with the image of him she couldn't get out of her head. But that didn't do him justice. It wasn't the same thing as sketching him from life beneath the bright morning sunrays, placing him in whatever position she wished.

Which was why she'd managed to pull her lips from his after only a brief embrace—before desire could consume them both and make her forget the whole endeavor—and whisper in his ear: *I want to draw you*.

Any current fidgeting aside, Jeremy had proven himself a patient subject. He'd let her guide him to sit at the base of the perfect oak tree, the one whose branches were spread out in a way that allowed light to shine down and hit his face and body at all the right angles. He'd let her rumple his hair, remove his cravat and waistcoat, and even undo the top buttons of his fall. All without touching her because that's what she'd insisted.

This was how she wanted to capture him. Thoroughly mussed, and maybe a little desirous, just like during a night of lovemaking. But not shut away in a secluded bedchamber, concealed by dimness. She wanted him with the world as his backdrop. Vivid, open, free.

Even if staring at him in such a pose while maintaining her distance put hefty demands on her self-restraint.

She pressed her back more firmly against the tree trunk she'd selected as her perch, trying to concentrate on the paper in front of her. She returned her pencil to the image of his left hand, freed from its bandage now that a country surgeon had performed an examination and proclaimed it well-healed. But instead of focusing on shading the straight pink scar that might always remain part of his palm, her mind went elsewhere, conjuring up another image. Jeremy, with a quill in hand, partaking in his own form of art. A couple times over the past week, she'd stirred from sleep to find the other side of the bed empty and him sitting at the writing desk by the window, his bare arm moving rapidly as he scrawled words onto the pages before him. Indulging in his own creative streak.

Each time, she'd thought of rousing herself and confronting him with the small truth she'd kept hidden. But each time, she'd also lost her nerve and remained in bed, waiting until he returned so she could roll against his body and begin the pleasure again.

That wasn't to say she believed she should never tell him. Indeed, what better time than now, when they were alone in a position of quiet intimacy but without the distraction of touch?

"I have a confession to make." She kept her voice low, creating another series of lines on the paper instead of looking at him. "I read part of your manuscript. Not intentionally, but I came across it in the schoolroom one day when I knocked some papers to the floor. I hope you aren't angry."

She swallowed, trying to draw another line but finding the pencil wavering within her hand. The fact that he'd inadvertently seen her artwork in return aside, she knew all too well from Samuel how secretive a person could be over their written words. However, when she chanced a look up through her eyelashes, Jeremy didn't appear displeased from this topic she'd so abruptly sprung on him. Rather, he seemed ... bewildered.

"Oh." His lips stayed open, rounded, for a moment. "Well, you're welcome to it, although it's only foolishness—"

"No." Theo gave her head a firm shake. She should have made her thoughts on that clear right from the start. "I didn't find it foolish. Humorous, yes, but not in a bad way.

Actually, I thought it was quite good. I'd love to read more some time if you would permit me."

"I ... yes, if you like. Thank you." Ignoring her instructions to keep still, he began twisting his hands and ... was he blushing?

She felt an unusually wide smile spread across her face while her heart gave a series of flutters. How was it that her back no longer rested against the tree trunk, but she seemed to be leaning forward in the direction of Jeremy where he reclined against his tree? She tightened her grip on her pencil and forced her eyes back to the paper, trying to appear nonchalant. "Have you ever considered submitting your work to a publisher?" She made another adjustment to his left eyebrow. There, that looked just about right. "I've known my share of poets and novelists over the years, and I think you could have success with it."

"Do you?" For a moment, his face brightened, but just as quickly, his jaw went tense. "I don't know. My father would say it's all a waste of time."

A stab of irritation surged through her at her hazy vision of the sour-faced Adolphus Clare. "But what do *you* say?"

"I don't know!" He threw his arms up, and suddenly, he was on his feet. His hair was still appropriately disheveled, and his breeches still hung loosely from his hips, but the pose was broken, and his eyes flickered with strain. "God, Theo, I don't know. I want to. Of course I want to. But where would it get me in the end? Likely not where I need to be. For, whatever happens, I *cannot* fail again. Not with you."

Flinging her drawing pad and pencil to the ground, she scrambled to her feet as well, about to rush to his side but then restraining herself, instead leaving a cautious distance. Now, it was her turn to gape with confusion.

"I don't understand." She watched his chest rise and fall

through the opening in his crisp linen shirt, trying to make sense of all he'd just said. Yet clearly, certain things about him remained unknown to her.

He blew out a deep, jagged breath, taking a careful step forward. When he spoke, his voice was low. "I was supposed to become a vicar. A *married* vicar, for I was betrothed, to another vicar's daughter, no less. All the plans were in place. A living had been provided for me, courtesy of my betrothed's—Caroline's—father. The wedding date was set. I renounced my fellowship at Oxford. I had everything I needed to live a comfortable, sensible life. Had I not brought it all to ruin."

"I still don't understand." She wished she had something more helpful to say, but sorting through all he'd just told her made it difficult to think straight. "How?"

"Because I didn't want any of it!" He stepped forward again, his face shadowed and intense. "I tried to do what was expected of me. A respectable occupation and marriage while setting aside any futile pastimes. I tried to convince myself that I could be content with writing nothing but weekly sermons. That I could grow accustomed to a vicarage if I gave it a chance. That if I merely adjusted my attitudes, I could find myself well-matched to a wife who thought novels frivolous and found any contact beyond a light brush of the fingertips shameful. Caroline, on the other hand, was smarter than that. In the end, she had the sense to confront the incompatibility between us that I'd tried so hard to ignore. She broke off the betrothal two days before the wedding."

She must have been unknowingly creeping toward him as he spoke, for she now stood closer to his tree than hers, but his last words made her muscles seize, adhering her to the spot. "I'm sorry," she muttered, her throat feeling tight. She'd always known he was a would-be vicar turned tutor, but as for the reason behind that—she supposed she'd been so caught up in her own struggles that she failed to ponder it. Never considering that he, too, could be dealing with loss.

A betrothed. It sounded like they'd been ill-matched, but nonetheless. Had he considered himself very much in love? Did he still mourn her loss and the well-planned, uncomplicated life that would have come with her? Something hot and insistent tugged at Theo's insides.

"I don't regret it." He shook his head, almost as if reading her thoughts. "She and I would have never made each other happy. I would have made a terrible vicar. And furthermore ... had I not lost everything from that life, I wouldn't have accepted a position as a tutor. I wouldn't have gained Ben and Alex. I wouldn't have gained *you*, Theo."

"Jeremy ..." She stumbled forward again, reaching her hand out but then snatching it back to fold it across her chest. One touch between them would end this. One touch and she'd be holding him, caressing him, and she wouldn't know how to stop. Yet he still looked like he had something else to say.

"That's why I cannot fail in this, don't you see?" He took a small step toward her as well but kept his hands at his sides. He must also recognize the danger of a touch. "Nothing with you is pretending. You're everything in the world I want, and I want to give you everything you desire. I need to find a way where I can be certain I'll succeed in doing that. I don't want to devote my time to something futile only to discover I've gone down the wrong road once more. Not if I run the risk of dragging you down with me."

In that instant, the self-restraint she'd been guarding so carefully snapped. She ran until the remaining distance between them vanished, cupping his face in her palms.

After Samuel's death, she'd been so certain she knew

what she wanted. A well-planned, comfortable, ordinary life. A life in which she made decisions only with her head and never let her heart get the better of her again.

She'd been wrong. So very, very wrong.

"Striving for what your heart desires is never futile." She stared into blazing green eyes, needing to draw him in with the power of her gaze and make him listen. "You aren't at fault for wanting something out of the ordinary. You owe it to yourself to pursue it and see where it takes you. I don't know what that means for the future ... for us. I only know I want you, Jeremy, exactly as you are. Yes, there are obstacles, but I also know we can overcome them, and ... and—"

Her lips met his. She'd used all her strength to hold off on touching him, and then she'd tried to explain what was in her heart, but now, she could only communicate in a manner that transcended words. She sank into the kiss, running her fingers down his neck to the hair at his nape, feeling the familiar sparks flare as he responded in kind.

How quickly their bodies—their mouths—entwined, connecting in a way that made it difficult to know where he ended and she began. Her movements lacked finesse; she was under no illusions to the contrary. But how could she help it when every nerve ending burned with newfound intensity, screaming with the desire to be near him? To feel his heat and strength and cling to it like she would never let go.

She shifted her weight forward, whimpering into his mouth as her breasts rubbed against his chest, hindered by the bothersome muslin of her bodice. Whimpering again as his tongue stroked hers, and the evidence of his arousal nudged her belly through his loosened breeches.

For as long as she'd sat by the tree trunk with her pencil and drawing pad in hand, they'd spent their time at a precarious sort of distance, holding their need for physical intimacy at bay. But after this turn of events, she no longer wanted to prolong things. She had to make him understand. She needed to show him, with her body, just how ardently she meant what she'd said.

Pulling her lips from his and twisting out of the embrace for even a moment was torture. However, she needed to glance behind her, to take stock of the carpet of grass and wildflowers and his discarded coat and waistcoat that lay rumpled upon it. It would make for the crudest sort of bed. Yet it was perfect. Any place she could be with him, free to act on the passion that consumed her body and soul, was perfect.

He understood the meaning behind the look. In the next instant, she found herself being lowered to the ground, her head hitting his bunched-up coat as a sort of makeshift pillow, grass tickling the backs of her arms and ankles. He pushed her skirts up high and out of the way, kneeling between her parted thighs. Looking down at her as if he'd just uncovered a buried treasure in the grass.

He tugged the shirt she'd already loosened over his head, causing sunlight to bounce off the sculpted lines of his shoulders and chest. She ran the tip of her tongue over her swollen bottom lip, every inch of her skin tingling in that moment of anticipation.

A fortunately short-lived moment, for then, he was stretching out and leaning down so his weight hovered just above her, his teeth grazing her throat, her chest, while his hand connected with her sprawled-out wrist, pinning it to the ground. She arched her back with a moan, closing her eyes to shut out the brilliant light above, so all that remained was sensation. The fragrances of leaves and vibrant spring-time earth, and most of all, a heady scent that was alluringly male. The feel of powerful hands, heated breath, and wetness as his tongue traced her nipples through her bodice.

The sounds of her own needy cries, and—oh, was that fabric ripping?

She didn't care because, suddenly, her breasts were exposed to the open air, and his lips closed over one of the taut points as his fingers pinched the other. A fresh wave of yearning shot through her, and her eyes flew open, needing to focus on him once more. Needing to watch as he left her breast and dragged his hand over her body, pushing past muslin until he came to settle between her legs, running a teasing fingertip down her slit and to her entrance.

She hissed in a breath as he repeated the pattern, his mouth rising to land beside her ear. "I love how you're always wet and ready for me."

His low, heated words sent a frisson of longing to her core as surely as his finger. He always knew what to say, what to do, to drive her out of her head until she became nothing but a puddle of nerve endings. But she wasn't too far gone to develop the overarching need to return the favor.

"And I love how you fill me." She waited until he jerked his head up, then pulled at the remaining buttons of his breeches, watching his eyes become glimmering pools of need. "I love how you're so hard and hot." She freed him, stroking along his rigid length as he bit back a groan, guiding him toward where they both most wanted him to be. "I love how it feels when your cock is inside—"

He plunged into her, and anything else she'd thought to say gave way to a strangled moan. The throbbing emptiness within her was replaced by hot, insistent pressure, and she *loved* it, just as she'd said. When he didn't move, she wriggled beneath him, giving her hips an inelegant thrust upward as she uttered a one-word plea. "Jeremy."

"Theodora." His hand went back to her wrist, holding her in place, as he withdrew until only the tip of him brushed her sex. He locked eyes with her, his body so close but not close enough. Pleasuring her. Torturing her. Torturing himself, if his quivering hips were any indication.

It wasn't fair that he still possessed the capacity for restraint when she lay yearning and aching. It wasn't fair, and she was going half mad, and—

He gave another powerful thrust forward, seeming to fill her to new depths. And this time, he didn't stop.

He pushed into her over and over again, her hips working to meet each of his strokes. The pleasure that had been just out of reach now hit her with full force, building to become something fierce and unstoppable. He had to feel it, too, for his breaths came fast and heavy, and the muscles in his jaw looked tight. Much like the muscles in her limbs, which had grown so taut it felt like a simple touch could break her into pieces.

How much more of this blissful torment could she endure? How was she to stand it when he returned his lips to her ear, catching the lobe between his teeth before whispering heated words. "I'll never tire of this." His thrusts became rougher, more hurried. Just as she craved. "I'll never tire of watching your face as you climax and feeling you pulse around me. There is *nothing* more breathtaking."

She didn't endure. She shattered, her body throbbing from the waves of her release. Doing the very thing he said he most desired.

With a groan, he wrenched himself away from her just in time for the product of his own climax to fall upon the grass. The muscles in his chest heaved with exertion while his features twisted into an expression of unabashed ecstasy.

She had to agree: there was no sight better.

After a moment, he lay down beside her, stroking her hair as they waited for their breathing to slow. Even then, tiny sparks danced low in her belly.

A while after that, hardness twitched against her thigh

again, and she climbed atop him, eager to take advantage of the fact that his shirt and breeches remained discarded in a heap. Eager to claim what she knew she wanted.

She'd always been told she was headstrong and passionate. Why try to deny that now? Why pretend to want something other than what had become engrained in the very marrow of her?

Once they found themselves spent and breathless once more, they may have dozed upon their earthy bed, although her mind had grown so hazy that she couldn't say for sure. It was only when he sat up, rifling through the pocket of his discarded breeches and proclaiming he hadn't brought his watch, that time came to exist once more. Indeed, the sun had traveled farther across the sky, and while it was by no means late in the day, they knew, by silent agreement, that the moment had come to leave their wooded sanctuary behind.

Jeremy busied himself with retrieving his various articles of clothing and pulling them on while she worked to straighten her gown, tucking in the torn neckline of her shift, before sauntering to the base of the oak tree and gathering up her drawing implements. She would have to finish the sketch later. By memory. Or better yet, she could bring it along when she visited his room that night. Unfortunately, she'd have to revert to drawing by candlelight, her wickedly captivating subject no longer brightened by the sun's golden glow. At least she would have the benefit of an *extremely* vivid mental picture.

She smiled to herself as they made their way out of the wood, heading in the direction of Beaumont's manicured gardens that would eventually lead them back to the house. Her limbs had turned weightless, her feet feeling like they walked on air. In fact, a satiated lightness washed over her whole body. It made it challenging for her to think of anything beyond contentment and pleasure. But as for the difficult bits—the details of what came next—she was filled with a surprising sense of calm. A certainty that, one way or another, they would figure it all out, and they *would* both get what they wanted.

All would have been well had distractedness not caused her to drop her pencil near another towering oak by the edge of the wood. She bent down to pick it up, and when she stood again, Jeremy was right there, waiting. He backed her into the tree, his palms pressing into the trunk so they framed her face, his body pinning hers in place.

Their lips connected at once, causing the sparks she'd thought satisfied to roar back to life. Did satisfaction even exist where her desire for him was concerned? Or would it just keep growing, keeping her in a perpetual state of wanting?

This was one more opportunity to find out. One more chance to be together before they parted ways on the garden path and the real world hit them once again.

Why shouldn't they? Branches and leaves concealed them from view, and they remained far from the house, and surely the day was still young. Besides, this wouldn't take long. Her mind already envisioned the way it would go. The way he would haul up her skirts, grip her thighs, and hurriedly thrust into her, bringing them both to a quick, rough release.

Heat pooled between her legs as they deepened the kiss and, just as she'd envisioned, he grabbed fistfuls of her muslin dress, sliding them upward—

"What in the blistering hell is going on here?"

The next moments elapsed as though time had suddenly slowed to a crawl. Jeremy's hand froze upon her thigh. Her breath hitched, and she forgot to exhale. And all the while, her brain tried to comprehend the fact that she'd just heard incensed words spoken by neither her nor Jeremy. That a shadow had appeared on the forest floor that hadn't been there before. That a figure loomed.

The haze of desire, followed by the sudden shock, had her head spinning, making pieces of this puzzle slow to insert themselves in place. She'd seen this man before. For that's what the figure who'd happened upon them and now stood glowering beneath a leafy oak branch was—a man. One with thinning brown-gray hair. A lanky frame. A crisp gray coat and breeches and a cravat knotted so tightly it looked like it must keep his face perpetually flushed and his lips in a permanent scowl.

All at once, the meaning behind the picture in front of her eyes clicked, and time seemed to speed up again, hurtling forward like a racehorse dashing around a track. Jeremy spun away, and she stumbled forward, letting her skirts fall to the ground.

It didn't make a difference. The damage had already been done.

Any swift movements or explanations they may find the power to undertake wouldn't change the fact that they'd just been caught in a passionate embrace by none other than Mr. Adolphus Clare.

16

Jeremy had done plenty of things over the years to earn his father's censure. Staying out past curfew at school. Carousing. Focusing too much time on his silly writing hobby. However, on none of those occasions when he'd stood before his father awaiting his wrath, even as a young schoolboy, had his heart sunk so low in his boots.

"Good day, Mrs. Prescott." Adolphus Clare, longtime man of business, bowed to her stiffly, his expression nondescript. Almost as if he *hadn't* just encountered them in the throes of passion. "I wonder if you might excuse us for a moment so I can have a private word with my son."

Theo's eyes shifted back and forth between Jeremy and the intruder, her face displaying something he'd never seen on it before. Uncertainty. The color had drained from her cheeks, her breaths coming too fast, and he wanted nothing more than to take her in his arms.

Yet that was impossible. As much as he might wish to proclaim his affections for her to the world, doing so to his father would require delicacy. Some *very* carefully chosen words, the exact nature of which he hadn't determined.

Above all else, he wanted to spare Theo any unpleasantness as he tried to figure it out while his father's outrage rained upon him.

He gave his head a slight nod, praying she understood. She must have, for she nodded as well, an abrupt, tense motion directed at his father. Then, with a final glance toward him, she spun on her heels, striding toward the house with brisk, unwavering footfalls.

Watching her go was akin to having a piece of him ripped away. He should have kept his damn hands to himself by the tree, and perhaps they wouldn't be in this predicament. It wasn't supposed to happen like this. They were supposed to have more time alone to think things through. To plan for the future ...

"Fuck!" He dug his fingers into his temples as if that could somehow clear his head. It seemed he'd begun pacing, for his boots dragged along leaves and grass, his vision filling with alternating sights of pristine oak trees and his father's reddening face. He needed to concentrate, to determine how to manage this appropriately. But only one word pounded through his head. *Wrong. Wrong. Wrong.*

"Fuck," his father muttered under his breath, his feet shuffling against the ground. He pulled off his top hat, wiping away a band of perspiration that had accumulated at his brow. Adolphus Clare, when angry, rather reminded Jeremy of a pot of vegetables that had been neglected upon a fire. Slowly simmering but building momentum all the time until, eventually, water spewed over the side and crackled upon the flames.

"Fuck!" Jeremy shouted at the cloudless sky, his voice echoing among the towering oak branches. What difference did it make if anyone else heard him now? He did one more turn over the uneven ground before forcing his legs to slow, coming to a stop in front of his father. It made not a scrap of difference because one of the worst people possible had already discovered him in the wood at the worst moment. Which raised a question. "What are you doing here, anyway?"

"What am I *doing* here?" His father's chin quivered as he quietly spat out the words, the redness in his face becoming more a shade of purple. The forgotten pot shuddered and hissed in the hearth, water boiling ever closer to the edge. Until suddenly, the lid shot clear across the kitchen and water erupted into the fire. "In case you've forgotten, I've been employed by the Marquess and Marchioness of Rockliffe for the past three *decades*," he roared. "As the dowager didn't feel well enough to continue with our previously scheduled meeting today, I thought I would seek you out instead. So perhaps the better question is, what are *you* doing here?"

Jeremy's eyes inadvertently darted to that one particular tree. The one where he'd spun Theo so her back rested against the trunk and his palms had pressed into the bark as he claimed her lips. "Do you really wish for an additional explanation?"

"No." His father made a strange, strangled sound, pulling at the knots in his cravat as if they'd suddenly grown too tight against his neck. "Forget that part. What I really want to know is *why*."

Jeremy opened his mouth to speak, but it seemed his father changed his mind on that, too, for he silenced him with an accusatory shake of his finger. "Do you have any idea how stupid you've been? This could very well lead to the ruin of us both. And for what? A quick tup in the trees."

"It isn't like that," he bit out, his own anger beginning to simmer. Toward his father? Toward himself? "You know nothing about what's between Theo and me."

His father's eyes bulged, his finger continuing to waggle with indignation. "*Mrs. Prescott* is none of your concern. You were hired to tutor her boys, nothing more. Anything beyond that, you must put out of your head *immediately*. The dowager has other plans for her."

"And what about what Theo wants? What I want?" Jeremy was yelling again, the sound pounding through his head along with his own heartbeat. Once more, the issue that constantly hovered over him came to punch him in the gut. He desired Theo with every scrap of his being, but he wasn't good enough for her. He couldn't provide all the things she needed. But there had to be some way ... some way he could remedy that.

"I could resign from my position as a tutor." Desperation clawed at his insides, causing the wheels in his head to start turning, for him to give voice to his half-formed thoughts. "I could go back to Oxford. Become ordained. Another living might come along. I should at least be able to obtain a position as curate. I may be far from a peer, but no one could say that a church profession was unrespectable or unfitting for a family—"

He was rambling. Vowing to return to that life, to the very thing he knew down to his core was wrong for him. Yet if it meant he could have Theo at his side, comfortable and provided for—stably if not richly—it would all be worth it.

"Dear God." His father's voice abruptly quieted, the color draining from his face and leaving it a sickly white. "Do you mean to say you're entertaining thoughts of *marrying* this woman? Of becoming a *father* to her children?"

Jeremy couldn't speak. The words, when put so bluntly, knocked the wind out of him. Yet that didn't mean the answer was anything other than a resounding yes.

The truth must have showed on his face, for his father

gasped, looking like Jeremy had just dealt him a blow. Fresh droplets of sweat coated his forehead, and his breath shook as he exhaled, the only noise in a moment of silence. Before all at once, the enraged red flush returned, sweeping from his neck up to his receding hairline, and he practically roared with fury. "No! *No*. You squandered a perfectly good marriage opportunity, yet now you fancy yourself in love with the last woman on earth you should have. Of all the idiotic things! I'd have never procured this blasted tutor position for you had I suspected for even a moment—"

"What do you mean?" Jeremy's body tensed, his skin prickling with something hot and unpleasant.

"Why do you think you were admitted to Rockliffe House so readily when you have no prior experience tutoring children? Why do you think you're compensated so handsomely for your efforts?" His father's green-gray eyes glittered with outrage. "Because *I* arranged it, on account of a favor owed me by the dowager."

Now it was Jeremy's turn to feel like he'd been punched. He held his legs stiffly, forcing himself not to stagger. Not even to blink. "Why would the dowager owe you a favor? And why would you ask for this?"

"I meant what I said, Jeremy." His father must have heard the question, although he chose to ignore it, instead glaring at him like he was about to spit poison. "Stay away from Theodora Prescott. In fact, remove yourself from this whole bloody house before matters have a chance to escalate. For if you hear nothing else I say, listen to this. The dowager will never, under any circumstances, approve of this match. And when things don't go as the dowager wishes, she will use any means necessary to make it so they do."

"No." Jeremy shook his head numbly, scarcely able to comprehend what he was hearing. "I won't be waylaid by fear of a bitter woman's anger, even if she is a former marchioness. Theo doesn't give a damn about it, either, I'm certain, and—"

His father cut him off with a curt, hollow laugh. "You know, Theodora Prescott herself was in a position to oppose the dowager not so long ago. Turned down all offers of assistance after her impoverished husband's death, said she and her boys would manage without help from the Prescotts, just as they always had. What a tragedy it was when, just a short time later, her printshop—her final hope at independence—burned to the ground."

The brilliant morning sun continued to streak across Jeremy's skin, but his insides turned to ice. "Are you saying—"

"Yes." His father wasted no time in forming a response. In confirming, with a single word, the worst of Jeremy's fears.

Horror made his throat so dry that it became difficult not to gag. But was there even the slightest chance he misunderstood? That his father had the wrong of it, that he overestimated the dowager's treachery? "How are you so sure that ..." Jeremy let the naive question die on his lips. Of course his father wasn't wrong. He was the dowager's longtime man of business. Ready to jump the moment she summoned him, no matter the time of day or night. Always prepared to fulfill his duty. Even if he came home afterward with his face pinched and his shoulders slumped.

He'd been with the Marquess and Marchioness of Rockliffe for so many years. Had worked his way into a position of trust. Was likely privy to all the family's secrets.

Jeremy choked back bile as he sustained what felt like yet another punch to the abdomen. He swallowed away the acrid taste, trying to form a final, detrimental question.

But no, he didn't need to pose that one, either. He had

only to peer at his father's face. Still reddened and lined with sweat, but at the same time, so oddly assured. And ruthless.

Theo's printshop had been reduced to ashes ... The dowager owed her man of business a favor ...

"You did this." Jeremy's voice came out as a stony, barely audible rasp. "The fire. You were the one responsible."

His father didn't flinch. He didn't so much as blink. And most of all, he didn't deny a thing. He merely stood there, waiting for Jeremy to absorb the whole sickening truth.

Jeremy turned abruptly, staggering to the nearest tree trunk for support. He pressed his palm into the bark to steady himself and looked at the ground, feeling dangerously close to casting up his accounts.

What was even supposed to come next? He could shout more oaths into the sky. Bellow his outrage at his father. Heave branches and stones until some of the ire flowed from his body.

Maybe. But that wouldn't change the fact that so much he'd believed was a lie, and everything he'd hoped for was shattered.

Even with his eyes planted staunchly on the tree roots below, as if they could somehow give him answers in a world turned upside down, he could feel his father's shrewd gaze boring into him. He didn't want to look at the man. Didn't want to be anywhere near him. Yet that unnerving sense of being watched continued until there was nothing left but to lift his head and lock eyes with someone who now felt more like a nefarious stranger.

"I assume you now understand how serious I am about this." His father knew better than to approach him. Yet even from a distance, the lilt of his voice and hard set of his mouth grated deep.

Jeremy wouldn't give him the satisfaction of nodding in

agreement. He wouldn't move a muscle. However, his father needed no further encouragement to keep going. "I don't want to see you hurt or cast down. You were meant for far better things. And if you're too thickheaded to walk away from this for your own benefit, then do it for hers. For the consequences she could face if you refuse. Do I make myself clear?"

Blistering fury surged through Jeremy's veins, and he lunged forward, grinding to a halt inches away from his father's face. He grabbed hold of the man's stupid, too-tight cravat, peering into those censorious eyes that widened just a shade from the sudden assault.

Jeremy was ready to scream and curse and tear the forest down. To unleash his vehemence for what his father had done, to avenge Theo ...

And then what? Would that make him anything other than the misfit tutor who had employment only because his father had ruined the woman he loved? Would that free Theo and her boys from the Dowager Marchioness of Rockliffe's clutches? Would that do anything to ameliorate this whole goddamn mess?

He released his father's cravat as if it had suddenly grown venomous teeth, jerking his body away at the same moment his father stumbled backward.

With what felt very much like a knife in his chest, he stomped over grass and wildflowers on a path that would lead him out of the wood. Snarling a single word before he went.

"Perfectly."

17

The usual gentle knock sounded upon Jeremy's door around midnight. It was the sound that ran through his head the whole time he paced about his bedchamber by candlelight, gathering items from his desk and clothespress. The sound his body longed for, his heart craved. While at the same time, the worst thing in the world he could possibly hear.

He dropped the crumpled shirt he'd been holding into the valise stretched out atop the foot of his bed, rushing to the door with brisk, silent strides.

Theo. He didn't need to open the door to realize it was her on the other side. Yet the moment he did, and she stood before him in the flesh, all soft curves and candlelit loveliness, his heart gave an excruciating lurch.

To say the remainder of the day had been hell would be a vast understatement. And instead of having the freedom to quickly address all that required discussion with her—so at least that first painful, inevitable step could be over and done—they'd been forced to wait.

No sooner had he stormed away from the wood and toward the house than Benedict and Alexander came rambling into the garden, eager to tell him about their new acquaintances in the village. From there, they'd asked if he could bring out a picnic blanket so they could complete their lessons outdoors. That much he'd managed. For their sakes, he'd read aloud, praised Benedict's Greek translation, and discussed the latest chapter of Alexander's story. Trying to ignore the fact he would never do so again.

But what had come after that was damn near impossible to abide. The dowager had risen just in time for dinner, insisting that Adolphus Clare and son must join the family in the dining room for the evening. Such an invitation—the opportunity to sit at a marchioness's resplendent table, to indulge in the finest food—could be considered nothing short of an honor. Yet when it forced him to spend several hours mere feet away from Theo, trying to keep up with the stiff conversation around the table while simultaneously feeling his father's discerning glances falling over them both, how could he view it as anything but a curse?

Stepping away from the table early—or more daringly, requesting a private word with Theo—would be impossible without rousing suspicion. And so, he'd sat in an uncomfortable state of numbness until the time came when he could politely decline joining an after-dinner game of whist in the drawing room, because he'd be damned if he spent one more minute in company with the rest of these people.

Which is what had led him to his bedchamber, where he began haphazardly throwing things in his valise, all the while wondering if Theo would appear. Half thinking it would be better if she didn't, that it would cut down on the ache for them both if he uttered his farewell in the form of a note.

However, now she was here, and he couldn't be sorry for

the opportunity to gaze at her one last time. Even if the words that followed were agony.

He motioned her inside, hurriedly shutting the door with a quiet click. He'd been such a blissfully ignorant fool, spending the week believing that if they just timed things correctly, they could do as they pleased. Yet he now knew that eyes could be anywhere.

In the safety of his bedchamber, he could truly take her in. However, what was he supposed to do next? Images of their time together in this room went racing through his mind. Of pressing her against the door, too impatient to wait another second before claiming her lips. Of lifting her in his arms and depositing her atop the bed. Of watching her remove each article of clothing, one by one, until she revealed every inch of her concealed beauty.

As he could do none of those things any longer, his body didn't know how to position itself. He brought a hand forward—and then retreated. Shuffled sideways a step. Locked eyes with her, stared at that little crease between her eyebrows that suggested, once again, uncertainty.

And suddenly, she was in his arms, her hands wrapped around his back as she dropped her warm weight against his chest.

He should never have allowed it. Each second spent like this—absorbing her heat, breathing in the faint scent of lilacs—would only make tearing away from her that much more gut-wrenching. But maybe these were the moments that would sustain him when he returned to his bachelor's lodgings, alone and purposeless.

He didn't dare envelop her in an embrace. He used a finger, though, to trace over one of the voluminous curls spilling down her back. To brush against the silk of her dressing gown. If nothing else, he could feel thankful for the fact that the night rail underneath was sturdy cotton that went up to her throat. Anything less would be torture.

She lifted her head, peering up at him with dark, expressive eyes, the crease above her nose deepening. "God, Jeremy, it was agony having to wait this long to speak with you. Please, you must tell me everything about your conversation with ... What's this?"

Her gaze fell to the other side of the room, to the valise stuffed with crumpled clothing upon his bed.

He cleared his throat. There was no use prolonging things. "I'm leaving. Going back to London. The mail coach comes through tomorrow evening, and I plan to be on it."

"You what?" Her eyes widened, and she took a step backward to better assess him from head to toe. To peer again at his hastily packed valise. "I agree we'll need to leave, but I need a little more time to—"

"No." He shook his head, to the extent he could. His body felt like it had turned to ice, ready to shatter from the slightest movement. "*I'm* going to London. Alone. I'm afraid I must resign my position at once."

"But I thought ..." She paused, a pinkish tinge sweeping over her cheeks. Until abruptly, her arms rose to cross her chest, and something flashed in her eyes, dark and dangerous. "*What* did your father say to you, Jeremy?"

He hated himself for what needed to come next. Hated the thought of causing her even a second of anguish. But if he didn't do this, what would be the consequences? Would the Dowager Lady Rockliffe invent some fresh way to make her conform—something that would cut even deeper, that would break her even more thoroughly? Would the dowager be so callous as to use the boys in her scheming? He couldn't take that chance, for any suffering Theo experienced as a result would rest on his shoulders.

"My father said nothing that wasn't true." His words came out dull, hollow. "It seems I must apologize for overstepping and make way for a tutor better able to stay within the necessary bounds. Like it or not, your marriage rendered you kin to a marquess, and there are certain expectations that go along with that. Ones with which I have no business interfering. You have your place, just as I have mine, and I was wrong to forget it. Therefore, I must thank you for the employment opportunity and take my leave. Had we been thinking clearly, we would have realized there was no other way for this to end. This is how it needs to be. And how I want it to be," he added quietly, as an afterthought.

Somehow, the words came out without breaking, even though the lie had torn him apart until nothing within him felt whole. He could only hope he'd been sufficiently emotionless while also thorough. For their relationship had to be severed, once and for all.

If speaking the words had been difficult, watching her reaction to them was so much worse. She drew in a sharp breath, emotions flickering across her face. First, the reappearance of that bewildered little crease. Then, a fire that seemed to ignite in her eyes, ready to unleash all the passion he'd come to love. And then ... nothing. A shadow spread across her features, and it was as if her face became a stone mask.

She took a rigid step backward, her fingers digging into the silk of her dressing gown as she clutched her arms more tightly around her body. "It seems I was mistaken on a few points." Her tone contained a hardness to match her expression. "How fortunate I had you—an accomplished scholar —to explain them to me, Mr. Clare."

She spun away from him, her hand flying to the door latch. Every grain of him yearned to reach out and stop her, to hold her in his arms, to get down on his knees and beg forgiveness for every untruth he'd just told.

But he couldn't. He had to let her go.

He staggered back to his bed, ruing the fact that his bedchamber was devoid of any sort of alcohol. With the mail coach not arriving until late tomorrow, what better way to pass the time than get drunk into oblivion? Then again, it seemed doubtful that even brandy could cure this ache.

He tugged off his cravat and threw it in the valise, then collapsed upon the brocade counterpane, staring up at the ceiling. Likely his view for hours to come, as he very much doubted he'd sleep a wink during his final night at Beaumont Manor. His final night under the same roof as Theo.

He closed his eyes, letting a vision of her float into his thoughts. Not the woman who'd just stormed out of his room, cold and distant, because of *his* actions. But the woman who'd peered at him over a drawing pad, and given him a brilliant smile to rival the sunlight around her, and clung to him like he made up her world.

He'd done it for her. Theodora Prescott, a woman of passion, determination, and strength. He'd wanted so much to be her rescuer, to carry her away from a life she didn't want. Yet of one fact, he was certain. Without him, she would find a way to get by. She'd made a friend—perhaps more—in a viscount. She was developing her talents as an artist. And above all, she'd more than proved her resilience.

She would move on from this. Somehow, she would find a way to achieve everything she wanted. And without him as an obstacle—his very presence bringing about the threat of condemnation—she and her boys *would* attain happiness, eventually.

He would take that knowledge and savor it. Use it to feel happiness on their behalf. For what else was left?

His eyes flew open, returning to the white plaster above, as his heart continued its dull thudding. A steady, throbbing ache that may lessen with time but never fully leave him.

From now on, any joy he eked out would come from whisperings of her well-being and success. As for hopes of obtaining his own joy—of moving on, of reopening his heart—well, those were already lost.

18

Theo had the dream again. The same one that had plagued her so often in the days following the printshop's destruction.

The dream where she trudged through the shop's entryway—devoid of its wooden door—and her feet brushed over a carpet of ashes. Soot had blackened the jagged glass in the windows, making the space dim. Yet it was bright enough to see what remained.

Or rather, that nothing remained.

She trod over cinders, as with each step, the horrifying truth sank in a little deeper. A useless array of metal pieces littered the floor. A few hinges and screws. Sorts, now devoid of their type case. But there was no more wooden press. No more stacks of paper. Everything that meant anything was gone. She was ruined.

Pungent smoke filled her lungs as she opened her mouth, a scream ready to rip from her throat. But then, a burst of flame and a brilliant flash of silver pierced her eyes, and she found herself transported back to her bed, breathless and perspiring.

The dream ended no differently when it returned to her today. She sat bolt upright, clutching her chest as she gulped in mouthfuls of fresh, uncontaminated air. This wasn't the printshop. She was in bed, wrapped up in a tangle of silky sheets, surrounded by delicate floral bed curtains and an intricately carved bed frame, in her room at ... Beaumont Manor.

No, this wasn't the printshop. But as the events of the previous night came rushing back, she found herself flooded with that same crushing sense of loss.

She scrambled from the bed, trying to ignore the dull throbbing originating in her head and traveling down her body. With a hand pushed to her forehead, she stumbled to the window, squinting at the burst of early morning light that hit her as she threw back the curtains. It was as if the sun were mocking her, rising with even more brilliance than the day before. Even though within her, there was only bleakness.

Judging by the lack of rustling in the corridor, it was still so early that she'd be best off flopping back into bed and letting sleep shut out reality a while longer. If only that were possible. However, she was under no illusions that she could drift back into a state of oblivion. Instead, she would lie tossing and turning while memories of the day before continued to build, mingling with the aftermath of her dream. She couldn't let herself succumb to that.

She went to her clothespress and pulled out the first dress she laid eyes on, a simple gray muslin without adornments. It would do. What she looked like didn't matter a whit as long as she could depart this room in all haste. She had to get away, to breathe air untainted by the smoke from her dream, to go someplace where she could think logically without having those thoughts break her.

A short time later, with the dress thrown on over clumsily laced stays and her hair barely contained in a loose knot, she slipped into the corridor, its tall, polished windows allowing sunlight to stream through. A fresh stab of pain hit her in the forehead at the added brightness, and she turned her eyes to the floor, taking a moment to get her bearings. Where was she even going? Downstairs, she supposed, was a sensible place to start, and if she just kept her head down to avoid looking directly into the light, and if she forced her too-heavy legs to keep moving, then surely, she could make it and determine where to go next—

"Mrs. Prescott."

A sharp voice called her name at the same time she crashed into something rigid. She blinked rapidly, trying to process the source of the collision. A spotless brown coat. A stiff white cravat, knotted too tightly around the neck. A face containing thin, pinched lips and green-gray eyes, peering down at her with an expression of mild disapproval.

Mr. Adolphus Clare.

She took a rapid step backward, careful to keep her face turned away from the blinding light of the windows. "Mr. Clare."

The name felt all wrong on her lips. She'd uttered it so many times in the past but for an entirely different person. One who exuded warmth instead of coldness. Tenderness instead of severity. Jeremy ...

She stiffened her shoulders, peering at this man who was Jeremy's kin, yet decidedly *not* Jeremy, with a scowl to rival his own. If he thought she would blush and cower before him after what happened yesterday—not to mention after her clumsiness just now—he had another thing coming.

"You're up early this morning." He stood assessing her for another moment, his eyebrow rising toward the thin wisps of hair above his forehead. "Is everything well?"

Of course everything wasn't well. Adolphus Clare had

tramped into the wood just as she'd allowed herself to believe good fortune would shine on her once more, sending all her hopes tumbling down. Driving Jeremy away. Revealing what a fool she'd been.

She swallowed down the lump at the back of her throat. "Quite well, thank you."

Her voice didn't waver. Her knees, however, chose that exact moment to grow weak, sending her pitching to the side.

Mr. Clare's arm shot out to steady her, his cold, slender fingers digging into her sleeve and jerking her upright. Yet in doing so, he'd turned them to face the windows so sunlight poured upon them both. She closed her eyes against the renewed pain in her head, and when she opened them, careful not to look toward the glass itself, even the silver and red glint of Mr. Clare's sleeve buttons created tiny but agonizing stabs behind her eyes.

Silver. A burst of flame. Again, the culmination of her dream came rushing back, only this time, it didn't feel like a dream but like a memory. Something she'd seen before. Something that filled her with a sense of alarm. It couldn't be ... Yet a chilling idea began to take hold, and she couldn't shake it.

Suddenly, she knew where she needed to go. She'd realized from the moment she woke up that she couldn't spend the day lingering under the same roof as Jeremy, just waiting for him to depart, but now, she had an exact destination selected. She needed to travel to the printshop immediately, which meant first going to see the person who could help get her there. He could help her with a great many things if she would only let him. Perhaps that time had come ...

She staggered again, wrenching herself free of his grip, letting her feet plod toward the stairs as fast as they would go.

"Mrs. Prescott, are you certain you're all right?"

She didn't take the time to answer. Any hopes of feigning normalcy were lost, and she had to get away. If he reported to the dowager that he'd caught her first thing in the morning displaying fitful behavior, then what of it? She would already be gone by then. As for any consequences, she would deal with them later.

If the butler found her early-morning request to have the carriage brought around at once strange, that didn't matter, either. For he complied with nothing beyond a slight twitch of his eyebrow, and within ten minutes, she was sitting upon the carriage's plush seat with the curtains drawn, meandering down the drive and away from Beaumont Manor.

She rested her head against the seatback, trying not to think of how each movement of the carriage, even in darkness, made it ache. Trying to quash the panicked urgency that swelled within her. Trying not to feel at all.

But some sensations refused to be quieted. Namely, the gnawing pain that engulfed her chest. The pain that provided a constant reminder of how wrong she'd been to make free with her heart.

She'd sworn she would never do such a thing again. She'd known better. Why, then, had she invested herself, body and soul, in Jeremy Clare when she knew it went against all reason? Why had she started envisioning a future with him where pieces of the world magically aligned to allow them to be together? Why had she thought their passion, their intimacy, signified things that couldn't be put into words? That he understood those things, and he wanted them as much as she did.

It hadn't, and he didn't. She'd thought for sure he'd hinted ... But at the same time, they'd never spoken of plans or made declarations of love or commitment. And whatever his father had said to him had been enough to make him walk away without a second thought. If that hadn't been his plan the whole time, once he'd sufficiently slaked his lust.

Her stomach roiled, and she leaned forward to rest her elbows atop her lap, grateful this part of the journey was only short. The carriage soon rolled to a stop, and a quick glance through the curtains revealed the stone steps of a resplendent manor house directly in front of her.

She let the accompanying footman help her down, careful to keep her eyes veiled from the sun. At least the awaiting portico was shaded, and a light perfume of roses and freshly clipped grass filled her nose as she mounted the steps, putting her stomach somewhat at ease.

She straightened her unflattering gray skirt. Smoothed back the hair that had fallen around her face. And knocked on Rosemead's stately front door.

The butler appeared in short order, unable to stop his mouth from gaping slightly as he took in the sight before him.

"Has Lord Pembrook returned?" She peered into the entryway, her heart beating with skittering thuds. "If he has, I need to speak with him right away."

The butler eyed her for a moment longer, his jaw twitching. But then, ever the efficient and exquisitely mannered servant, he stepped aside, motioning for her to enter. "Follow me, please."

She scurried inside, wasting no time in trailing after him as he led her down a corridor and into a cheerily decorated morning room adorned with sunny yellow wallpaper and furniture upholstered in shades of pale blue.

"If you could wait here a moment, Mrs. Prescott, I'll see if Lord Pembrook is free to receive visitors." The butler delivered a courteous bow, then swept back through the doorway, the sound of his increasingly hurried footsteps echoing down the corridor. Likely in a rush to tell the viscount, using the gentlest terms possible, that a deranged woman awaited him in the morning room at whatever ungodly hour it was.

She went to each window, pulling the curtains just enough to block out the worst of the direct sunlight, and collapsed upon a blue and white striped settee. Then, she got to her feet again, pacing up and down the room. Looking at anything to distract her from her racing heart. The ormolu clock upon the mantel. The vase of white lilies ...

"Theodora! What a surprise." Percy strode into the room wearing his customary gentle smile, giving no indication she'd done him the inconvenience of rousing him from bed. Everything about his attire was flawless, as usual—his blue coat even matched the stripes upon the settee. Only the stubble lining his jaw gave her cause to suspect he'd been unprepared and forced to rush downstairs for this unexpected visit.

He approached a cerulean velvet sofa—which, thankfully, sat in a corner outside the sun's direct path—and motioned for her to join him. "I returned only last night, so I must confess, I anticipated having to wait a little longer to see you—but, is something the matter?"

Their eyes locked as she came up alongside him and his immediately filled with concern. She sank onto the sofa cushion, feeling his gaze continue to evaluate her. No doubt taking in her unsightly tangle of hair. The shadows beneath her eyes. The pallor of her skin. But when he lowered himself beside her, there was no scorn in his expression. Simply calm, unaffected caring.

Her heart pounded. Her head did, too, and she rested it within her clammy palm. She took a breath, ready to utter the short speech she'd prepared.

"I cannot marry you."

Had she really allowed those words to cross her lips? They were the opposite of the ones she'd intended to say, but she must have, for the echo of them rang through her ears, and Percy shifted beside her, biting down gently on his lower lip. Her fingertips began trembling beneath her head, and she straightened her neck, daring to meet his eyes again. "I'm sorry."

All at once, her hand was within his, and he clasped it lightly, unfazed by any dampness. "It's quite all right, Theo. The arrangement I proposed was merely a suggestion and in no way an obligation on your part."

She squeezed her eyes shut a moment, feeling tears rising dangerously close to the surface. "It's not because I don't value you and the kindness you've shown me—"

"I know." He patted her hand once more before carefully releasing it, bringing his own hands to rest clasped atop his lap. "I understand."

She swiped quickly at the corners of her eyelids, swallowing back a thick thump. Indeed, the new small smile he gave her had a look of ... knowing, somehow.

Which was ironic, given that she struggled to comprehend it all herself.

She'd come here to seek help, and with only a few differently arranged words, she could have obtained it.

Yet, in the end, some little revelatory piece inside her had broken free. It had always been there, really, subtly nudging her, but when the pivotal moment came, she could no longer contain it.

Despite everything that had happened, she couldn't deny what was in her heart. Even if that heart was now shattered. Even if Percy desired a marriage involving nothing beyond friendship. Their union would be convenient, but it wouldn't be real. She couldn't live that lie.

Not when, for better or worse, so much of her was driven by passion. That passion may have gotten her in more trouble than she cared to remember. It may have nearly snapped her in two. Yet passion—*love*—had also fulfilled her in a way nothing else could, to the point the aftermath was almost worth it.

Perhaps this time, her heart had been damaged beyond repair. It pounded agonizingly enough in her chest to make it feel that way. But if there was even a tiny chance it could become whole again in the future—in the very, *very* distant future—she had to leave herself open to it.

Of course, that revelation did nothing to soothe her at present. Nor did it assist her with the other problems that still needed solving now that she'd rejected the easiest solution. A way to print Samuel's manuscript and begin earning a steady income. The means to procure a home, just for her and the boys. And most pressingly at the moment, a method of getting to London.

She shuddered as a wave of weariness swept through her, and pain darted behind her eyes once more.

"Is something else wrong?" Percy kept his voice low and calming, as if she were a frightened animal he didn't want to scare away. "If anything is troubling you, I hope you feel you can confide in me. And if there's anything I can do to assist you, anything at all you require, you need only ask."

He ... still wanted to help her? Even though she'd turned him down? Tears threatened again, not born purely from sorrow but from the tiniest flicker of hope that emerged from beneath the crushing weight of desperation and despondency. In a world that shattered around her, she still had one person left to trust. That knowledge made all the difference.

"Some headache powder, if you have it." She started small with her requests, trying to smile between clenched teeth. She should really go back to Beaumont Manor and rest before her condition had a chance to worsen and the remainder of the household noticed she was gone. However, doing so would mean ignoring her intuition in favor of lying about in her bedchamber while thoughts of Jeremy consumed her. Not to mention, in traversing the corridors, she would run the risk of *seeing* him. Or, God forbid, having another encounter with Adolphus Clare and his scrutinizing gaze.

The stifling smoke and flash of light from her dream hurtled back to inundate her senses again, and her limbs went tense. Once again, suspicions tugged at her with a strange insistence. She needed to go to the printshop, looking for answers, because something wasn't right.

"Also ... if you sincerely mean I may ask for anything ..." She paused, waiting to see if the absurdity of the idea would hit her and make it vanish. But it didn't. The idea swirled through her thoughts, calling to her, until her words came out in a tumble. "I wonder if I might borrow your coach. To travel to London. Only for the day. For I need to go urgently, and the Rockliffe coachman would never accept such a request from me without the dowager's permission. If you'd be willing to assist me ..."

Percy tilted his head to the side, unable to stop himself from staring at her, causing the crease in his brow to deepen. And how could she fault him? She'd shown up at his door far earlier than good manners dictated, looking a fright and behaving peculiarly. Yet she lacked the ability to explain herself more clearly, for voicing her fears aloud would make her sound nonsensical. She had no proof. She only knew there was a force within her driving her forward, and she needed his help.

"Very well." He straightened, rising to his feet in one seamless motion. "One moment, please."

He'd said ... oh, he'd said yes. Relief swept over her, putting a temporary pause to the tumult within. Her eyes followed him as he went to a nearby end table, ringing the brass bell upon it, and strode out of the room. In another moment, indistinct murmurs sounded on the other side of the door, followed by footsteps. Then more murmurs. Setting her plan—if she could call it that—into motion.

It didn't take long before he appeared in the doorway again, carrying a small velvet bag. "I've asked for the coach to be made ready, and my housekeeper will return from the stillroom in a minute with your headache powder."

She scrambled to her feet as fast as she could without jostling her head, moving to meet him in the middle of the room. "Thank you. Truly. A thousand times."

"Yes. Well. I have a feeling trying to dissuade you would be futile." He attempted a small smile, though his face still contained traces of worried lines around his mouth and forehead. "I can accompany you should you require assistance."

"Thank you, but that's unnecessary. I'm certain I can manage." Her response came quickly, without the need for thought. Whatever awaited her at the printshop, she needed to face it alone.

"I suspected as much. In that case, you must take this."

She gasped as he dropped the bag into her hand, and the unmistakable weight of coins filled her palm. "No. You've already done more than enough. I cannot accept your charity besides."

She tried shoving the bag back at him, but he encircled his hands around hers, firmly pressing it into her grip. "It isn't charity. Consider it payment for that painting of yours you showed me. That one with the garden that I said reminded me of Rosemead. I'd like to purchase it."

"I cannot—"

"You can, Theodora." He took a long step backward before she could make another attempt to forcibly return the money. "I trust you'll see the painting delivered to me after your return from London?"

She stayed unmoving for a moment, the velvet weight continuing to push into her skin. Every part of her hurt. All of her was lost, except for the stanch, terrified, foolhardy part that insisted on this journey. But in front of her stood a single spot of comfort.

She lurched forward, wrapping her arms around his neck, grateful for the hand that offered a gentle pat against her back. "Thank you."

That word alone felt insufficient. However, if she lingered, letting all the reasons for her gratitude to him on this horrific day pour out, the tears would start, and she wouldn't have it in her to make them end.

She straightened herself quickly, taking a few steps toward the door. Any minute now, the housekeeper would arrive with the remedy for her headache, and word would come that the coach was ready. From there, she would need only to send her own coachman back to Beaumont Manor with a message for Amelia asking her to look out for the boys and another message for the boys themselves so they wouldn't worry. Then, she'd be on her way.

Partially afraid that she'd misunderstood something and this journey was all for naught. But more afraid that the suspicions blossoming within her signified truths too terrible to fathom.

19

Jeremy took a final look through the desk by his bedchamber window, ensuring that none of the pages of his writing remained behind. Not that he particularly cared. At present, they felt exactly like what his father said they were. Foolishness.

Perhaps someday, more foolish ideas would fill his head, and he'd find the motivation to scribble them down. Currently, there was nothing but a void.

He ambled over to the bed, eyeing the valise he'd carelessly stuffed with all his belongings. He could rifle through it again, confirming he hadn't forgotten to pack any of his shirts, or his shaving kit, or some equally insignificant item. However, there was little point to the exercise, given he'd already performed it twice. But the mail coach wouldn't arrive in the village for several hours yet, and how else was he to pass the time?

He'd undertaken the disagreeable but necessary task of speaking with the Dowager Lady Rockliffe earlier in the day, as soon as word came that she'd risen and was available to hold an audience in the study. He hadn't missed the way her silver brows rose and her fingers tightened around her cane when he announced his resignation, effective immediately, and his plans to return to London. For a moment, her lips had parted, and she appeared on the verge of demanding an explanation. Or perhaps even ... protesting? That small lapse in her usual staid demeanor had quickly vanished, though. Instead, she'd informed him that he could consider his duties completed and focus his remaining hours on preparing for the journey. Then, she'd dismissed him with a flick of her hand and turned her attention to some papers upon her desk, mumbling under her breath about the inconvenience of finding a replacement in short order.

Hence, he'd spent the time since in his bedchamber, unable to face the prospect of whom he might encounter should he choose to venture beyond. At this point, walking all the way to London was beginning to feel like a better idea.

A rapid succession of knocks pounded against his door, and his heart lurched before commencing its own accelerated pounding. He'd sequestered himself in here because it seemed the wisest—safest—thing to do. Because he didn't know if he had the strength to look upon Theo's face again and then walk away.

That didn't stop the sensation flickering through his chest that bore a strange resemblance to hope. For the first time that day, he crossed the room with hurried strides. What if, against all indications to the contrary, there was still some way they didn't need to separate? If there was some detail he'd overlooked, and she could forgive him for what he'd said—

He flung open the door, his head swirling with images of dark eyes, full lips, flawless skin.

And immediately had to adjust his gaze downward. A set of brown eyes, much like Theo's, indeed appeared in front of him, but about half a foot lower than expected. Accompanied by a set of blue ones, a couple inches lower again.

"Benedict. Alexander." He nodded in greeting, doing his best to muster a smile. Difficult, given the flicker of hopefulness in his chest had transformed into a dull, nagging ache. He'd known all along this moment would come but had tried pushing thoughts of it away, not yet ready to deal with another cause for remorse.

"Are you well, Mr. Clare?" Benedict looked him up and down, his dark brows drawing together. With a little more practice, his abilities to aloofly scrutinize would soon rival his grandmother's.

"I am." It wasn't a lie, insomuch as he hadn't developed some debilitating illness. As for the way his life had fallen apart and he'd never been brought so low, he needn't trouble the boys.

"Why, then, is nothing about this day going as it should?" Alexander pushed forward, needing no invitation to enter the bedchamber, and began pacing along the floor. "First, we hear that Mama has gone off somewhere in Lord Pembrook's coach. Then, Aunt Amelia develops a grippe and cannot leave her room. Then, Grandmother won't stop muttering to herself and shuts herself away in the study. And *then*, you don't come down for our lessons on time, and Grandmother says we're to leave you be. It was all well and good to go to the pond with Achilles for a while in search of frogs, but we didn't find any, and that got tiresome, and besides, you promised to read aloud to us from *The Iliad*. So, if you're not unwell, why didn't you come?"

Jeremy remained frozen in the doorway, taking in Alexander's animated face—the way he tilted his head, making his curls flop, and scrunched his nose with bafflement. Jeremy had told himself the boys wouldn't view his departure as a hardship. After all, hadn't they rolled their eyes and complained about the tedium of his lessons enough times to make it clear they didn't want a tutor? That had been in the early days, though. Now ... was it possible he'd misjudged?

He could make up some excuse, delay the revelation of the truth a short while longer. But what would be the point? The boys didn't deserve lies and were likely too clever for them besides. Indeed, Benedict was staring through the open doorway, his eyes fixed expressionlessly on the bottom end of the bed. On the valise.

"You're leaving." Benedict took a single step into the room, his voice coming out like flint. "Aren't you?"

Jeremy hadn't expected it to be like this. Hadn't expected another blade to come in and sever him where he'd already been gutted to within an inch of his life. He would gladly take a real knife to the chest if it would spare them all this despondency. But as that wasn't an option, what was he to do but clear his throat and force out words? "As much as I may wish otherwise, the time has come for me to return to London."

"Do you mean ... permanently?" Alexander came to an abrupt halt, peering up at him with two saucers for eyes.

"Yes. I'm afraid so. Although I'm sure a new tutor will arrive in no time, who can continue with your lessons—"

"I'm sorry about your hand." Alexander's chin began trembling. "We didn't mean for you to get hurt when we ran after Achilles, I swear. And I'm sorry about the mouse, and the worms, and for saying your Greek history book was stupid, and—"

"No." Jeremy rushed over to him, placing a hand atop his slender shoulder, feeling about as tall as the specks of dust beneath his boots. "My departure has nothing to do with any of that. I've enjoyed my time as your tutor more than I can say. I do not *want* to get on the mail coach today and leave Beaumont Manor for good, but we always knew this was only a temporary arrangement, and—"

"This is rubbish," Benedict snapped, pulling Jeremy's attention back to where he remained standing just inside the doorway. His arms were folded tightly across his chest while a glower Jeremy hadn't witnessed for weeks now darkened his face. It was the look from the early days, suggesting he very much wished for his tutor's demise.

"Ben …" Jeremy started, but it was too late. In a sudden flash of motion, Benedict turned and bolted, flying into the corridor.

Damn it. Jeremy ran, too, reaching outward, forcing his legs to sprint. He couldn't leave without making sure the boys understood—

"No." Benedict's body shuddered the moment Jeremy's fingers connected with the back of his coat, and he jerked the offending hand away from him. Yet the disruption made him come to a sudden stop—obliging Jeremy to do the same to avoid a collision—and he whipped his head around, shooting Jeremy one more blazing-eyed, bared-teeth glare. "Don't you *dare* follow me."

And then, he was fleeing again, his feet pounding down the corridor and around a corner, out of sight.

Goddamn. Bloody. Hell.

Jeremy's breaths came too fast. His body felt too heavy. But that was all secondary. He turned toward the soft noise rustling behind him. Alexander, quietly tiptoeing down the corridor.

"Alex." Jeremy rushed back the remaining few steps to his side, starting to reach for him but then thinking better of it. Whatever he did, he couldn't afford to botch this. As he'd already done with Benedict.

Perhaps it would help if he crouched down, positioning

himself at the same level as Alexander's widened eyes and the mouth that drooped uncertainly.

Slowly, he began sinking toward the floor, hoping to God he would say the right thing. Alexander's feet shuffled, and his hands balled into fists that quivered against his sides. "Alex, I—"

Alexander's coat brushed against his as he shoved past him. His shoes hit the floorboards with rapid thumps. And in an instant, he was down the corridor and out of sight, just like his brother.

Leaving Jeremy crouched down in a silent corridor, alone.

His legs didn't want to raise him back up again, but he made them, eventually. With stiff footsteps, he managed the short distance to his bedchamber, looking behind his shoulder the whole time. Half ready to bolt himself, Benedict's admonition be damned. Yet what would that accomplish beyond creating additional ire?

Once the boys had a little time to cool down, perhaps they would deign to speak to him again. He would have to try—to *make* them—for he couldn't let the last time they saw each other end like this.

He pressed his fingers into his forehead, throwing his head back so he gazed at the ceiling as he paced. As if he still had thoughts of becoming a vicar and could find the answers if he only turned heavenward.

That path, of course, was lost to him. Just like the other paths he'd legitimately wanted before they'd slipped away.

What was left? *Nothing*.

Nothing, except one persistent, accursed piece of knowledge.

This knowledge was nothing new. He'd experienced it in more ways than he cared to remember, and dealt with it, and tried to move on and do better.

However, never had it hit him so thoroughly or seemed more true. Never had it built and built, crushing him until it became difficult to breathe.

This knowledge beat him down, stared him in the face, and refused to let him get back up.

Refused to let him forget that, simply put: he'd failed.

20

The sun followed Theo all the way to London. Its rays glinted into the coach when she eased back the curtain during their brief stop to change horses in preparation for the final leg of the journey. If anything, it shone even brighter when she peeked through the window near midday, when the passing blur of fields and farmhouses changed into rows upon rows of buildings, and the coach slowed to accommodate the increasingly congested streets.

At least her headache had lessened to a manageable dull throb, sparing her the need to conceal herself in darkness. Perhaps because of the headache powder and tisane she'd accepted back at Rosemead or the cold cloth she'd pressed against her forehead for the first hour of the ride. Perhaps because she was now about twenty miles from Beaumont Manor, not to return until the reason for the raw ache in her chest had made his own departure. Perhaps because she approached the printshop, and her urgency to get there numbed the fear.

She ran her fingers over the velvet bag from Percy, its weight in her lap a constant reminder of possibilities. It wasn't an exorbitant sum—he knew better than to try humoring her too excessively—but it provided a starting point. As soon as she was able, she very much intended to pay him back every shilling, and he could keep the painting as a gift. But first ... first, she needed to consider how to best use the money to her advantage, along with the other meager savings she'd accrued, so she could turn the money into more.

Eventually, she would come to London and look at buildings for lease. Ones that had rooms up above and plenty of open space down below. Maybe she could walk by printshops in operation as well. Look through the windows to see the equipment at work and distract herself with hopes for the future. Even if she couldn't fully put her heart into it.

But before she did any of those things, she had to take a tour of *her* printshop—or what remained of it. The place that had been calling to her since she woke up in a cold sweat that morning, the lure of it growing ever more insistent since her bizarre encounter with Adolphus Clare.

She kept the curtain open as they turned onto the Strand and pulled up before the familiar building. Well, not so familiar anymore, given the boarded-up windows and soot blackening the stone facade. However, it was still recognizable as the version she always saw in her dreams.

The coachman was kind enough not to look at her strangely as he helped her down before the burned-out shell of a building or to question if she'd made some mistake when she gave him this address. He simply saw her safely to the ground, got back on his perch, and drove around the corner to tend to the horses.

Leaving her alone, observed only by nameless passersby, to approach the front door of the printshop. Well, the spot where the door had once stood. Now, only a few haphazardly nailed planks remained in its place. A new addition since she'd last been here.

She took a step back. Paused. Then rammed her body forward, where she was rewarded with the crack of splintering wood. She did it again, adding her fists this time, doing away with the lingering fragments of board like a woman possessed.

The irony of the moment didn't escape her. How many times, as the years of her marriage wore on and Samuel's dependence on alcohol grew, had she chided him for doing things that were reckless and erratic—the acquisition of the printshop being a prime example. On each occasion, he'd insisted on the soundness of his actions and seemed so certain he did the right thing, even if no one else could understand the logic.

Now, she was the one behaving erratically—taking a full morning's journey in a borrowed coach just so she could visit a shell of a building that had nothing left for her. Except the flash of light from her dream kept returning to her, followed by the startling glint when Adolphus Clare had grabbed her. Insisting that, somehow, there was a connection. She would tear this place apart until she discovered once and for all what that connection was.

With the boards lying in a pile at her feet, she crossed the threshold, immersing herself in the cavernous ruins still enclosed by impenetrable stone walls. The tang of smoke had drifted out of the building even before she'd broken the first board, but inside, it was cloying. Only marginally diminished from that first morning she'd shown up to survey the destruction.

She put her arm up to shield her mouth and nose, waiting for the same agonizing jolt to hit her as her eyes adjusted to the dimness and the charred remains of the shop came into focus.

The jolt, though, didn't come. It had been replaced by something different. The sensation that went through her was more of a mild pang, accompanied by a renewed throbbing in her head.

She needed more light. Sunrays flowed through the doorway, providing a condensed stream of brightness upon one bare patch of floor, but with the sooty, boarded-up windows, it wasn't enough. She needed more, so she could gaze upon every last inch of this decimated shell.

She rushed to one of the front windows, ripping away thin pieces of board. Rubbing the sleeve of her spencer against a jagged piece of glass that remained, wiping away some of the soot. Allowing a fresh burst of light to illuminate the wreckage. But still not enough.

She ran to the opposite window, desperately clawing at boards. Pulling and heaving, and scrubbing furiously with her sleeve, until scraps of wood lay in a heap on the floor, and brilliant yellow rays lit every corner of the room.

It was the same scene she'd encountered before—both in real life and in her dreams—only bathed in cheery sunlight instead of a gloomy haze. There was the same coating of cinders beneath her feet. The same blackened pieces of metal littering the floor.

The image hurt, but not to the point of bringing her any closer to the answers she sought. She had to keep going, to take one last turn about this room, to witness every scrap of the damage.

Her chest, heaving from exertion, burned as she took in breaths of acerbic air. Still, she crept across the floor, farther into the wreckage. Her eyes stung now, too, water accumulating at the corners. From the smoke, surely. Or from …

Dear Lord, was she crying? She'd tried to do away with such foolishness long ago, for what good had tears ever done her? Yet with each step, the hurt began to increase, and she couldn't hold back.

She reached the back wall, brushing her finger across a section of the stone. At one point, a small table had rested here. It was the spot where, on that final evening before the fire, she'd laid her completed copy of Samuel's manuscript. The manuscript she'd so painstakingly tried to revise, convincing herself it was her ticket out of debt. That its posthumous printing would make it that much more valuable, that Samuel would be honored rather than appalled with her interference in his writing.

No traces of it remained but the ashes below her. She'd lost it.

Just like she'd lost Samuel. The man who'd claimed her heart when she was a girl of eighteen. The father of her children and the man who, despite any turmoil they'd experienced, would always have her love, even if that love had changed.

Just like she'd lost her belongings, one by one, as the creditors came. As she pawned off what they didn't take to gain money that was never enough.

Just like she'd lost Jeremy.

The air continued to sting her eyes, and her tears overflowed, running down cheeks that felt too tight. This journey was a fool's errand. Sorrow had let her imagination get carried away, had made it conjure up fears and misgivings beyond the realm of probability. Really, what did she expect to find besides burnt piles of useless rubble? She should depart at once—even if it was too late to pretend she hadn't taken leave of her senses. Act like this had never happened. Go back to Beaumont Manor and figure out what came next. That would be the logical thing to do.

Why, then, couldn't she break out into the fresh air, feeling like this visit had served its purpose? Instead, her legs remained stuck in place, wobbling but unable to propel her forward. Her head ached again, along with her chest. The air was far too smoky in here. But she couldn't leave.

Very well. She sank to the floor, finding a seat in a pile of cinders. She would stay here a moment longer, then. Let the tears fall. Wait for the world to stop spinning.

She trailed her fingers through the ashes, watching her white cotton glove grow increasingly black. Much like her skirt, which was no doubt ruined, but she didn't have it in her to care. Around and around her fingers went in an almost trancelike rhythm, tracing spirals through the remnants of her old life and what perhaps could have been if not for a neglected candle.

Until suddenly, she connected with something hard, breaking her out of her daze. It was only a small object, like the screws and bolts strewn across the floor. However, this was something a little different, with a metallic edge peeking out of the ashes that glinted in the brightness, along with a little flash of red, just like a flame.

She screwed her eyes shut against the abrupt flash of pain that hit her head.

No. Not this headache again. She forced her eyes to open and face the brightness, willing the pain to remain at bay. *Focus.*

Putting one hand to her forehead as a shade, she plucked the object out of the ashes, letting it rest within her palm. There were two tiny discs connected by a thin pair of shanks. Sleeve buttons.

Her rapid breath caught in her throat. *Focus.*

She lowered her makeshift eyeshade, using a finger to wipe away the thick layer of blackness coating much of the buttons. They were solid silver, with some sort of intricate etching and a tiny ruby at the top—not the buttons of a printer or his apprentice. With a shaking hand, she ripped off her blackened glove, furiously rubbing a clean finger against the remaining soot.

Another painful, blinding flash shot through her head. The same flash that had startled her out of her dream that morning.

The same flash that had pierced her when she'd stumbled and Adolphus Clare grabbed her, turning them toward the light and making the silver at his wrists gleam.

She'd been wrong to doubt herself after all. Yes, heartache consumed her, making her thoughts feel hazy and irrational. Nonetheless, she'd *known*. These buttons had been here the whole time. Perhaps her slippered feet had passed over them, or they'd glinted in her eye when she'd done her tour in the hours following the fire. Not fully registering with her amidst the sickening, crushing sense of loss, but still there like a little flicker in some buried part of her mind. Brought to the forefront now that loss hit her again.

Despite the pain, her eyes remained wide open, unable to shield her from the brightness. The last bit of grime had come away from the buttons, and in the brilliant stream of sunshine, the silver glimmered proudly, leaving no place to hide the truth. The ornate whirls etched within were actually letters. Initials, one on each button. Not that she needed to read them to know.

AC.

Adolphus Clare.

21

"Ben! Alex!" Theo couldn't stop the note of panic from creeping in as she yelled into Beaumont Manor's vacant top-floor corridor. "Boys!"

She'd already shouted the house down on her single-minded quest to find them without delay. The kitchen. Dining room. Drawing room. Library. Up to the schoolroom, even though they no longer had cause to be there now that their tutor had left.

All the while, she'd called out with a sort of firm, unwavering flatness, unwilling to let the storm raging within her break free. She couldn't lose her head yet. Not until she'd located them and they'd all gotten far, *far* away from this godforsaken place.

However, now that she'd surveyed their bedchamber, only to find their beds made up and their belongings untouched, and the lone sounds in the corridor surrounding it came from her own voice and footsteps, a little of her hastily stuffed-down panic rose closer to the surface. She *needed* them to appear. To have them pack their things so they could leave at once.

She went back down the corridor in a half-run toward the stairs, the sound of her heartbeat pounding through her ears. The rapid beating had started all the way back in London when she'd flown out of the printshop and screamed for Percy's coachman to rush her back to Beaumont Manor as if their lives depended on it. More than three hours later, her pulse continued to race. Her head kept pounding while her breath came in short, shallow pants.

But she couldn't allow herself to get distracted by any of that. If the boys weren't indoors, they must have gone somewhere on the grounds. After all, it was a beautiful day, with the blinding, revealing sun shining high in the sky.

She raced down two flights of stairs, back through corridors she'd already traversed, and into the drawing room. Giving it one final scan—in case she hadn't gone through earlier with as much levelheadedness as she hoped and had inadvertently missed some sign of the boys—she cast open the doors leading to the terrace, stepping out into the afternoon sun.

The frisson of pain that came as the brightness hit her eyes barely registered. *Nothing* would waylay her until she found the boys. "Ben! Alex! Boys, please—"

"What in heaven's name?" A harsh, affronted voice pierced the air as the sound of wood hitting stone echoed across the terrace.

Theo's body tensed even before her head whipped toward the source of the commotion. Bile rose in her throat even before her eyes fully adjusted to the light, revealing the Dowager Lady Rockliffe reclining in a cushioned chair on the shaded side of the terrace, a glass of lemonade and a few biscuits resting on a silver tray beside her. Once more, wood hit stone as the dowager gave her cane another thump against the terrace, her eyes widening with disdain.

Theo swallowed back the bitterness that threatened to

choke her. Tamped down the fury that filled her veins, ready to explode. She chanced one rigid step forward, keeping her voice low so there was no chance it would waver. "Where are my boys?"

"Oh, for God's sake." The dowager gripped the elegantly curved arm of her chair, using it, along with her cane, to propel herself upward. She arched her back, seeming to rid herself of the stiffness that follows a lengthy repose, and fixed Theo with a decided scowl. "Have you gone mad? You went off to Rosemead at barely the crack of dawn, likely frightening Lord Pembrook out of his wits, and now you've returned hours later covered in filth and smelling like a hearth. Seeing the boys in your state should be the last thing from your mind. You'll frighten them, too. In fact, I forbid you from going anywhere near their bedchamber until you've ordered a bath and—"

"They're not in their bedchamber, and I need to see them *right now*," Theo burst out, the words ending with a strangled cry. She threw her neck back, giving herself one moment to face the sky, because even having sunrays pierce her aching head was better than looking at the dowager.

She needed to keep her composure. To think. Yet the same sense of dread she'd experienced the day the boys had vanished from Mayfair was creeping in again. Only this time, there was no one to jump in and come to her aid.

"Get ahold of yourself." The cane rapped against the terrace again, and when Theo snapped her head back down, the dowager was still looking at her with eyes like ice. "The boys not being in their bedchamber is hardly a cause for panic. If they're not in the house, I imagine they decided to amuse themselves outdoors now that Mr. Clare has decided to shirk his duty and Amelia is too unwell to entertain them. In any case, why this sudden urgency? It's unseemly."

"Because." Theo clenched her teeth, taking another step

closer to where the dowager remained in the shadows. And another, and another, until every disapproving line on the dowager's face became visible, and she drew close enough to stab an accusatory finger into the dowager's chest. Not that she would do such a thing and give the dowager additional cause to act like the affronted party. Instead, she stood with her hands clenched into fists at her sides, refusing to let anger make them tremble. She leaned in slightly, just enough so there could be no missing her vehement whisper. "I'm going to have them pack their things at once so I can take them the *hell* away from here."

For a split second, the dowager's face slackened, her body lilting slightly to the side. Just as quickly, though, she stiffened her frame, and the expression of pinched displeasure swept over her once more. "Really, Theodora. While there may be a great many things I could say about you, I never took you as a woman prone to hysterics."

Outrage pounded through Theo's head and churned in her stomach, straining to break free. Still, she forced herself to stay exactly where she was, speaking in that same dangerous whisper. "That was *before* I traveled to my printshop and discovered your role in committing arson."

The dowager was prepared this time. She didn't so much as twitch, aside from a bony finger that stroked the top of her cane. Something in her icy blue eyes flashed. She was calculating, considering how to best proceed so she could emerge unscathed. Considering to what extent she could throw around further accusations of paranoia and how much her daughter-in-law really knew.

"Don't demean either of us by trying to refute it." Theo's voice became louder. Unsteady. How could she help it when the woman who'd ruined her stood mere inches away, contemplating further deceit? The sleeve buttons remained where she'd tucked them into her bodice before she flew out of the printshop, providing a cool weight against her skin. *Proof.* "Although perhaps you should have a conversation with your man of business about taking better care the next time he commits a crime on your behalf."

To the dowager's credit, she made no affronted exclamations or additional claims about Theo's hysteria. She merely stood there, eyeing her levelly. Adopting her own quiet, steely tone. "What is it you want from me, Theodora?"

"I want to know why!" Theo was shouting now, and biting heat swept over her face. She was doing nothing to help her case as to not appearing overwrought. However, she could no longer hold back.

"Why would you do this?" Fury surged out of her. Fury, combined with shocked, sickened despair that made it difficult for her to keep her knees from buckling. "You made it clear you wanted no association with me from the moment Samuel first brought me through the door of Rockliffe House. He estranged himself from you, and for years, you seemed perfectly content to pretend we didn't exist. Why did his death change that? I'm still the same unsuitable trollop you always deemed me to be. Your grandsons are still tainted with my baseborn blood. Why couldn't you accept, after everything that had passed, that I didn't *want* your help? Why couldn't you have just left us alone? Why ..."

She couldn't keep going. Her throat had grown tight, and while her eyes stung, she refused to let the dowager see a single tear. She could only stand there, trying to catch her breath, while reconciling herself to the fact that the dream that had startled her awake in the morning had now become a living nightmare.

The cause of which stood stiffly before her, her pinched lips slightly quivering in a very un-dowager-like way before she finally let out an exasperated huff of breath. "Why is everyone too blind to see what is right in front of them?"

"What could you possibly mean?" Theo snapped, although even without clarity, a fresh pang of dread hit her in the stomach.

The dowager emitted a sharp, beleaguered sigh. "I suppose I should make accommodations for your ignorance, given your lengthy estrangement. Very well, then. Let me put this plainly, for it is imperative you understand. Benedict is to become the next Marquess of Rockliffe. Until he marries and sires an heir, Alexander will be the spare. Over my dead body will the Rockliffe heirs grow up in an impoverished poet's hovel or set their sights only as far as becoming compositors or pressmen. They need to go to Eton, and be amongst the ton, and embrace what is their birthright. Just as they need a mother who will marry well so she won't bring them shame."

"Benedict will not be a marquess!" Theo glared at the dowager, who could now be accused of taking leave of her senses herself. "Have you forgotten about your oldest son? He already has a daughter, and presumably, he went chasing after his wife in hopes of siring sons. In fact, I heard whisperings she was with child at the time she ran off. I regret if that situation is fraught with complications. Nonetheless, it has nothing to do with me and *my* sons."

"Nicholas cannot sire children, and the Marchioness of Rockliffe is dead."

"Excuse me?" Theo's body went rigid as her mind fought to keep up with the meaning behind the dowager's tersely uttered declaration.

Another momentary flash of something—regret?—flashed across the dowager's face before she abruptly wiped it away to glower once more. "Listen carefully, Theodora, for I will only explain this once. Many years ago, Nicholas was involved in a hunting accident. He took a hit from a malfunctioning rifle, after which he was lucky to be alive. Due to the location of his injury, a physician at the time suggested there may be complications ... But what did the physician know? Newly arrived from Edinburgh, with all these newfangled ideas. Nicholas proved him wrong as soon as he got married, for the new marchioness announced she was increasing mere weeks later. A happy event, to be sure, and a cause for great relief. That is, until a daughter arrived in only six months, as plump and healthy an infant as you ever saw and bearing not the slightest resemblance to either of her so-called parents.

"That Nicholas chose to condone such wantonness was beyond my control." The dowager curled her lip as, for a moment, her contempt was redirected to the memory of another daughter-in-law. "Feelings aside, I suppose he thought there was no irreparable damage done. That the marchioness would go on to bear his own children—heirs—in time. Except she didn't. Years passed, and we all sat foolishly waiting for an infant who never came."

The dowager's knuckles turned white from the grip she placed upon her cane. "Would you like to know the cruelest part of all? Not long before Samuel's death, the marchioness announced she was increasing again. This time, however, duplicity proved too much for her. She admitted the unborn child belonged to another, and just as quickly, she and her lover were on a ship bound for India with her by-blow daughter in tow. One could claim that her contracting fever shortly thereafter was no more than she deserved. Regardless ... she succumbed to it quickly, and any hopes to rectify that catastrophe of a situation were lost. It's almost too horrific to fathom. Yet why waste time focusing on matters other than how they truly are? The degenerate Marchioness of Rockliffe won't be coming back. Nicholas cannot sire heirs with another, and whenever he's finished licking his wounds and returns home, I'll be damned if I sit by and watch him be cuckolded again. Benedict has true Prescott blood in his veins. He's the future marquess."

"No." Theo's vision blurred as she rapidly shook her head. If only the motion could cause her thoughts to blur, too, so she could make the dowager's words go away. *Benedict ... the future marquess ...*

The possibility, while always in plain sight, had never fully dawned on her. It was too surreal, too far removed from the life they'd always led. So opposite of anything Samuel would have wanted for his son.

"Yes." The dowager's voice came out as a sharp bark. "You would do well to accept the truth yourself, for any aversion we have to it won't make it different. Besides, if anything, you should be pleased. Your son is to inherit one of the most esteemed marquessates in the kingdom. You'll have wealth and prestige like you never could have imagined when you were toiling back on the Strand."

Pleased? The air had been sucked from Theo's lungs. This wasn't right. None of it could be true; there had been some mistake—

"I hope you now see the necessity of you and the boys residing with me," the dowager said, cutting into Theo's whirling thoughts. "And before you decide to shower me with further ire, let me remind you that I *did* offer you the opportunity to come to Rockliffe House and have your debts erased with no strings attached. It's regretful you so foolishly turned me down and I had to take additional measures to make you realize the benefits of accepting. In any case, you did come crawling back to me, eventually, and we're now exactly where we need to be. I suggest we all let go of bygones and look to what needs to happen in the future."

Theo's stomach heaved. Her position in the shadows,

far too close to the dowager's frosty glare, had turned her body to ice. But when she staggered backward a step, turning her face away, she was immediately hit with a burst of sunlight that triggered the pain of her earlier migraine.

There was nowhere left to turn. This vast, beautiful, seemingly perfect estate closed in on her, consuming her with all its secrets and unwanted truths. "I feel like I've sold my soul," she choked out, fighting back a sob. The Dowager Lady Rockliffe may have rendered her desperate enough to come here. But in the end, Theo was the one who'd taken the bait.

She gripped her forehead, trying not to let the dowager see how she fought for breath. Trying to find purchase as the world spun around her, her head throbbed, and a deep, harsh sound began ringing in her ears.

That sound. What started as low background noise intensified, becoming a steady, insistent bark. She peered across the lawn to see grass flying and Achilles's stocky white and brown body bounding toward the terrace.

"Oh, what now?" The dowager's scowl turned in the direction of the uproar, and she hobbled into the sunlight toward the terrace steps. "This, after I paid one of the stable boys extra to ensure *that dog* remains out of trouble. If this is the care he takes, he better not think he's getting a single coin more from me ..."

She trailed off, ready to brandish her cane in self-defense as Achilles barreled straight for her, his pace unrelenting. But instead of causing a collision, the dog abruptly veered to the side, brushing past the dowager as if she didn't exist. Instead, he came to a stop by Theo's feet, looking up at her while emitting another series of urgent barks.

The boys. Her mind instantly flashed to all the occasions she'd strolled across the grass or looked out the window to see Ben and Alex running with the dog at their side. Yet as she stared out at the sweeping expanse that stretched before the terrace—the formal gardens, the pond, the oak wood off in the distance—there was no sign of them. Not so much as the rustle of leaves.

She'd been so hell-bent on finding them before the dowager's revelation obliterated everything in its path. However, now that the unwanted admissions had done their damage and ceased, that same nagging sense of unease at the boys' absence filled her once more.

She tried reaching for Achilles to pat his head, but he spun away with a whine, hurrying back toward the terrace steps. He paused only to look behind him, giving her a pointed look.

Her legs remained shaky, but she managed a couple small strides forward, approaching the steps. Encouraged, Achilles jumped down onto the grass, turning his head again and letting out another demanding bark. She may have little experience with dogs, but she'd have to be blind not to see how he wanted her to follow.

"Ben," she whispered, peering into Achilles's expressive eyes and taking another step forward. "Alex." Because maybe, somehow, the dog understood the meaning of those names.

"You really have gone mad," the dowager muttered behind her, rapping her cane against the stone as she stalked back to the shade.

Perhaps the dowager was right, but what did it matter? What more did Theo have beyond a dog who wished to be followed, a pressing need to find her sons, and a sense of dread?

A faint shuffling noise came from behind one of the tall hedges lining the garden path, followed by a flicker of movement. She whipped her head toward the path, her heart giving a hopeful lurch.

However, the figure who emerged from behind the hedge wasn't Ben or Alex. Indeed, it was only one figure, tall and unquestionably adult. That of Jeremy Clare.

Under different circumstances, the sight would have undoubtedly reopened a wound and left her body raw. At the moment, though, her stomach had no farther to sink. Her heart couldn't race any faster than it already did. Indeed, she no longer had time for anything beyond her one critical question. "Have you seen the boys?"

She must have had the ability to absorb a little more sensation, for her chest constricted painfully as he shook his head, his eyebrows drawing together in concern. "I've been looking for them. I couldn't leave without saying goodbye."

At the disruption to their progress, Achilles began pacing in the grass, low whines coming from his throat as he shot looks between Theo and Jeremy both.

Theo rushed the remaining distance to the terrace steps, taking hold of the railing. And abruptly froze.

The sky had been a perfect blue all day, dotted with small puffs of clouds. Off in the distance, though, in the direction of the corn fields, something else filled the air. Rather like a cloud, except too gray and hazy for the weather and too close to the ground.

The smell of smoke had followed her all day long. First, from memories of her dream. Then, from her clothing, still covered in the printshop's ashes. However, her nose now twitched from something new. A fresh whiff of smoke—just a hint, but enough to trigger her brain into making a connection.

"Fire," she yelped, taking a split second more to gaze toward the fields, trying to form a map of this land she barely knew and what buildings might be in the vicinity.

She turned back to Achilles where he stood pawing at

the grass, his whines growing louder as he waited. Then, she turned to Jeremy.

He looked at her, too, with a face as bloodless as hers felt.

He understood.

Panic made additional speech impossible for her, and perhaps there were no words to rationally explain her unfounded but overwhelming sense of dread. Nonetheless, he understood.

His green eyes remained fixed on hers a moment longer, promising so much that couldn't be put into words, either.

And then, in an unspoken agreement, they ran.

22

Jeremy's lungs burned in protest as he sprinted across fields, the air surrounding him growing increasingly more pungent with smoke.

It didn't matter. In fact, he welcomed the ache, for it meant he was gaining ground, approaching the necessary destination. Not that he knew for sure where that was or what he'd find there. However, hearing Theo yell *fire*, and seeing the terror in her eyes, had been all the explanation he needed. The boys were missing, and she believed they were in danger. He trusted her instincts, enough that he would run over every flame-engulfed inch of this estate until he saw Benedict and Alexander safely returned to her.

Especially because their decision to run off felt very much like his doing.

The sun shone so brightly, even through the haze, that he nearly missed the first lick of flame that shot up in the distance. It appeared only as a brief flash in the corner of his eye but was accompanied by another spurt of barking from Achilles, followed by a renewed burst of speed.

That's when Jeremy truly saw it. Achilles bolted diagonally across a wheat field toward a rundown barn, where smoke poured out of the roof and orange flames danced in one of the lower windows.

"Theo!" he shouted, glancing behind him just as he moved to switch course. She'd noticed, too, and was already on the way, her face awash with panic as she frantically tumbled through the field.

A lone man—a farm laborer, presumably—appeared from around the back of the building, tossing a bucket of water toward the blazing window and the surrounding boards that had begun to scorch. It had all the effect of a single raindrop. The approaching sound of persistent barking caused the man to turn, and his expression, already pinched with worry, turned to a gaping look of horror as Achilles lunged toward the barn.

"What's happened?" Jeremy called, pulling every bit of strength he had left to give his legs an additional boost so he could catch up with the dog. He darted forward, taking hold of the collar the boys' had bestowed upon Achilles and using it to temporarily hold him back. The last thing he needed was for the man to bolt for fear of an agitated bulldog.

"I don't know." With Jeremy acting as a barrier, the man relaxed enough to shake his head. Up close, it became clear from his gangly frame and the faint dusting of hair above his lip that he was really more of a boy. "Makes no sense how a fire could have started. This barn hasn't been used in an age —not since the new one was built over by the south field— and the door's jammed besides."

"My boys." Theo came up behind Jeremy, her chest heaving with exertion, just in time to catch those final words. She paused only to suck in a ragged breath, then darted forward again, grabbing hold of the barn doors. Just like the farm laborer said, they shuddered but didn't come open.

"Boys!" she shrieked, her voice disintegrating into a fit of choked coughing as she violently tugged the door handles, to no avail.

"Go get help," Jeremy snapped at the laborer with his ineffective bucket, releasing his hold on the keening Achilles so he could run to Theo's side. He gripped the door handles along with her, jerking them back and forth, but still, the doors wouldn't give way. It was as if something had sealed them shut from the inside.

"Ben," Theo croaked on a strangled breath. "Alex." The name turned into a sob, which became another fit of coughing that left her struggling for air.

And no wonder. Even with the panic surrounding the boys, it hadn't escaped his notice that he'd come upon her looking like she'd already been through a fire. Covered in soot, her eyes wide and haunted. Something had happened, and even though he was supposed to stay far away from her, he couldn't go anywhere without talking to her and assuring himself of her well-being.

But that would have to come later. Presently, he had not even a second to stop. Nor would she want him to.

He spun away, snatching up the farm laborer's discarded bucket. Even in the past few moments, the flames swaying in the window above it had grown. In the window on the opposite end of the barn, though, nothing showed through the glass but an opaque haze.

That was his best chance.

With Achilles at his side, barking his approval, he made it to the window in four long strides. He took the bucket in both hands, hefting it above his head, and swung. The tiniest shred of relief flickered through him at the accompanying sound of shattering glass. He was one step closer. For though the window was small, he should still manage to squeeze through.

"Jeremy." Theo's raspy voice sounded behind him just as he rose onto his tiptoes, ready to launch himself through the cramped space and into the smoke. She grabbed his shoulder, pushing herself in front of him to stand by the window, gasping as smoke billowed out and filled her already struggling lungs.

"No," he roared, grasping her by the waist and spinning her away. Knowing the boys could be trapped and in imminent danger was the worst kind of torture. But having Theo join them and facing the very real possibility he could lose all three of them ... He would run through a thousand burning buildings before ever allowing that to happen. "You need to stay here and catch your breath. I mean it. You'll put us both in peril if you go in there like this. Wait here, and I'll be back in a moment. I promise."

Her lungs wouldn't allow her to protest. Yet something else appeared on her face, faintly visible through the panic. The tiniest shadow of doubt. As if she'd perilously steered him wrong, asking for something to which she had no right.

But nothing had changed. He still trusted her instincts. He trusted *her*. He loved her, just as he'd come to love the two boys whom he'd so fatefully been charged with tutoring. *Not* going in the barn wasn't an option.

"A moment," he repeated, giving one final look into the dark, glittering depths of her eyes. Praying, above all else, that she would listen. Then, he hurled himself through the window opening, into the flaming, smoky abyss.

Jagged glass cut at his palms and tore through his clothing as he maneuvered himself through the tight space. The pain was but a hardly discernible twinge, not enough to slow him for even an instant. It couldn't. Not when, through the cloying haze and sound of crackling wood, a muffled but urgent voice emerged.

"Come on, jump!"

Giving himself a final push, he scrambled onto the floor, hauling his cravat up over his mouth and nose as he hastily surveyed the scene. At the other end of the barn, fire consumed the wall and floorboards, casting a dangerous red glow across the space and sending sparks shooting into the air. The flames were ravenous, traveling quickly thanks to the stray bits of hay littering the area. They currently approached the only object in the otherwise empty space: a sturdy wooden ladder that lay discarded in the middle of the floor. A ladder so tall it must have been intended to give access to ... the hayloft.

The hayloft. His eyes darted upward, squinting from the sting of the smoke that billowed toward the rafters. There, peering through the haze, was a small, terrified face.

"Alexander!" he shouted, his chest swelling with both relief and horror at the same time. He hadn't just imagined that voice. He'd really and truly located Alexander and presumably Benedict along with him. Now, time was of the absolute essence.

He dove across the floorboards just in time to kick the ladder away from the path of the encroaching flames. For now. How the boys had ended up in the hayloft while the ladder rested flat on the ground was a matter about which he had more questions than answers. But for the time being, they were all irrelevant.

He heaved the ladder upward to lean against the edge of the hayloft's floor, then leaped onto the bottom rung and barreled to the top. Sure enough, Benedict sat huddled in the far corner of the loft, his face just as stricken as his brother's.

"I'm sorry," Alexander croaked, launching himself against Jeremy's chest and clinging to his arms for dear life the second he hopped off the ladder. Whether from smoke or otherwise, Alexander's eyes shone with tears. "I didn't mean to knock over the lantern or the ladder. Ben and I were arguing, and it all happened so fast—"

"It's all right." Jeremy rushed to crouch down, pulling Alex's collar over his nose so he would have at least some form of shield. "It doesn't matter anymore. You just have to go down the ladder so we can leave."

"But Ben." Alexander shot a glance toward his unmoving brother before leaning in close to Jeremy's ear. "I told him our only chance for escape was to jump, but he wouldn't. He's secretly afraid of heights," he added in a raspy whisper, mindful of his brother's feelings even under the circumstances.

Jeremy chanced a quick look behind him to assess the flames below. Soon, they'd come to claim the ladder once and for all, along with the beams holding up the hayloft. The seconds ticked away.

He bolted across the hayloft, sinking to his knees and fixing his hands tightly atop Benedict's shoulders. "We need to leave, Ben. Right now. I fixed the ladder, so you need only climb down it."

Benedict's glassy eyes were off in space, not seeming to focus on anything at all. Jeremy shifted, quickly assessing the easiest way to heft him over his shoulder. But suddenly, Benedict's head twitched, and he appeared to fully absorb Jeremy's presence.

"You didn't go away," he choked out, his voice weak and ragged from the smoke.

"No." Jeremy shook his head, feeling the sting in his own eyes and throat. "Of course not. I would never go anywhere without knowing you're all right."

He moved to take one of the clammy hands clasped tightly around Benedict's knees, giving it a slight tug. It was the final thing he could do before picking him up and carting him away.

All at once, though, Benedict was clambering to his feet, keeping pace with Jeremy as he pulled him along, sprinting back to Alexander at the edge of the hayloft.

"Go," Jeremy shouted to Alexander, peering back down at the ground below them. Just as he knew it would, the blaze had intensified, swallowing up more of the wall and floorboards and setting its sights on the ladder as well.

At least with Benedict now standing beside him, Alexander didn't need to be told twice. He hopped onto the top rung and began a rapid descent, his body nimble despite being plagued by both fear and the sweltering heat.

"Your turn, Ben." Jeremy gave his hand a final squeeze before releasing it, silently willing him to go.

Fortunately, Benedict didn't hesitate this time. With a determined nod, he dropped himself down and clutched the ladder's rails, following in his brother's hurried footsteps.

Oh, thank God. Alexander was already halfway across the blazing barn, with Benedict quickly catching up. And a good thing, for the flames grew higher—closer—by the second, eager to consume every board.

Jeremy began scrambling down the ladder's rungs two at a time to the sound of an angry pop and crackle that made him halt. The fire had come, latching onto the ladder's rails where they rested against the floor, eager to begin its journey upward.

This was it. No more climbing down, then. He took a split second to assess the space below him and the path least obstructed by flames.

Then, he jumped, landing on the ground with a heavy thud, narrowly escaping the burgeoning inferno. He would process the effects of the knocks to his body later. What did they matter while he was alive, back on the ground and able to run, urgently needing to get the boys to the broken window.

The boys, however, had run to the jammed door, pulling at something that rested between the handles. A stick of some sort. A shovel? Whatever it was, they heaved it away, and Benedict grasped the handle, shoving his weight against the door.

It gave. The door slowly creaked open, and Benedict pushed it again until the sun's natural brightness flooded in to mix with the hellish red inferno of the barn.

The boys paused only long enough to make sure Jeremy was following. And oh, was he ever. He darted along the rapidly disintegrating floor, trying to yell at them to go, but the smoke had made that impossible.

In the end, it didn't matter. They all burst out of the barn together as something behind them snapped and then collapsed with a roar.

The barn would be gone soon, but they were here, staggering into the sunlight. All of them shaking, coughing, struggling to get fresh air into their lungs.

But most importantly, free.

23

Was it possible for a person to keep on living even if their heart stopped? For Theo's heart, so rapidly pounding for much of the day, had seemed to cease the moment Jeremy dove headfirst into the blazing barn. It was as if her body had tried to numb itself because focusing on what could be happening in that barn had the power to crack her open and destroy her.

She'd stood beside the broken window, waiting for the coughing to stop but not able to take in breaths even when it did. How much time had passed? Seconds, likely, which felt more like days. Nothing appeared through the jagged glass besides a covering of smoke, and nothing was audible besides the crack and roar of flames. Blistering heat poured from the building, and still, her body had turned frigid.

That was, until the door creaked at the other side of the barn. Until it flew open, and two small figures stumbled out, with a taller one hovering behind them. Ragged and ash-covered, but still upright. *Alive*.

That's when the ice within her thawed instantaneously, and the emotions she'd been holding back washed over her like a flood. With shaking legs, she ran across the untamed grass, putting herself in the doorway's path. She didn't make it all the way before her weight became too much and her knees buckled, leaving her sitting in a heap on the soft ground. She could still outstretch her arms, though, and peer at the three faces approaching her, unsure whether the tears pouring down her cheeks were from anguish or laughter.

Two small bodies crashed into her arms. So much larger than the days when she'd first cradled them but still little enough for her to remember them as the tiny infants who'd changed her world. She squeezed tight and closed her eyes, letting herself simply feel their warmth and remember they were safe.

Only when their chests stopped heaving against her and they responded to her murmured questions about their welfare did she pull away, wiping her eyes so she could fully take in their solemn, grime-streaked faces. "What happened, boys?"

Benedict bit his lip, his dark eyes troubled. "We were trying to run away."

Her heart took the hit, aching for the many things he'd already gone through. For the changes he'd have to go through still. "I was so worried," she whispered, feeling the sting behind her eyelids once more.

"I'm sorry, Mama." Alex dropped to the ground, clambering into her lap in a way he hadn't done for many years. "We didn't know what else to do. Nothing was going right. Grandmother was muttering about you running off, and then Mr. Clare said he was leaving, and we wanted to leave as well. To stow away on the mail coach and go back to London, because Beaumont Manor would be insufferable with only Grandmother for company. But then, we overheard a chambermaid say the mail coach didn't leave until near dinnertime, and we needed somewhere to hide until then because, of course, Grandmother would never *allow* us to get on the mail coach. So, we found this old barn, which was a very clever hiding place, and we were even smart enough to bar the door, just in case someone happened along."

Alex's face nearly displayed its usual animation before suddenly clouding over again. "But then, as we were waiting up in the hayloft, I told Ben we should sneak down to the house and see if you'd returned because you might want to run away to London with us. I wanted to be sure we left plenty of time to seek out Achilles, too, because we couldn't find him when we first went to hide, and we could hardly run away without him. But Ben said you hadn't come back and probably wouldn't for a long time, and that leaving the barn would spoil our chance to get away, and that we'd have to wait and send you along a note in time. He said that finding Achilles would have to wait as well, and that with any luck, the dog would turn up as we were leaving the estate. And as we argued about it, I accidentally knocked our lantern to the ground, which gave me such a fright that I jumped and toppled the ladder, and I'm very, very sorry."

"Alex, I'm so sorry, too ..." Again, a lump rose in her throat that felt somewhere between a burst of laughter and a choking sob. She reached out a hand, running it through his dusty tangle of hair. Russet brown, just like his father's. Just as his blue eyes were Samuel's, and his enthusiastic grin that could light up a room, and his vivaciousness when it came to the things that truly mattered to him. Above all else, she needed to ensure that he, along with his brother, felt loved and protected no matter what. That she always did what was best for them.

"You don't need to be sorry, Mama." Alex managed a tiny smile. Not the usual expression that lit up his eyes but a smile nonetheless. "In the end, *I* was correct, not Ben, because you did come back. For that matter, Mr. Clare didn't leave, either. He was still here, and he rescued us, and he's the whole reason we're still alive. Again."

He turned to look behind him, still with that half-grin, and she followed his gaze, her heart giving a small lurch. Jeremy sat on the grass a short distance away with the now-dozing Achilles sprawled out beside him. His skin was dusted with soot, his clothing torn, and a trickle of blood spread over both hands. But even so, he returned Alex's smile with an abashed one of his own. "I'm not certain I deserve all the credit. Your mother and Achilles provided a great deal of help."

Her breath hitched, and when she tried to speak, the words caught in her throat. Yes, she'd been the one to spot the fire and feel in her gut that the boys were in danger. But Jeremy was the one who'd listened. Who'd been willing to act, without question, based only on the instincts of a frantic mother and a barking dog.

Her world, which had been temporarily reduced so nothing remained but her two children safe in her arms, began expanding again. There was activity all around them. Footsteps and hooves pounding over grass. Voices shouting. Water sloshing and then sizzling as it connected with flames. However, none of it fully came into focus. Her eyes were solely on Jeremy.

Jeremy, who gave Achilles a final scratch behind the ears before the boys rushed over to greet the other, canine hero of the day. Jeremy, who slowly rose to his feet, brushing stray grass off his breeches—not that it made much differ-ence, given the fabric was singed and in tatters.

Jeremy, whose green eyes didn't leave hers for an instant as she rose along with him. Not able to look away.

The distance between them was but a few feet, yet also

endless. This was the man who'd so suddenly turned cold and walked away, making her believe she'd been careless with her passions and foolish with her heart.

Except ... he hadn't walked away. Not from her boys.

He'd thrown himself into a burning building without a second thought, just because they *could* be inside. He'd risked his life for them. He'd seen them safely returned to her.

That came above any wounds to her heart.

Gratitude swelled within her to the point that her knees wavered again, and she wished for nothing more than to stumble forward into the safety of his solid chest. Only ... perhaps he didn't want that. He'd made it clear he viewed their relationship as a mistake. His heroics with the boys didn't mean that had changed.

But what *did* it mean, and what did he want from her? A passionate kiss? A handshake? Where did they go from here?

He spared her the need to ponder it further by stepping forward and gathering her in his arms. His hands pressed against her back, holding her close. Every bit as sturdy and comforting as always, even though he and she both smelled like ashes and had spent the day traveling to hell and back. He rested his chin against the top of her head, his breath a calming rustle in her hair, his arms continuing to hold tight as if he'd never allow danger to befall her.

All the while, she let herself cling to him, uttering the same words over and over. *Thank you.*

The world undoubtedly kept turning around them, a frenzy of shouts, movement, and flames. None of it registered. Nothing poured through her but the sensation of a warm, strong body and a steady embrace. She would keep it that way as long as possible. Savor it, in case when time came to exist again, the embrace vanished, never to return.

Too soon, Jeremy's muscles stiffened, breaking the spell. His grip on her slackened, and his chin rose from her hair. That's when the world came back again, in the form of wheels creaking and hooves barreling toward them. She lifted her head from the shelter of his chest, shifting her gaze toward the commotion.

A chair back gig careened through the field, grinding to a halt as its driver—the Dowager Lady Rockliffe—set eyes upon Ben and Alex where they reclined with Achilles in the grass.

Theo's body tensed, ire sparking within her, ready to ignite like the timbers in the barn. Jeremy, however, barely seemed to notice the dowager. Instead, he stared at her red-faced, wide-eyed passenger. Mr. Adolphus Clare.

Had the dowager paid heed to the illicit embrace happening mere feet away from her, perhaps a new blaze of a different kind would have exploded right outside the barn. But as it turned out, her attention appeared fixed solely on her grandsons. As for Adolphus Clare, though, he regarded nothing but Jeremy, even as he hopped to the ground and helped the dowager descend from the gig. The brief glint of relief in his eyes quickly gave way to something darker. A question that became a pointed look of censure.

Jeremy swallowed, his jaw going rigid as he took a hesitant step away from her. He still focused on his father while so much flickered through his own green gaze. Ire to match her own. Uncertainty. Regret.

She stared, too, back and forth between father and son. The older man who'd done the dowager's bidding and ruined her. The younger man who'd rescued her boys and captured her heart.

Even after all the flailing about she'd done, the sleeve buttons remained tucked securely inside her bodice. So subtle but *there*, a little metallic reminder.

Something flashed inside her head. Not the spurts of pain she'd experienced for much of the day, for the migraine seemed to have dissipated for good. No, this was something different but equally as gripping.

Unfettered clarity.

"You knew." Her voice became a whisper, meant for Jeremy's ears only. She started backward a step so she could fully take him in as she absorbed the implications of her discovery. "Your father told you about the printshop fire. About what he did."

Jeremy's gaze snapped away from his father, coming to land on her instead. No doubt Mr. Clare—father, man of business, and arsonist—continued to watch them, assessing their every move. But it didn't signify. The world had shrunk again, leaving her with nothing to focus on but Jeremy's face. The widened eyes. The parted lips. The gray cast to his skin. And then, the slow, regretful shake of his head.

"I would give anything to change it." His words were raspy, and his hand began reaching for her before abruptly becoming a fist at his side. "You're my world, Theo. I couldn't let you get knocked down again because of me. I wanted to protect you."

It was a good thing his fingers didn't connect with her skin, for her heart did enough tumbles without the addition of touch. She didn't need that distraction right now. For suddenly, the next step in the path became crystal clear, and she wouldn't let anything stop her until she'd seen it through.

She spun away from him, traversing the short distance to where the boys were languidly rising to their feet amidst an animated lecture from their grandmother.

"Hurry along, into the gig," the dowager was saying as she hovered above them. "We need to get back at once so I can call for the physician, along with arranging for some sorely needed baths to be sent up—"

"Boys?" Theo stepped forward, inserting herself in the empty space between her sons and the dowager, effectively blocking them from the dowager's view and cutting her off mid-sentence. An incredible lack of politeness on Theo's part. Yet why pretend? She had a single purpose in mind for this encounter and no time for extraneities.

Looking at Ben and Alex helped the nerves in her stomach calm, and she placed a hand upon each of their shoulders. "I've been thinking about what you told me regarding your plans for the day, and I agree. It's time for us to run away."

"Oh, for heaven's sake," the dowager muttered behind her, the accompanying scowl apparent even though not within Theo's line of sight.

It didn't deter her in the least. She merely peered at the boys, whose faces creased with bewilderment, and managed a small smile. "If there are any effects you'd like from the house or perhaps some provisions for the journey, I suggest you get them now. Then, we'll be on our way."

"This is madness!" the dowager spluttered. "You cannot possibly mean to—"

"Oh, we do." Theo's smile broadened, her chest filling with a surprising note of lightness as she gave each boy's shoulder a squeeze. "Yes?"

Brightness washed over their features in unison, accompanied by two firm nods. They trusted her. They relied on her. Now, it was time for her to set things right.

She released her grip on them, her heart growing lighter again as they ambled away with Achilles trotting at their heels. Both of them—appearances aside—unscathed. It was miraculous, really. But then again, hadn't the past months challenged them just as arduously? Yet they were resilient, all three of them—four, if she counted Achilles. And no matter what the future had in store for any of them, that wouldn't change.

"I forbid this." The dowager's cane hit the grass, and she propelled herself forward, occupying the space where the boys had just stood so she could glower at Theo. "You're still overwrought and are not thinking clearly—"

"On the contrary, my head is clearer than it's been in a very long time." Theo squared her shoulders, pulling her spine up tall. Eventually, the day's events would take their toll and exhaustion would set in. At the moment, though, energy coursed through her veins. Perhaps because, after so many months of feeling powerless, she now had the ability to take back control. "You can disagree with my decision to leave. You can forbid and make threats. You can come up with some other nefarious way to make me bend to your will. But I suggest you think long and hard before doing so."

She took in a breath, fighting against the heat that pricked her skin. This wasn't going to become another shouting match, nor would she allow herself to be accused of hysterical anger, even if she had good cause to feel that way. She simply needed to state the facts. The reason she had power. "We were *incredibly* lucky the barn didn't burn with the boys still inside. As their decision to hide there came about from a long string of events set in motion by *you*, any unfavorable consequences would have fallen on your head."

She swallowed back the lump rising in her throat, forcing herself to remember the boys as they were just a few moments ago, striding across the grass. Unharmed. "I hope you've come to know them well enough over the past weeks to realize they aren't the sort to back down. You may think you can keep pushing, and eventually, you'll break us all, but you're wrong. If you force us into something we don't want, the boys will continue to rebel. They'll run, just like they did today. And then what? What happens when you push too hard, only next time, the outcome isn't so lucky?" She leaned in close to the dowager's stony face, quietly uttering the coup de grace next to the silver curl above her ear. "Then, you'll have neither heir nor spare. You'll have *nothing* but the knowledge that the Prescott line ends here."

She stepped away only after hearing the dowager's slight but still audible gasp, staring into hard blue eyes with a ruthless intensity of her own. "So, here's what is going to happen. The boys and I are returning to London to establish our own home, wherein I'm going to carefully consider everything you told me today. You're going to remain at Beaumont Manor and do the same. It could be, at some point far in the future, that I deem it best, for Benedict's sake, for us to come to some sort of reconciliation. But until that happens—*if* it happens—you're going to stay away from us."

Inside, her body trembled with the force of the words she'd just hurled the dowager's way. Outside, though, she stood stock-still, watching the dowager's eyebrows rise and her pinched lips fall open. It would seem the former Marchioness of Rockliffe had just been rendered speechless.

Temporarily, anyway, for she was quick to recover herself, wiping away every trace of shock in the blink of an eye. The expression that replaced it, though, wasn't her typical glower. She may have intended to appear scornful, but that glint in her eye ... it was desperation. Subtle, but Theo had seen it too many times in her own reflection to let it go undetected. Except now, the tables had turned.

"You need to see reason, Theodora." The dowager managed a commanding tone that no longer had any power over her. "Your home was taken. Where, exactly, do you intend to go? How do you mean to accomplish this?"

The same questions niggled deep inside her. She would

be foolish if they didn't. However, the sensation was secondary to the freedom that stretched out before her. To the possibilities and new beginnings. No, she didn't have all the answers yet, but one step at a time. And as for the next step? That, she did know.

She spun away from the dowager, getting another glimpse of the scene around them. The blackened barn in the background, ruined, but with the flames now contained within. Adolphus Clare, unmoved from his position by the gig, his face pale and horrified by the exchange he'd just witnessed.

But most importantly ... Jeremy.

Jeremy, who'd heard the non-whispered parts of the exchange as well. Who stayed just where she'd left him standing upon the grass, peering at her with widened eyes and a poorly concealed smile.

She went forward, step by step, returning to the spot where she'd fallen into his embrace and let gratitude—and much more, too—pour from her body. His clothes, of course, were still torn, just as ashes still coated his face and hair.

He was perfect.

She reached forward, lacing her soot-covered fingers with his. Holding tight, feeling a smile of her own struggle to break free as she peered into the green eyes that had captivated her from the moment he leaped from the errant hackney in the rain.

She answered the dowager's question. But mostly, she spoke to him. "I thought the boys and I might start by procuring seats on the mail coach."

24

The mail coach wasn't built for comfort. To maintain its tight schedule, it barreled down the road, seeming to hit every rut on the way.

It didn't matter. In fact, Jeremy welcomed each sway and bump for the way it sent Theo's thigh pressing into his.

The only other passenger—an elderly gentleman prone to motion sickness—had opted to take the outside seat, leaving the interior as a private space for just the four of them—Jeremy, Theo, Benedict, and Alexander. And Achilles, too, Jeremy supposed he should add, given the extra coin it had taken to sneak the now-dozing dog on board.

In any case, this was precisely the arrangement they needed. A place to sit uninterrupted and unwind. And when the chaos of the day caught up with the boys, causing them both to press their heads to the windows and fall into a deep sleep, the explanations between him and Theo began.

First, his, for he needed her to understand every detail of what transpired between him and his father yesterday in the wood.

And then hers. He listened as she spoke of the many hours she'd already passed in a coach that day and the destination she'd traveled to in London. Watched, with his stomach in his boots, as she procured the evidence she'd found there. Held her, with his hands pressed firmly against her back, as she explained the confrontation that had awaited her back at Beaumont Manor. The secret that had come to light.

For a while, he said nothing, simply let her catch her breath as her words traveled through his smoke-addled brain. Across from him, the future Marquess of Rockliffe continued sleeping soundly, his body—not yet entirely free of soot—curled upon the seat. While in Jeremy's arms, the future Marquess of Rockliffe's mother rested, tilting her head against his shoulder. Her life had been fraught with complications before, but now ... now, they'd escalated to a whole new level.

"What will you do?" he murmured into her hair after a period of silence had stretched between them. She still smelled faintly of flowers, even amidst the lingering ash.

She gave a curt laugh that became a sigh, burrowing more tightly against his side. "Do you mean next month? Next year? In ten years? Whenever Ben becomes the marquess? Because the answer to all those questions is, I don't have the faintest idea. At this point, I'm taking it one day at a time. One hour at a time, really. I suppose the first step is to locate an inn for the night and then find more permanent lodgings. Lord Pembrook did me the kindness of purchasing one of my paintings, so at least the funds from that can tide me over for a short time until I establish a permanent means of income."

Under different circumstances, the revelation would have caused a tight pang of envy to vibrate through his chest. How could he feel anything but glad, though, knowing she had a way to provide for herself and the boys after their abrupt and unexpected departure from Beaumont Manor? The source of the funds was irrelevant.

The tightness in his chest came mostly from issues with *himself*. From his dreary bachelor's lodgings. From his arsonist father. From his newfound lack of employment and the month's salary that had landed in a villain's pocket.

He had the opposite of everything she needed. Had so much work to do …

But still. Still, he couldn't pretend anymore or let her walk away with misconceptions. Not that she needed him handing her another complication. But she deserved the truth to do with what she would.

"You'll figure it out. I have every confidence. And in saying that, I want to make something clear." He inhaled once more at the top of her head, then pulled back, peering at the way the setting sun streaked through her hair. "I meant what I told you in the wood yesterday, more ardently than I can express. I love you, Theodora Prescott, with every fiber of my being. Nothing would give me greater happiness than spending the rest of my days with you by my side. Yet so much has changed since yesterday, and—"

"Maybe, but other things have stayed the same." She scrambled to pull herself upright, gazing upon his face with intense, flickering eyes. She reached out, allowing a lone finger to trace over his jaw, causing the normal rhythm of his breathing to grind to a halt. "I meant everything I said yesterday, too. About wanting you and finding a way forward together. The revelations that have since come to light have no bearing on that—"

"But they do." He reached up to his jaw, capturing her soft, gloveless hand against his skin. He didn't want to interrupt her. Indeed, nothing would feel better than listening to her keep going, of hearing his sentiments returned.

However, the longer he did that, the more he risked having his resolve crumble entirely and reaching out to take hold of her, never to let go. That couldn't happen. He needed to do this right. "Before we make plans for a future together, I need to ensure I can prove myself worthy."

"Worthy?" Her dark brows rose high on her forehead. "You're the hero of the day. You just rescued my sons from a burning building. I could receive no better proof than that."

The tips of his ears grew hot, and he gave his head a small shake. "This wasn't a matter of heroics. Doing any less was never a possibility. I was their tutor, and I had a responsibility to them. Furthermore ... I hope you know how much I care for them, too. I'm not entirely sure how it came about, but somewhere between the mouse in my chair and the salt in my tea, the boys wheedled their way soundly to my affection."

Theo bit her lip, looking like she was about to let a smile escape. "If you're still trying to convince me of your unworthiness, you're saying all the wrong things."

His own tight-lipped smile appeared in return. If only it were that simple ...

"It goes beyond that, angel." Reluctantly, he brought his hand down to clasp it with the other in his lap. "You and the boys cannot live on my affection alone. Nor can you live in a couple of dingy rooms in a building that allows neither women nor children. I need to change some things. Seek new employment. Find new lodgings. Only when I have a clear path forward, with a steady means of providing for a family, will I ask you to tie your future with mine. It's the least you deserve. And in the meantime ..."

He swallowed, trying to ignore the faint stabbing sensation in his gut. This was the hard part, but also the part he needed to feel certain she understood. "In the meantime, I want you to consider if, after everything you learned today, a life with me is truly what you desire. If you can look at me the same knowing what my father has done. And if you feel my station is still suitable, given Benedict's position and the expectations that will fall upon him—"

"Jeremy." She spoke his name in the same gentle tone she used when Alexander had gone on a tirade about the story he wrote not being good enough. "Ben may be unavoidably destined for the peerage. I, on the other hand, am a writer's daughter first. And regardless, all three of us want you just as you are. I'm already certain."

"Nonetheless." A spurt of lightness dared to soar through his chest, but he couldn't let it get carried away. "I'd feel better if I knew you'd taken some time to think about it when we're farther removed from the chaos of today. Just as I'd like a little time to better establish myself so I can feel confident I deserve you."

She blew out a long sigh, flopping her head back against the seat and then onto his shoulder. "Very well."

The coach hit a particularly large rut, and he threw his arms around her to keep her from slipping away. Yet even when they'd left the rut behind and the coach resumed its usual bumpy swaying, his arms remained fixed in place, relishing every bit of her warmth and softness they could.

The sun grew ever lower in the sky, casting shadows across the coach's interior that signaled the impending arrival of nightfall. Before they knew it, the familiar streets of London would come rushing past, and the journey would reach its conclusion. Theo and the boys would seek out an inn. He would return to the cold starkness of his bachelor's lodgings.

And then, a new chapter would begin.

His body ached from the mere thought of parting with her. Self-doubts abounded. But at the same time, her words planted a seed of confidence within him. A tiny, whispered belief that, in the end, this would all turn out exactly as it should.

Theo shifted against him with a yawn, pressing the side of her face into his coat. "You're stubborn, you know," she murmured, her eyelids fluttering closed. "But I suppose you're right. It will be good for me to take a little time to get my own affairs in order, too."

Her hand draped across his chest, and he gently caressed it before bringing his fingers up to stroke her hair. Listening as her breathing slowed, feeling the final words she uttered clutch his heart.

"I hope we can then arrive at the conclusion that we deserve each other."

25

Theo pulled her pelisse tight to her body as a sudden gust of wind came up, pushing her sideways on the pathway she traversed through St. James's Park. She hurried her footsteps, taking extra care to secure the satchel containing her drawing implements at her side. A quick glance at the sky revealed an onslaught of darkening clouds, getting ready to release a deluge. Yet even the thought of an imminent drenching couldn't erase the lightness in her limbs. Not when amongst the pencils and sketchpad in her satchel, there was now also a small pile of coins.

Once more, she owed Percy her eternal gratitude. No sooner had she sent a note back to Rosemead the day after the fire, thanking him again for his assistance and explaining her permanent departure for London, than another note arrived—this from another viscount, looking to purchase a painting for his redecorated study. Then came another, from the sister of the baroness who'd already engaged Theo to sketch her portrait when the new Season began. As it turned out, said sister hadn't yet departed for the country and also wanted a sketch, which is why she'd summoned Theo that very afternoon.

And while he never wrote anything to confirm it, all this was Percy's doing, of that she had no doubt. She may have abandoned her tentative place amongst the ton—at least for the foreseeable future—but he still wanted to help her succeed.

"Theodora!" A deep voice called to her, mingling with another fierce blast of wind. Her eyes darted over to the nearby street, where a curricle had pulled to a halt, and its driver waved in her direction.

"Percy?" She went forward a few steps, taking in the face partially shaded by the elegant black top hat. It was almost as if her thoughts had summoned him to appear before her. She grasped her skirts so she wouldn't trip, running the remaining distance to the side of the curricle. "I didn't know you planned to be in London."

"May I give you a ride to your next destination?" He extended a gloved hand to help her up. "With any luck, we can get ahead of the rain."

"That would be much appreciated." She hopped into the curricle, settling herself on the seat beside him while clutching her satchel tightly in her lap. "I was just on my way back to my new lodgings in Essex Street. The ones I wrote of in my letter. But what are you doing here?"

He prodded his identical black geldings into motion, setting off down the busy street. "Truth be told, I was hoping to catch you as you made your way home. I believe you also wrote of spending the afternoon sketching at Mrs. Salisbury's town house?"

"And I believe I have you to thank for that." She peered at the neatly angled profile of his face, the set of his mouth giving nothing away. Not that she needed it to in order to realize all he'd done to help. "Once again, I'm in your debt."

He kept his eyes focused on the road, giving a subtle flick of his wrist. "It was nothing. A gesture from one friend to another, and certainly not anything that warrants repayment. I merely wanted to assure myself of your well-being before I depart."

"Depart?" She felt her eyebrows draw together. "Are you going somewhere other than Rosemead?"

"Yes." Despite the clatter of hooves surrounding them, he lowered his voice just a shade. "After careful consideration, I've decided to go north. I have a hunting lodge in Yorkshire, which, outside of shooting season, has the distinct advantage of being quiet. Secluded. I find the older I get, the more I seem to desire such things. I'm not sure when I'll return."

She reached out, placing her fingers against the fine blue wool of his sleeve. "I'm glad for you if that's what will bring you happiness. For you deserve it more than anyone else I know."

Finally, he turned, managing a shadowed version of his usual pleasant smile. "As do you. I hope we can still write to one another, and I'll do what I can to help from a distance should the need arise. Do you think you'll be all right?"

She blew out a long breath, letting her weight drop against the curricle's seatback. What a question.

A week had passed since the day of her printshop discovery, and the fire, and her hasty retreat to London. Since she'd reclined in the mail coach, nestled in Jeremy's arms.

A week in which so much had changed. She and the boys had gone from an inn to a modest but passable set of rented rooms. Her savings slowly grew thanks to her artwork, and with any luck, word of mouth would help her continue to expand her reach. The next step was finding a suitable school in London for the boys, so they could continue their education and be prepared for ... well, whatever came in the future. But little by little, they figured it out.

Just as Jeremy did in another part of London. And despite what she already knew in her heart, she gave him the time he insisted he needed, subsisting on only a couple of brief exchanged notes. In the end, if they could both come together feeling whole and worthy, the wait would be worth it. And in the meantime ...

"Yes." She nodded, filled with a certainty that grew a little more each day. "Please don't worry about me. I'm going to be fine. Although ..." She turned from Percy, gazing at the bustle surrounding them as the first fat raindrop splashed upon her cheek. "As for getting home, we've driven too far and have missed our turn."

Percy's hand went to his neck, smoothing a nonexistent flaw in his cravat. "Actually, I was hoping you wouldn't mind if we made another stop first."

Slowly, she shook her head, watching the faint tinge of color that spread across his cheek. It wasn't that she minded doing anything he asked. However, for him to make such a request on a whim, just as the rain began to fall, was exceedingly odd.

They zipped down Fleet Street at a steady trot, the wind rippling through their hair, before he veered to the side and slowed the curricle in front of a tidy brick building—a shop or office of some sort, by the looks of things. He came to a stop behind a black lacquered coach that was just pulling away, giving her the briefest glimpse of the elaborate crest painted upon the door.

That's when her stomach sank, and her skin prickled with something that felt uncomfortably close to betrayal. "Why are we here? What is the meaning of this?"

He turned, then, his eyes darting to one of the building's windows before coming to rest on her. "I'm sorry, Theodora. Please don't be angry."

She brought her own gaze to the window, and although the departing coach had given her a warning of what was to come, a cold weight still hit her in the chest at the sight of the Dowager Marchioness of Rockliffe standing behind the rain-streaked panes of glass.

"She came to me," Percy said, his voice even and gentle. "She explained a little of what happened last week and said she had an urgent need to see you. Asked if there was any way I could assist in arranging a meeting. After hearing her out, I agreed to help. I hope I haven't done wrong."

Theo said nothing, merely continued peering at the unwanted view. Whatever version of events the dowager had given him, she highly doubted it included mention of the marquessate's future or of the lengths to which the dowager had gone to make Theo submit to her will. The dowager should have known better than to interfere so soon, or at all. Theo thought she'd made that *very* clear.

Yet there the dowager stood, a rigid figure peeking out to survey the street. From this distance, the coldness of her eyes and the hard set of her mouth weren't visible. In fact, the burgeoning rain blurred the view more and more until all that remained was the silhouette of a slight, elderly woman with her body stooped toward her cane.

"If you don't wish to go inside, I'll take you home without saying another word about it." Percy's words finally caused her to turn away, and when she met his eyes again, they were soft and imploring. "However, I believe it would be to your benefit to speak with her."

She sighed, folding her arms across her chest. If he were anyone else, she'd be furious at him. Yet he'd shown right from the beginning that he only ever had her best interests at heart. She trusted him. And if whatever the dowager had said made him think Theo should entertain a conversation with her ...

"Very well." With heavy limbs, she pushed herself off the seat. "I suppose I'd best go see what she wants and get it over with."

"I'll wait right here until you're through," he said, his coat beginning to darken from the raindrops pouring upon it. "Or I can accompany you inside if you don't want to go alone."

She gave her wet skirts a shake and adjusted the satchel's strap upon her shoulder. "Thank you, but that's unnecessary on both counts. You should go home now, too, out of the rain. Prepare for your longer journey. I've managed Lady Rockliffe before, unassisted, and presumably possess the stamina to do so again."

"Of that, I have no doubt." He flashed her a rueful smile, letting his hand rest upon hers. "As I lacked the foresight to travel in my coach today—or at least in my phaeton with the hood—I suppose I'll take you at your word and be on my way, as long as you're certain you'll be all right getting home."

"Of course. It isn't far, and I don't anticipate taking long here." She squeezed his hand, letting her features soften. "Farewell, Percy. While I'm not certain I should thank you for this, you've given me so many other reasons to feel gratitude that it hardly signifies. In any case, I wish you a safe journey, and I hope you find the happiness you seek."

"Farewell, Theodora. I have every confidence good things are in store for you."

"Thank you." She uttered the words a final time as she jumped to the ground, watching with a small pang in her chest as he turned the curricle and went on his way, back toward Mayfair.

That was that, then. All that remained was the brick

building with the figure in the window. A sight that made the pang become a constant thudding of her heart. Yet Percy had brought her here, wanting to help. Thinking a meeting with the dowager was for the best.

"As long as she hasn't deceived us both," Theo muttered, marching up to the polished red door. She threw it open, bursting into the space with her shoulders held high and rigid, ready for battle.

"Theodora." The dowager nodded curtly, pulling her own body upright as she moved a few steps closer to the doorway.

Theo couldn't speak. Her jaw went slack, and she found herself blinking at the scene before her, unsure of which way to look first as she tried to take it all in.

The space was only small, poorly lit thanks to the cloud-darkened sky, but so many familiar things jumped out at her. A large table, piled high with paper, rested against the back wall, above which hung several shelves containing bottles and ink balls. A sturdy wooden cabinet stood next to the window, containing rows of type cases stacked neatly upon their racks. And in the center of it all was a printing press. Not the wooden machine from her memory but an apparatus made entirely of iron.

She snapped her attention back to the dowager, pinching her lips in a straight line. "What is this? And why would you coerce Lord Pembrook into bringing me to meet you here?"

The dowager arched a thin silver brow. "It's a printshop. I thought that would be obvious. In any case, it's yours."

Theo's head spun, her eyes darting around to reexamine each element of the room. *Press. Type cases. Ink. Ink balls. Paper*. Everything needed to print a manuscript. "Mine?"

"Yes, yours." The dowager gave her a pointed look, almost as if she were trying to explain something complex to a young child. "I procured it for you. This is what you wanted all along, is it not?"

Anticipation dared to flicker within her. Yes. *Yes.* This was where she'd pinned all her hopes. Envisioned her future. Her independence.

But just as quickly, an icy blast of reality came to douse it. "Thank you, but I'm finished accepting charity from you. Never again will I place myself in your debt."

"This isn't charity." The dowager appraised her with pale, shrewd eyes, her posture as regal as if she were the queen receiving a subject. In the next moment, though, she slumped. Not drastically, but enough to cause her shoulders to drop and make it clear she'd shifted her weight to rest against her cane. Enough to make Theo detect what she'd first spotted when the dowager appeared as an obscured shadow through the window. Vulnerability.

"This is repayment," she continued, her jaw staying stiff as she spoke. "It isn't anything more than what you're owed. Merely a building. The staffing and management of the establishment will still fall to you, and if you run it to the ground, the responsibility will rest solely on your shoulders. However, I took something from you, and now, I'm giving it back. I hope we can consider any debts between us erased."

The distinct oily fragrance of ink filled Theo's nose. This was what she'd been striving for—this inane venture of Samuel's that had turned into so much more. It now dangled in front of her face, hers for the taking. Except, it seemed rather like bait, waiting for her to snap it up, only to find herself ensnared. She would *not* make that mistake again.

"Take it, Theodora." For the first time, a hint of weariness to match her posture crept into the dowager's voice. "There's no catch. You made it clear all ties between us were severed, and this isn't an attempt to change your mind. Carry on as you see fit, and whatever opinions I may have on the subject, I'll find it within myself not to interfere."

The dowager didn't wait for a response before pivoting stiffly on her cane. She shuffled forward, coming to a stop beside the cabinet at the front of the shop and reaching into her reticule. Her hand emerged with a folded piece of parchment and a key, setting them atop the type case. For a moment, she simply stood there, her fingers running over the key's grooves. Until suddenly, she turned again, capturing Theo's gaze. "If you feel you cannot accept my offering, then throw these in the Thames and forget you ever came here. I hope you don't do that, though. In fact, I hope very much you succeed. For the boys' sake."

Theo's pounding heart squeezed tight. That's what she'd wanted all along. To do right by them. To give them all they deserved.

"And finally, I hope you remember what I told you before." The dowager lectured as usual, but her words didn't contain their typical hard bite. Nor was her face creased with a scowl. Why, her demeanor showed tendencies in the range of ... gentleness. "Your dislike of the circumstances won't make them different. One way or another, Benedict *will* become the marquess. You need to ensure ... You need to prepare ... Oh, just take *care* of him, whatever you do. Alexander, too. That's all I ask."

The dowager moved before Theo could blink away her surprise, rushing onto the rainy street in a sudden burst of speed. Theo, on the other hand, was still frozen in place. Surrounded by a printer's wares.

Hers.

She blinked again, slowly. None of this felt real. Yet when she opened her eyes, the printshop still surrounded her, small but efficient. Ready to be put to use.

Hers.

She tried the affirmation again. It was still surreal, but this time, it sank a little deeper. Tentatively, her feet moved across the floor—which didn't float away on a dream—until she stood where the dowager had stood, beside the type case cabinet. She unrolled the parchment—the deed. Saw her name scrawled in black ink. Ran her fingers over the key. The dowager may not have it in her to utter the words *I'm sorry*, but these items spoke of a thorough apology.

Perhaps some small, spiteful part of her would like to do as the dowager said and sink them in the murky waters of the Thames. Yet her mind brimmed with other possibilities.

26

For a moment, when Theo returned to the address on Fleet Street the next afternoon, her breath hitched with the expectation that her key would no longer open the printshop's door. Yet when she put it in the lock, it turned just as smoothly as it did yesterday, admitting her back into the well-stocked room that had previously left her speechless.

Not a dream, then, despite how far it seemed from reality. The printshop was still here and still hers. And after staying up much of the night, her thoughts racing far too quickly to allow for sleep, she knew what she wanted to do with it.

She glanced through the windowpanes at the rain that had yet to relent. Regardless of the weather, the street remained filled with pedestrians, all clutching umbrellas or with their faces turned to the ground. However, none belonged to the person she awaited.

Jeremy had filled a prominent place in her mind ever since this key first fell into her hands and her future changed. She burst with the need to tell him. To find comfort in his arms as they talked through the situation and everything it meant. Yet she'd vowed to let him come to her first when he felt established enough to prove his worth. Not that this was in any way necessary, but it was so important to him, and she wouldn't risk interfering if it meant he would go forward considering himself still lacking in some way.

But then, the hastily scrawled note had come that very morning.

Theo,

There's so much for us to discuss, and in truth, I'm not sure how much longer I can manage the separation. May I see you?

Yours,

J

The timing couldn't have been more perfect. With newfound lightness, she'd crafted a note in return, giving him the Fleet Street address and requesting he join her at three o'clock.

She swept away from the window, letting her eyes adjust to the shop's dim interior as she tried to put her fluttering heart to rest. The hour still hadn't arrived. Indeed, she'd purposefully come here early for the task she needed to see to before he showed up. Soon enough, she'd lay eyes on him again and speak the words she'd imagined throughout the night. But in the meantime ...

She crossed the floor, going to the small stove at the back corner of the shop. The rain and wind left a damp chill in the air, unbefitting of a summer's day, to the point of necessitating another heat source. Of course, she would require the stove today regardless.

She made quick work of locating the tinderbox and getting a fire going, watching the flames as they sprang to life within the cast iron. Perhaps at an earlier time, the sight would have made her stomach roil and her lungs struggle to fill with air. At the moment, though, nothing came but an unyielding sense of certainty.

Just like yesterday, her satchel remained a steady weight against her shoulder, although no longer filled with art supplies and coins. She shrugged it off, placing it on the table next to a stack of printing paper and unfastening it. Removing the hefty pile of writing paper that rested within, each piece marked from top to bottom with her hand-writing.

Samuel's manuscript. Well, not the original copy he'd worked so zealously to create, which remained tucked safely inside the drawer of her bedside table, but her version. It wasn't yet complete, thanks to the numerous distractions that had come her way over the past weeks, but contained hours' worth of work nonetheless. The words she'd somehow found the will to reproduce and revise again after her first attempt had been lost.

She picked up the title page she'd so carefully copied—*A Descent to the Underworld: a novel by Samuel Prescott*—running a finger over the ink before crumpling it within her palm and letting it drop into the fire.

The first page was the hardest. However, once it fell, instantly snatched up by the growing flames, she added another and then another, her hands developing a rhythm that didn't relent.

She'd tried so hard to simultaneously work her way out of debt and do what Samuel would have wanted. Yet these pages were filled with her words, not his. She'd done her best, but she was no writer, and she certainly wasn't Samuel Prescott. Any book she managed to put out into the world would be a lie. And he *wouldn't* have wanted that.

These pages upon pages she threw in the fire were based on words that had faced rejection from publishers all over

London. He'd created them at a time when he was already so far removed from his former self, gripped by a strange fervency fueled by endless bottles of whisky and opium.

She'd clung to the words regardless, as her final piece of him, as her hope for the future. However, she now had a different path forward. And while maybe a tiny piece of her heart had closed, keeping her memories of Samuel locked tight inside, the rest burst wide open, ready for all the love she could both give and receive.

"Theo."

When the voice called out her name, her state of anticipation had shifted into a sort of trance as she watched the last of the pages wilt beneath the orange glow. Yet that single word, uttered by that specific voice, had her spinning away from the fire immediately, rushing across the shop.

Jeremy stood in the doorway, looking so much like he had the day she'd first laid eyes on him. A water-logged hat and topcoat. Hair darkened by rain. Green eyes that pierced her. On that first day, though, they'd been full of apology. Now, they were wide with awe.

She stopped just short of him without allowing herself the luxury of crashing into his arms—a position from which she'd be hard-pressed to remove herself. Instead, she grasped his hand, leading him a few steps farther into the unlit shop. He said nothing as he took in the scene, but his face had become a giant question.

She didn't make him wait. She let the whole unlikely story come tumbling out—its telling helping to prove to her, too, that it truly was *real*—ending with the question that continued to prod her. "Do you think I'm right to accept it?"

"Yes." He didn't hesitate for a second in answering her. While she spoke, he'd simply held her hand and listened, not giving away anything of how he felt. Now that she'd finished, he pulled her close to him, encircling her waist in his arms and offering a grin that shot straight to her heart. "While I may be disinclined to agree with the dowager, she *is* right about this being nothing more than what you're owed. I'm so happy for you, Theo. This is what you've worked for all along. You'll finally see the manuscript printed."

She gave her head a small, barely perceptible shake. "Not that one." The corners of her eyes stung at the thought of the farewell she'd just experienced beside the fire. But at the same time, a smile crossed her lips for what was to come. "I want to print *your* manuscript. It's time that *Peregrine Plumtree* found a place in the world. If you're willing, of course ..."

She trailed off as his hands stiffened around her waist and his eyes grew large once more. He glanced over her head toward the iron press and the stack of blank paper. The things she herself had stared at in disbelief and then pondered over and over again as she planned for the future. His jaw twitched with the onslaught of thoughts that must now be racing through his head.

But then, his gaze returned to her, filled with bright green intensity. "I'm willing. More than willing. As long as you're certain. If you truly think the manuscript suitable—"

"I do. I'm beyond certain." She slipped her fingers up around his nape, pressing her palms against skin still damp from raindrops. "I have every confidence in you. I want this for you. For us."

The pulse jumped in his neck, and he leaned in, brushing the faintest kiss against the bridge of her nose before pulling back so they could fully hold each other in view. "I've been so eager to see you. There are things I need to tell you about my week and to ask you, too."

He paused, spending a moment to take a breath. To smooth the wrinkles from his wet coat. He could take all the time he needed. He'd stood here, unwavering, as she told the story of her time since they'd parted ways after arriving in London. Now, it was her turn to do the same, whatever he had to say. She clasped her hands in front of her, determined to stay that way, without distractions, until he was through. But in the meantime, her heart dared to flutter with something suggestive of hope.

"I had an unexpected encounter this week as well." A shadow spread across his face, and his brow rumpled. "My father showed up at my lodgings. I didn't want to see him, but he was extremely insistent I take a minute to hear him out. In the end, he didn't stay long. He merely wanted me to know that he'd resigned from his position as the dowager's man of business and that she'd given him something for me before he left. It was the remainder of my salary, wrapped up in a letter of recommendation."

Theo's lips parted, allowing a small sound of disbelief to escape. Had they entered some sort of alternate existence in which the dowager *didn't* seek to crush whatever displeased her? But maybe the theme of the week, as far as it related to the dowager, was to expect the unexpected.

He shook away his own brief expression of bemusement, clearing his throat so he could keep going. "I procured employment at a grammar school here in London. It might not have the prestige of Eton or Harrow, but it's respectable enough, and I believe the position will suit, at least for the time being. If you haven't made other arrangements, I thought perhaps Benedict and Alexander could attend. It would at least give them a good introduction, should you later decide to send them for schooling elsewhere."

"That sounds like a wise plan, indeed. Until the printshop is fully established, at any rate." She'd intended to stay where she was, unmoving, until he finished speaking, but as always seemed to happen in his presence, her body must have inched forward, for her skirts brushed against his breeches. How could she help it when, once again, he proved how he always kept her *and* the boys in mind?

"I've been looking at lodgings as well." He moved, too. Just a little, but enough for his knuckles to connect with her sleeve. Enough for her to experience a tiny jolt and to desire so much more of his touch. "I have a few possibilities in mind, although I haven't selected anything yet. I thought you might first like to survey them along with me. That is ... assuming I'm correct to imagine that bachelor's apartments may no longer suffice for my situation.

She bit her lip, although her smile still insisted on breaking through. "I should certainly hope they would not."

That brilliant, heartwarming grin reappeared, and he reached for her hands, pressing them against his own so their fingers intertwined. For a moment, he glanced at the floor, exhaling as he collected his thoughts. When he looked up again, his green eyes focused on her so intently that their surroundings once more melted away. "I wish I could give you more. I wish I constantly knew all the answers. But I promise to always be by your side as we figure them out together. I told you before, but I want to tell you again, now and every day for the rest of my life. I love you. I love your passion, your determination, your strength. I love who you are to me, but also who you are as a mother, and I hope you know I'll always care for Ben and Alex as if they were my own. Will you marry me, Theo? For there would be no greater honor than having the three of you accept me into your family."

Her body was floating. Her heart soaring. Yet the pressure of his fingers held her in, reminding her what she needed to say in return. "We don't require more. Only you. Don't you see how you already give us everything we need?

Some future association we have with the peerage won't change that. I know Ben and Alex may be short on words at times, but it's clear to me how deeply they both adore you. As do I. I love you, too, Jeremy. With you next to me, I feel I could conquer anything that comes my way. So yes, I will marry you. Yes, yes, *yes*."

Their lips collided, bringing a surge of heat to her body, which had already absorbed more elation for one day than she thought possible. Her fingers were in his hair. His hands cupped her chin. As surrounding them, in this dusky space where rain tapped against the window and subtle warmth drifted out from the stove, the printing equipment sat waiting. Ready for the next step forward.

She gave herself another moment to absorb the sensation of his kiss before pulling her head back and gazing into green eyes and then at the printing press, which somehow still hadn't vanished. "I'm convinced this must be a dream," she murmured, the words of his proposal floating through her head.

"No, not a dream. This is even better." He pressed his mouth alongside her ear, the heat of his breath sending a shiver down to her core. "But why don't we see what we can do to make it all feel a little more real?"

Epilogue

Six weeks later

Jeremy wasn't quiet as he rushed up the stairs of their home in Buckingham Street. In fact, eagerness made his boots pound against each wooden step, to the point it was a wonder their cantankerous neighbor didn't bang on the wall. However, when he traversed the short hallway, reaching the open sitting room door—silence. The commotion he made didn't cause anyone within to so much as stir.

He halted in the doorway, suddenly feeling overlarge and overloud. The scene before him was so peaceful—so perfect—that he scarcely dared move a muscle for fear he'd make it dissolve.

On the sofa nearest the doorway, Benedict sat curled up with his spectacles perched atop his nose and the rest of his face buried in a book. That pair of spectacles had turned him into so voracious a reader that Jeremy had a hard time keeping him supplied with literature. Achilles, always glad for a companion and a warm place to doze, lay sprawled out with his head in Benedict's lap and his legs dangling over the sofa's arm. Not that Jeremy or Theo encouraged him in becoming too familiar with the furniture, but the dog seemed to have other ideas.

Alexander lay on his stomach on the floor nearby, a pile of paper spread out in front of him, along with an inkpot. His quill moved furiously across the page, making only the briefest pause each time he raised it to dip it in the ink, leaving a steady stream of words in its wake. After finishing the dragon story he'd started all that time ago back at Rockliffe House, he'd done a second, featuring a cyclops, and now worked on another with sea serpents. Always aided by a few illustrations from Theo, of course. His tongue pressed against the edge of his mouth as he worked, while his expression appeared faraway as if he were lost to another world. A feeling to which Jeremy could sometimes relate during those late hours after the day was done when he had his own quill in hand.

Not that he ever drifted into his head for too long a stretch anymore. Why would he when the most exquisite woman in the world made up his reality?

She currently sat at one of the most frequently used areas of their home: the sturdy oak desk by the window that received the brunt of the evening light. Sunrays streaked over her, casting her in a golden glow and making her hair glisten like polished obsidian. It was funny, really, how closely her position resembled Alexander's. Ruby lips slightly parted, her tongue pressed to the corner. Dark eyes locked downward, absorbed in the paper before her. Fingers clasped around a paintbrush, letting it drift over a section of illustrated leaves. Not in a frenzy like Alexander, but making slow, meticulous strokes, dotting the paper with watercolor.

It had now been a month since they'd married by common license and combined their lives into this single dwelling, but his heart would never stop clenching each time he came upon that sight. Nor would his mouth ever cease twitching upward. Helping her get the printshop up and running, and watching the words he'd written be copied over and over as they went through the press, had felt like the greatest accomplishment. However, having the publisher of a botany guide approach them for printing, and then request that Theo color the illustrations to make a few special edition copies, had brought the feeling of success to a whole other level. Word of her skill as an artist was obviously traveling, undoubtedly in part due to her continued commissions from members of the ton. If that could end up driving more interest toward the printshop, who knew how far the venture could go? His wife was formidable, and this was only the beginning.

He could have stared at the scene for the rest of the evening until the sun sank below the horizon and the room became shrouded in blackness. But in the end, although his pounding up the stairs had done nothing to disturb them, the slight creak in the floorboards as he shifted his weight caused Theo's head to snap upward.

"Jeremy." She smiled—the sight that made coming home each day the best feeling imaginable—and carefully set down her brush before pushing herself to her feet.

"Good evening." He ruffled two curly heads—and a set of furry ears—as he crossed the room, stopping before the desk and pressing a kiss to Theo's forehead. "Did everyone pass a pleasant day?"

"Yes, although it seems to have gotten away on us." She leaned in to kiss his cheek in return, her eyes traveling to the clock on the end table and then to the boys, lounging contentedly while still half-absorbed in their tasks. "I think Hyde Park tired those three out."

He grinned at the two sets of rosy cheeks and the tangles of hair that hung over their foreheads. Now that he took a closer look, Benedict and Alexander did appear somewhat windblown.

Perhaps his only regret with this new situation was that he and the boys were often confined to a schoolroom, no longer free to move their lessons outdoors whenever they wished. As soon as circumstances allowed, he hoped to leave his position at the school and resume teaching them at home. In the meantime, however, Theo had arranged with Lady Amelia—recently returned to London, despite the Season coming to a close—to meet at the park twice a week, as long as the weather was fine. A plan that also seemed to agree with the boys, as they were always pleased to report that their aunt did *significantly* less complaining than their grandmother.

A gaping chasm still existed between the life Theo had chosen for them in these rooms here on Buckingham Street and the future that loomed ominously at Rockliffe House. Yet Lady Amelia provided a sort of bridge between the two. Maybe, in time, they would all feel ready to cross it.

"Did you have a good day as well?" Theo pulled his hat off and set it on the corner of her chair, then brought her hand up to smooth his cravat and waistcoat. After the extra excursion he'd just done, perhaps he was windblown, too. "You're late getting home today."

The idyllic scene he'd encountered upon reaching the sitting room had put everything else on pause. But suddenly, the reason he'd bolted up the stairs in the first place came rushing back, and eagerness coursed through him once more. "I did. Apologies for the lateness. I had to make a stop at the lending library along the way. Now, I have something to show you."

He unfastened his satchel and reached inside, his hand immediately connecting with the object he sought. His fingers ran over smooth leather and the soft edge of paper, and he pulled it out, dropping it into her hands. He had to bite his lip as he eyed her, no doubt looking as enthusiastic as Achilles at dinnertime.

Recognition filled her features as soon as the book hit her palm. Like him, she traced over the brown leather binding for just a few seconds before surveying the letters stamped on the spine and flipping open the cover to the title page. *The Peculiar Exploits of Peregrine Plumtree: Volume 1. A novel by Jeremy Clare.* The last time she'd seen this, it had been fresh off the press, unbound.

"Jeremy, this looks ..." She paused, taking another moment to examine the leather and the pages secured neatly within. A real, finished book. "Wonderful."

"I want to see!" Alexander, suddenly returned from his faraway world, scrambled to his feet and hurried across the room. Likewise, Benedict tossed his book to the side, darting forward to keep pace with his brother. Which encouraged Achilles, who'd been unceremoniously robbed of his pillow, to amble along behind them.

Benedict reached them first, and Theo put an arm around his shoulder, handing him the book. "Well, what do you think?"

He rewarded them both with an infrequent wide smile as he took in the title on the spine. "I think this is very impressive. Given that *our* printshop helped make it and all."

Beside him, Alexander bounced up and down as he awaited his turn, filled with a fresh burst of energy. "You're right, Mama! It does look wonderful."

"It does, doesn't it?" Jeremy was grinning nonsensically, but he couldn't seem to do otherwise. Too many dreams that had once felt impossible had now come true.

Even after he'd completed his fair copy of *Peregrine Plumtree* and brought it to the shop, and Theo had hired a compositor and printer, the idea of becoming a successfully published novelist often continued to seem surreal. Because what if no one showed interest in the book or the story was deemed abysmal, and it was all a waste of ink and paper ...

As it turned out, though, the real-life story of Theodora Prescott spurning the Dowager Marchioness of Rockliffe and running off to marry a tutor turned novelist had generated a great deal of talk and curiosity amongst the ton. And it happened that talk and curiosity sold books. Enough that they were now doing a second print run—five hundred copies this time—before they moved on to volume two.

Of course, the book he'd just held in his hands made up only part of the dream. It would all become meaningless without everything else that surrounded him.

He took another glance around the sitting room at the scene now in motion. Benedict, studying the book's first page through his spectacles. Alexander, nudging in to take a closer look as Achilles's spindly tail swished against his leg. And Theo, looking on, her cheeks nearly glowing, her eyes shining bright.

All here in front of him in a home of their own. No, it wasn't an elaborate Mayfair town house, but this small space was theirs. Perhaps in time, as their finances increased—and maybe the size of their family did, too—they would move on to somewhere bigger and better. For now, though, this collection of rooms was just what they needed. A place to be together. A place filled with love.

This was the rest of the dream.

This was happiness.

THE END

Bonus Content

Sign up for Jane's monthly newsletter to get access to free extra content, including a subscriber-exclusive bonus scene for *A Study in Desire*. You will also be the first to know about new releases, giveaways, special promotions, and more.

Join now at: www.janemaguireauthor.com/newsletter

About the Author

Jane Maguire is a Canadian author whose lifelong passions for history, writing, and love stories inevitably led her to begin penning historical romance novels. While her love of historical fiction spans all eras, she focuses her writing on high society in the regency period. She enjoys crafting stories with lots of angst, which makes giving her characters their happily ever afters all the more satisfying.

When she isn't at her computer writing and researching, you can find her vacationing in the Rocky Mountains, playing classical music on the piano, or simply curling up with a cup of tea and a good book. She lives with her husband, two kids, and a very floofy cat.

You can find Jane online at www.janemaguireauthor.com.